THE
YOUNG
Chieftain

⚬⚬ KEN HOWARD ⚬⚬

Tamarind

THE YOUNG CHIEFTAIN
TAMARIND BOOKS 978 1 848 53033 1

Published in Great Britain by Tamarind Books,
a division of Random House Children's Books
A Random House Group Company

This edition published 2010

1 3 5 7 9 10 8 6 4 2

The Random House Group Limited supports the Forest Stewardship Council
(FSC), the leading international forest certification organization. All our titles that
are printed on Greenpeace-approved FSC-certified paper carry the FSC logo.
Our paper procurement policy can be found at www.rbooks.co.uk/environment.

Mixed Sources
Product group from well-managed
forests and other controlled sources
www.fsc.org Cert no. TT-COC-2139
© 1996 Forest Stewardship Council

Set in 11.5/14.75pt Minion

TAMARIND BOOKS
61–63 Uxbridge Road, London, W5 5SA

www.**tamarindbooks**.co.uk
www.**kids**at**randomhouse**.co.uk

Addresses for companies within The Random House Group Limited
can be found at: www.randomhouse.co.uk/offices.htm

THE RANDOM HOUSE GROUP Limited Reg. No. 954009

A CIP catalogue record for this book is available from the British Library.

Printed and bound in Great Britain by
CPI Bookmarque, Croydon, CR0 4TD

A large wave knocked Jamie flat and he floundered towards some rocks that formed a wide, flat ledge at the base of the cliff. With an effort he hauled himself up onto the shelf.

'Jeez. Duncan never said nothin' about this,' he said aloud. He consulted his watch. 4.30 p.m. He peered out over the dazzling, empty ocean. 'So where are you, dude?'

He scrambled to his feet and looked along the bay. The sandy beach had all but disappeared and the tide was still rising fast. Already waves were breaking powerfully over the ledge. Jamie retreated towards the cliff face, looking desperately for some way of climbing higher. The cliff was composed of crumbly chalk and offered few hand- or footholds. Jamie searched in his pocket and brought out some sweet wrappers and the Stone of Doran. He was about to replace the stone in his pocket when something made him examine it more closely.

Jamie raised the blue stone to eye level and looked closely at the glass inserted into it like a lens. Something cloudy within seemed to move and swirl . . .

To Ben

For their invaluable help in preparing this book
I would like to thank my agent, Sheila Ableman,
Diana Webb and Joyce Sachs in Los Angeles;
Alan Blaikley, and the great team at Tamarind/
Random House – Verna Wilkins, Patsy Isles,
Chimaechi Ochei and Sue Cook.

1

MacDoran

Has it ever happened to you? Has life ever ganged up on you, hit you from behind when you least expected it, and catapulted you into a totally new direction? Into a new person? Perhaps someone you never knew you were, or could ever become? Some stupid action that started a train of events that would change your whole world?

No? Well, maybe not – yet. But keep a wary eye open, because it might.

It happened to Jamie. It all began as a silly prank; it wasn't even his idea, although as usual he went along with it. And of course in a way it was *because* of him. Because of who he was. Jamie MacDoran. Now that's a fine name for a fifteen-year-old kid from Vego Park, California. A fifteen-year-old *black* kid, from The Valley but still a part of Los Angeles where you have to pull your own weight.

His buddies at University High School often had a good laugh at the strange surname. 'Mac-*Dough*-ran' they would intone like some exotic mantra, or just 'Big Mac'. Well, let's face it, that's what you get with a Scottish dad in the American aircraft industry.

There we have young Jamie MacDoran, growing strong under the flawless blue Californian skies, surfing in the sun-kissed blue Pacific Ocean, hanging out with his friends, without a care in the world. Of course, that last bit is nonsense – put about by those who want to believe that childhood is a blissful prelude to the real grim grown-up world of business, stress and responsibility.

There's plenty of stress and worry when you are a kid – just of a different kind.

But on the face of it, Jamie did have many of the good things in life. He was tall and slender, with a brilliant smile that lit up his face. He was intelligent, although he didn't always let it show, and a gifted athlete.

The boys were walking off the basketball court with wimpy noodle legs after their gruelling practice. It was important to drive themselves hard because of the upcoming big game against Martin Luther High, their arch-rivals. University High was a small private school with a great sports history, demonstrated by the ageing championship banners hanging in the gym. The school

2

also paid the tuition fees of promising young athletes from poorer families and so attracted kids not only from the nearby Valley but also from right down to South Central LA.

The downside was that many of the students had to travel long distances to get to school. Jamie lived in The Valley so there was no problem. He was a first-year student, but was already one of the best players on the team. He sat on the bleachers, towelling his face and arms, shaking from the exertion. The gym smelled of stale sweat and echoed to the incessant squeak of trainers against wood.

'Man, that was a good practice,' he mumbled as Lester approached, greedily slurping the water out of his bottle. Lester, the junior forward on the team, had smooth dark skin and long, bony arms and legs. He sported a small Afro, which hadn't really grown out yet but he felt it made a statement about who he was. He was half yawning, half sighing. 'Man, I'm tired. We'd better win this game!'

Jamie looked up sharply. 'Is there any doubt in your mind? 'Cos there sure ain't in mine.'

Lester drained the bottle. 'There you go, Mr Optimist – but it's all good. I know we can win if you're on your game – that's the difference-maker.'

'What y'all talking 'bout?' Jeroo called out as he ambled towards the bleachers, tearing off his shirt and splashing water liberally over his body. 'We gonna win this game, 'cos this kind of workout can *only* mean we winning!' Jeroo's crackling voice had a southern lilt even though he was raised in Los Angeles. He played guard with his stocky body. He was quick though, his legs blurring in double motion when he ran up the court.

Chico slotted himself beside Jamie on the bleachers. 'Sho, you right!' Despite his short legs, Chico played point guard because of his speed. His bright eyes darted back and forth, registering every man on the court like real-time GPS. He was good-looking and always thinking about girls and dates. He pulled a foil package out of his bag and regarded it sadly. 'Man, I'm so tired I can't even eat my mama's tacos right now, and you know how good they are!'

Jeroo wiped himself dry and sat heavily in between the others, who again shifted to accommodate him. 'But you know, Rob Lewis is gonna be tough to defend, he's so damn quick and agile.'

'He's just one guy,' scoffed Lester. 'He ain't no LeBron, and anyway that's Jamie's man. You can handle that, can't you, Jamie?'

Jamie punched the air. 'Yeah, just let me at him; he don't scare me an' I'll be ready for him. Real question is, will he be ready for *me* when I change into second gear?' They all laughed and picked up their things to go.

Chico threw a discarded towel at Lester. 'What time's your bus, Les? You gon' make it?'

'I'll make it all right. Just hope I don't fall asleep and miss my stop like last week and end up in Gardena.' Lester picked up his backpack and headed towards the exit. 'See you tomorrow.' He grimaced. 'So we can do this again!'

'Later, man, and no dreaming.' Chico grinned as he packed his bag.

The boys left the gym and walked over to the parking lot where Chico's sister, Anna, had agreed to pick some of them up. She was late – as usual. They were sat at the senior patio table when Lester reappeared. He had missed his bus and would stay at Jeroo's place instead.

Lester slumped dejectedly into the seat. 'So that means I ain't gonna see my girlie tonight.' He shaded his eyes against the filtered sunlight. 'I was at her house the other day, and her pa had rented that old movie, *Braveheart*.'

'Ain't that Mel G?' asked Jeroo.

'You got it. It was R-rated 'cos of all this cussin' and violence.' He turned to Jamie. 'And they were all in Scotsdale . . .'

'Scot*land*, ape-ass,' muttered Jamie.

'Same difference. An' Mel Gibson had red hair, you know, like down to *here*.' He pointed towards his knees. 'And he was wearing this sort of skirt.'

'He gay or something?' Chico wanted to know.

Lester thought about it. 'Don't think so. It had something to do with their beliefs and stuff.'

Jeroo became interested in the story. 'Hey, Jamie, your dad's from there. He like that? Look like Mel Gibson?'

Jamie smiled. 'Oh, sure, with a number two crop.'

'But he is the chief?' demanded Jeroo. 'Like with the Indians?'

'Not Indians, knucklehead.'

'So what are they?' Chico crossed his eyes. 'Aliens?'

'C'mon,' persisted Jeroo. 'Stay serious. Your dad is the main man? My brother told me 'bout your report in history, when you talked 'bout him, so don't go cold on us now, my man.'

Jamie shook his head. 'It ain't like that. Not now.' He stood up. 'Anyway, I don't know. He don't talk much about it. Just spends hours yelling on the phone in his den, and comes out real mad.'

Lester piped up. 'But he got the gear?'

'What?'

'You know – the dresses and stuff?'

Jamie zipped his jacket. 'I guess.'

Jeroo's eyes widened. He pointed a finger at Jamie. 'Whoa, hold up, wait a minute, somethin' gotta go there. Your dad wears *dresses*?'

'No! . . . Yeah – sometimes, maybe.' He caught them staring open-mouthed at him. 'For ceremonies, but I've never seen—'

Jeroo leaped to his feet with a cry. He and the others surrounded Jamie and danced in a tribal ring, chanting and throwing their hands in the air, slowly gathering speed. When they eventually imploded in a laughing heap of flailing arms and legs, Jamie had to fight his way up for air.

Jeroo surfaced next to him, eyes gleaming. 'Show us, Jim-Jam. You *gotta* show us.'

2

The Den

Anna pulled up in her beat-up Jeep, trailed by a cloud of toxic emissions. The boys raced towards her. 'Front,' yelled Lester, and nobody complained as he jumped into the front seat. He didn't want to be crammed in with the others, sticky with sweat and smelling from b-ball practice. Jamie, Chico and Jeroo all squeezed into the back; the cracked 'pleather', which at one time probably matched the green of the exterior, scratched your legs if you were wearing shorts so the guys lowered themselves gingerly onto its surface.

Anna scowled at them in the rear-view mirror. 'You think this is some kinda bus, huh?' The boys remained silent, not wanting to do anything that might change her mind. 'OK, you can all ride this time, but I'm only taking you one place. That's it. You hear me, Chico?' Anna screamed as she pulled away.

Jeroo grinned. 'No problem, Anna darling. We're all going to Jamie's.' Jamie protested as the over-burdened Jeep rolled out of the parking lot and belched noisily down the street.

Zee Diamond was on the stereo and Jamie was sitting squashed on the back seat, eyes half closed, enjoying the vibe. They all yelled each chorus tunelessly:

'Gotta get it right, hold tight, hold tight.
When I feel you close to me,
That's the place I want to be.
Get it right, hold tight, hold tight.
Come tonight, hold tight, that's right.'

The Jeep stopped with a jerk. They were at Jamie's. 'Thanks, Anna,' he said, and waved. He opened his door and got out. 'See you, guys.'

But Chico, Jeroo and Lester had already piled out the other side.

'No way. This is a definite no-no,' Jamie tried.

Anna shouted something that was drowned out by the music, and the Jeep pulled away in its fog of exhaust. The boys stood on the sidewalk and looked at Jamie.

'And what is this supposed to mean?' he asked.

Jeroo put an arm round his shoulders. 'We could not be so disrespectful as to ignore the generous offer of hospitality that you have extended to your best buddies.'

'*My* offer?'

'Sure thing. To learn first-hand the history and customs of a people whose existence until now we had woefully been in ignorance of.'

Chico smothered his laughter with his hand and picked up his bag. 'Which way, O leader?'

Pacific Drive, Vego Park, ended abruptly in a cul-de-sac several miles away from the ocean. Jamie often wondered why names had to be so misleading. Vego Park contained no hint of a park. You could be sure that an apartment block named Ocean View would overlook a container depot; a Riverside Inn would nestle against a railroad track and High Gables would be a nasty, squat concrete box. Did nobody else notice?

Families like the MacDorans settled in Pacific Drive because it was quiet and considered a safe place to bring up kids. At the end of the drive there was a turning circle backed by some wooden picnic tables and a few rusty swings. The houses had been built at speed by a developer, with the choice of two styles – the basic Georgian or the more expensive Monarch. The MacDorans', at number 27, was a Georgian.

The group turned into the empty drive. This was unfamiliar territory. Chico lived fairly close, so Jamie often got a ride to school with him; otherwise he would take the bus. His bus ride was nothing like Lester's, though – two and a half hours into South Central to the Elm Estate (no elms, naturally). Lester's home was close to a noisy shopping centre in an ugly cluster of apartment blocks that was patrolled by the police at night. Even Jeroo lived one hour north in Sylmar at Rodeo Heights (don't ask!).

This was a first – because in the few years since he had arrived in Vego Park, Jamie had somehow managed to avoid inviting any of his friends home. He realized it was a defence mechanism – but why? Today, despite or maybe because of Jamie's increasingly desperate attempts to foil the visit, the guys were intent on penetrating the MacDoran homestead. And no one had any real plans for getting home. They would worry about rides later.

The house was silent. Jamie's mom, Marcia, was at the clinic where she worked each day as a psychotherapist; his dad never got back from the air-base before dinner was on the table, and often not until it was finished. Jamie dropped his backpack on the floor beside the hall table, the other boys followed suit and fell silent. All eyes were on Jamie. Sweat trickled down his neck as they walked down the hallway towards the den.

The wooden sign tacked on the den door had been a birthday gift.

JAMES MACDORAN

it read, and then beneath, in smaller letters:

Hail to the Chief!

They all waited, watching Jamie.

'Look, I'm not sure . . .'

'Open up, Jim-Jam.'

From habit or superstition, Jamie tapped on the door.

'Who that for, man?' asked Jeroo. 'Your old man's at the base. He sure ain't gonna answer.'

They pushed past Jamie, spilling into the room, looking around.

Lester gave a low whistle. 'Nice. Very nice.' He picked up a glass paperweight and touched some silver trophies.

Chico peered at the framed certificates, pursing his lips with the effort of deciphering them. 'For services to the aero – aero-naut-ical industry.' He whistled. 'Big cheese.'

'Look.' Lester had discovered a large framed photo on the wall – black and white and fading. 'Is this the tribe? Which one is your dad?'

It was hard to tell, because the rows of stony faces were as frozen as the mountain range in the background. Jamie's finger finally found a tall, blond man standing slightly apart in the back row. 'That's him.'

'You bin there?'

Jamie shook his head. 'Nah. It's a real long way. Dad goes sometimes.'

'Guys, look what I got.' Jeroo was halfway into a large chest, pulling out a swathe of tartan material and wrapping it around his shoulders.

'No,' cried Jamie. 'I said we could look, not—'

Lester was beside Jeroo. 'That's what I'm doin' . . . I'm *lookin'*. Where is it, the skirt thing? Ah . . .' And then he was wrapping round a kilt, over his trainers and baggies, hand on hip, sashaying across the room, 'Now, listen here, my men.'

Jamie forced a smile. 'OK, guys, that's it. Put it back. Game over.'

But it had only just begun. Jeroo dug down into the chest again and pulled out a sporran, the chain of which he looped around his neck. Lester held up a dirk and was fencing with it like a musketeer, and Chico pulled out a set of bagpipes and was trying to milk them.

The noise of their laughter and shouting obscured the sound of the den door opening. It was some time before, one by one, they fell silent as they became aware of the figure standing framed in the doorway.

Lester was the last to realize. He was playing blind man's buff, with the kilt now around his head, whirling like a dervish . . . until his outstretched fingers came in contact with the cold, unyielding face of James MacDoran.

'Woo. Touched ya! That means, honey, you is *dead*. D-E-A—' One eye peered from between a fold of material. 'Oh, shoot! I mean . . . *sir*?'

James's silence was worse than any explosion of anger. His gaze slowly panned across the boys' faces, finally coming to rest upon Jamie.

'Dad.' His grin was lopsided. 'Thought you was working.'

His father's compressed lips were a cold, white line. 'And is this what you do when you think I am working?'

'No, Dad. I mean, look, I sure am sorry.'

'*Sorry?*'

'We were just . . .' Jamie trailed off and hung his head.

His dad strode forward and thrust his face close. Eyeball to eyeball. 'Just what, son? Just bringing your pals to invade my private space, to mock and despoil? Is that it? Have a good look around, guys, while the coast is clear. The old man is really loopy – belongs to some sort of cult, straight out of *The Da Vinci Code*. You should see the weird stuff he's got stashed away. Is that what you told them, eh? Son?'

Jeroo stepped forward, with a huge conciliatory smile. 'Oh, c'mon, Mr MacDoran, don't go hitting on Jamie. It was nothin'. Only a laugh . . .'

'What?' James whirled round and glared at Jeroo. 'I don't believe we've been introduced.'

Jeroo recoiled. 'Er, Jeroo Kowalski, sir. We and Jimbo, we're all buds at school an' . . .' He looked around desperately at the others.

'It's the truth.' Lester finished unwinding his headgear. 'We didn't mean no disrespect. No, sir. Just havin' fun.'

'Fun? Is that it? Fun and games? Childish pantomime? Eh?' James's American accent, acquired slowly over the years, disappeared and the short, sharp words were aimed like darts. 'Well, you listen now and listen well. Do not ridicule what you do not understand. These are not playthings.' He snatched the proffered articles one by one from their guilty, outstretched arms. 'These are not for amusements. Not for laughs. Not for *fun*. And most certainly not for children.'

He gently placed them back in the chest and closed the lid. He turned to face the boys, his arms folded, head held high. 'They are to be worn only by he who has the right. By history. By birth. By duty. By the true chieftain alone.'

'Hail to the Chief!' muttered Jeroo under his breath.

'Jeroo, you have something to add?'

Jeroo shook his head. 'No, sir.'

Jamie's dad watched with a laser-like stare as the boys slunk awkwardly out of the room. Lester paused for a moment, thinking about going off on him, and then decided to just let it go – it wasn't his business anyway. Chico was already on his cell, begging for a ride home. Only Jeroo looked up briefly as he passed Jamie and rolled his eyes. 'Hey, man, we're with you,' he whispered.

Jamie flung himself down on his bed. What a stupid, no-brainer thing to do! What was he *thinking*, letting them talk him into such a jackass stunt?

He pressed fingers against his eyelids. Oh, c'mon, who was he kidding? He knew he could have stopped it anytime. He had just wanted to act the big-shot son of the chieftain and get off on the Scottish weirdos as though he knew *something*. But the fact was he knew *nothing*, and Dad had made him look like he *was* nothing.

Shamed him in front of his friends. Who needed that? Why couldn't he have told him off later? Hit him after? *Anything.*

James looked up at the ceiling. There was the scrape of a chair from his son's room, some footsteps and then the accusing thump of the stereo. Zee Diamond was screaming:

> *'Why'd you have to go and say those real mean things?*
> *Why'd you have to go and act so cruel?*
> *'Cos you know you have the power to bring me down*
> *Like a clown who always plays the fool.'*

'You think I was too tough on him?'

Marcia was clearing the dishes from the table, scraping Jamie's uneaten portion into a bowl. She was tall and slim with high cheekbones and dark, smooth skin. Her long braided hair framed her face. 'Sure scared the heck outta *me.* But I'm sure he'll realize . . .'

James sighed. 'I'm not so sure, Marcie. I don't like his attitude. I don't like those so-called school friends he hangs out with. I think they're a bad influence. He never brings anyone home, and when he finally does, why these hoodlums? Why not some nice, decent kids?'

'What are you talking about? Jamie's old enough to decide what and who he wants . . .'

'Well, at the moment he seems to want to fool around. His grades are down. What's happened to him? He's a bright kid, was always near top in his class. Why can't he find some decent mates who are nearer his . . .'

'Background?' Marcia arched an eyebrow. 'I think that might be a little difficult.'

James put his head in his hands. 'Oh, I don't know.' He sighed deeply. 'Do you think he hates me?'

Marcia looked at him sharply. She put down the bowl and leaned her hands on the table. 'No.'

'He looked at me as though he did. There was such anger in his eyes.'

'C'mon. You're his dad. Why would he hate you . . . ?'

'But?'

Marcia looked puzzled. 'Excuse me?'

'Why do I feel there is a "but" coming?'

Marcia undid her apron and hung it over the chair. She had changed out of the formal tailored clothes she wore to work into jeans and a cashmere sweater. She sat down at the table again.

'No, it's just that . . .' She reached out and touched James's arm. 'I think maybe neither of you know each other very well.'

James laughed bitterly. 'What you really mean is that I don't spend enough time with him. Eh? That I'd rather spend hours buried in that den trying to sort out those Scottish crackpots. Busying myself with clan nonsense that must seem like a lot of mumbo jumbo to you . . .'

'I have never said—'

'No, you've never *said*, but you must *feel* it. And rightly so. And it's not fair on you or on him. I am so bound by ancient ties that I don't have time to – what's

16

the word you psychologists use? *Bond?* That's it, bond with my son. That's what you mean.'

Marcia shook her head slowly. 'What I mean is . . . you have many claims on you, including a tremendously demanding job, which you are very good at, and which puts the smart clothes on Jamie's back and the food on our table . . .'

'But . . . ?'

'But . . . relationships need feeding too. And a teenage boy needs to spend some time with his father.'

'Doing what?'

Marcia stood up, exasperated. Her eyes flashed. 'Well, *exactly*! If you even have to *ask* that question, it shows how little you really know about your son. Just be with him, find out what makes him tick. It will be good for him too, being able to see you as . . . well . . . who you are, instead of . . .'

James nodded. 'Instead of this jerk who's always bawling him out?'

Marcia looked down.

James sighed again and ran a hand through his hair. 'I suppose you're right.' He gave Marcia a weary smile. 'Is this what you tell your patients?'

Marcia looked up at him, her eyes steady. 'Everyone needs different things. But, yes, I do think we all need to be reminded that we are loved.'

3

In the Blood

It was stiflingly hot in the classroom and a large fly batted insistently against the glass in an attempt to reach the shimmering blue sky outside. Mr Steadman sensed from their glazed expressions that Shakespeare and *Macbeth* were definitely not uppermost in his students' minds.

Jamie yawned. He had always been a top student, but the twelve-year-old who had devoured literature was now content to flip through graphic novels instead. He should still have been in the top class, but his persistently poor grades meant he now shared one of the lower classes with some of his team-mates. It was as though he had turned off his mind, shut down a whole part of his being to fit in.

'So, what is Shakespeare trying to tell us about ambition? Anyone?'

Shakespeare's message was evidently not coming in loud and clear and the class remained silent.

Mr Steadman sighed. 'Look, Macbeth is a murderer. This is a gruesome and bloody play. He and his wife have blood on their hands. What *should* he do?'

'Wash up?' Jeroo suggested as he sat back in his seat, pleased with his humour.

'Thank you, Mr Kowalski. In fact, his wife – Lady Macbeth – tries to "wash up" as you suggest, but finds that she can't get the bloodstains off . . .'

Lester's hand shot up, a cheeky look on his face. 'She should try Plumber's Mate, sir. When I was spraying my bike, I got all this black gunk—'

'Mr Thomas, Shakespeare was writing in Elizabethan Britain. Date, anyone? Mr Lopez, can you tell me when Shakespeare was writing?'

Chico wriggled and looked desperately at the open text for any clues. 'Er . . . well . . . I guess it was quite a long time ago . . .'

'*How* long ago, Mr Lopez?'

Chico scratched his head and appealed to the fly. 'More than . . . fifty years?' he ventured. Mr Steadman walked round his desk and sank heavily into his chair. 'Look. This is a blood and guts story about greed and murder and envy – it's straight out of *The Sopranos.*'

There was general disagreement. *The Sopranos* was *much* better.

'. . . and it was written four hundred years ago.'

'Oh, man,' said Chico, shocked. 'That is *really* old. What we doin' filling our brains with stuff that is so old?'

'Because great literature is eternal. It shows that human nature does not change; people's problems and desires don't change. In this play, which is also called the Scottish play, Shakespeare— Mr MacDoran?'

Jamie, gazing at a tiny wisp of cloud as it passed the front of a palm tree, did not hear the altered tone.

'Perhaps you more than anyone in this class should be able to tell us what this play is really about?'

There were snickers of laughter as Jamie stifled another yawn. It was only when Jeroo kicked him hard in the shin that he was aware of Mr Steadman standing over him.

'Sir?'

'Mr MacDoran, you must feel some empathy with Shakespeare's Scottish play? Perhaps you would like to simplify it for us?'

Jamie cleared his throat and swallowed. 'Er . . . well . . . it's . . .'

'Yes, Mr MacDoran, we hang on your every word.'

'Macbeth is . . .'

'Yes . . . ?'

Jamie looked around at his buddies, who were willing him to pull a rabbit out of the hat and somehow redeem the pride of the entire class. He wanted to show solidarity but not appear a smart-ass.

He thought for a moment, then the hint of a smile crept across his face and his eyes focused. 'Well, sir, as I see it, it's about this five-star general, bad-assed dude, who's freaked-out by these crazy old women, who tell him if he plays his cards right he can be the main man. So with his own lady, who suffers from real bad insomnia, he starts to snuff out the opposition and soon is controlling all of the action. But the nutcase ladies have spooked him real bad, tellin' him he'll surely be top gun unless the trees start walkin' like the Ents in Middle Earth or he meets some brother who wasn't born from a woman. You'd think he had it cut and dried but, 'cos it's a play, it all kinda comes true. Malcolm's troops creep up camouflaged with twigs and leaves and it turns out that Macduff was delivered by Caesarean, which I personally reckon is a *real* cop-out, so he skewers MacB in the big sword fight. The End.' Jamie looked up innocently. 'Did I leave anything out, sir?'

Even some of the girls in the class giggled while Jamie's buds gave him high fives.

'Steadman didn't like it,' said Chico. 'You could tell.'

'He laughed,' said Lester. 'He did laugh.'

'Yeah, but there's laughing and there's laughing. The laugh was on him, and teachers don't like that.'

The boys made their way along the sidewalk, soaking up the heat that rose from the slabs. 'Anyhow' – Lester turned to Jamie – 'how in the heck did you come up with all that stuff?'

Jamie shrugged. 'Dunno. It is a pretty weird story. It

must have stuck somewhere in the back of my mind. Perhaps my old man told me once.'

Jeroo suddenly halted and folded his arms. '*They are to be worn only by he who has the right*,' he said in a remarkably accurate impersonation of Jamie's dad. '*By the true chieftain alone.*' The buds fell about laughing.

'Speaking of which, is the Screaming Skull talking to you yet?' asked Lester.

Jamie pulled a face. 'I guess. Never seen him like that before. It's usually Mom who flips. You don't want to be around when she goes off . . .'

'They're the worst,' agreed Chico. 'My mom throws things when she gets really mad. She threw the cat once. You're pretty safe if it's you she's aiming at. Anyone else is in *real* danger.'

At The Dime Diner they swung onto the chrome stools and ordered Coke and Mountain Dew. Above them a TV screen showed a basketball game in lurid green and magenta. Jamie glanced up. 'It's a replay. Last night's game. Pirates won forty-nine to thirty-seven.'

'You up there one day, Jim-Jam!' Chico punched Jamie's shoulder. Jamie curled his lip into a modest smile. 'No, I mean it. You're good, man, and you know it; just don't want to brag.'

'We're not doing so good at the moment,' Jamie reminded him.

'Be easy. You're just finding your top form, and when you do, it's all over.'

Jeroo winked at Chico. 'He gets the girls though. *Real* mack-daddy.'

22

Jamie mimed. 'Who, *me*?'

'Yeah, you.' Jeroo drained his Coke. 'She's always givin' you itty-bitty looks outa the side of her eyes.'

'And who is this?'

Jeroo mimicked Jamie. '*Who is this?* As if you didn't know, man. Carol Masters is all over you. She is the number one fan in the Jamie MacD Appreciation Society and she wants to claim her prize.'

Jamie swirled the remaining liquid in the bottle. 'Your imagination is almost as big as your ass.'

'OK. Don't believe me.' Jeroo fumbled inside his bag for his cellphone and punched some keys.

'What are you doing? C'mon, man . . .'

Jeroo put his finger to his lips. 'Shhh, she's on the line.'

Jamie groaned and held his head in his hands.

'Yo, Carol? Yeah. That's right; it's me, Jeroo – the Big J that ends in an "oooh"? No, hang on. Just hang on in there a moment, hear me out, huh? Yeah, I'm not calling for *me*. Nope. Someone else wants a word – urgently. Another Big J. Yeah, he's standing right by me.' Jeroo grinned. He put his hand over the phone and mouthed, 'She's hooked. I can tell.' He put the phone back to his ear. 'You got a minute, 'cos if not maybe he'll call you later, but who knows when.' Jeroo held out the cell. 'Signed, sealed and delivered.'

Jamie shook his head, reluctantly took the phone and glared at Jeroo.

'Hey, what's up? Yeah. I know, Jeroo's crazy. What? No, it's not like that either. Sure I'd like to talk, but we're 'bout to get into somethin' so I'll have to catch you later. When? Well, I don't know. Tomorrow? OK. Later.'

Jeroo grinned as he took the phone back. 'Just call me your fairy godmother.'

Jamie sucked gloomily at his soda. He wished Jeroo wouldn't push him into things he didn't want to be pushed into. He could handle his own love life. *Love life?* Huh, that was one big joke. Not much action coming his way recently. Not *any* action to be honest, except a fumble after the prom with – what was her name? He couldn't even remember. Lucille, maybe?

Carol was nice. Really nice. Too nice, he guessed, with a religious dad breathing down her neck. A pastor or something. Try anything and the heavens would part and the wrath of God would rain down on you.

He looked over at his friends, who were whispering together and laughing. They thought he was on it all the time, a lover boy. But they were the ones always shooting their mouths off about how much they were getting. *She's wild for me. Can't wait to get her top off. Didn't see any No Entry sign.*

Truth be told, they were probably all in the same boat – dreaming, and sinking fast.

4

Joshua Tree

The white Subaru SUV sped along the Valley Interstate 10. Its green and purple pennant – the colours of the Aeronautical Department – fluttered in the breeze.

Jamie snuck a look at his dad, his face set, eyes trained steadily on the road. This had come as a bit of a surprise: his dad's sudden invitation for a weekend trip to the desert, delivered gruffly, almost offhand. It wasn't a terrific surprise either. To be honest, Jamie had been looking forward to hanging out with his buds. Chico had downloaded some tracks, which he said were amazing. But given the showdown at the den and a recent very average set of grades, Jamie reckoned he was in no position to refuse.

Predictably, his dad had drawn up a long list of supplies and provisions, methodically checked them off, then stowed them in the trunk and on the back seats. Everything he did was always assessed and itemized. Jamie guessed it came from his job. You couldn't be a few parts short when you were testing an aeroplane.

His father caught the look. 'OK?'

'Sure.'

Jamie punched on the radio and scanned through the channels. He found a hip-hop station and mouthed along to *Jump In It*.

The mountains were shimmering in the heat as they turned off the I-10 onto a narrow, twisting road and began to climb. There was little sign of any habitation. A stone slab in the scrub ahead read WELCOME TO JOSHUA TREE NATIONAL PARK. Jamie stifled a sigh. It was going to be a long two days.

Jeroo held his hands clamped over the earphones and swayed.

'Wow,' he shouted. 'North Star are awesome.'

'What'd I tell you?' said Chico. 'Ain't they the bomb?'

The rest of the gang were sprawled in Chico's room in The Valley. Mrs Lopez had brought them in a dish of fiery home-made salsa and Doritos, which they dipped and munched contentedly.

'Something else . . .' said Jeroo, unplugging the earphones. 'They just get better.'

Chico was flipping through *LA Weekly*. 'They got a gig at the House of Blues comin' up.' He sighed. 'Which we are gonna miss. *Fifty dollars.*' He whistled. 'How come it's only old people who got money? You know, real old guys around thirty or more? What they need bucks for? Should be the other way round. It's young guys like us that really need the big cheese.'

'I wish I was loaded,' said Lester. 'I'd go to all the big gigs, flash my triple-A backstage pass and get to meet with all the big stars. Get invites back to their mansions and swim in their infinity pools.'

'You can't swim,' Chico pointed out.

'You don't have to swim, you just kinda crouch in the water sipping margaritas.'

'I'd get my own band,' said Jeroo. He jumped up, snatched a battered old squash racket from the wall and began to play air guitar. 'I'd buy me a Fender Stratocaster, butterscotch blond, and take lead.' He arched his body and reached for a painfully high chord. 'Lester, you could play bass.'

Lester shook his head. 'I can't even play *Cranium.*'

'Bass is no big deal,' said Jeroo, who was leaning back, throttling the racket. 'It's only got four strings. Chico could be on the kit, and Jimbo could take vocals since no one else can hold a tune.'

Lester pulled a face. 'These days you don't need to be able to sing. Just gotta do the rap and make with the movements . . . The chicks go wild for it.'

Jeroo stopped playing and rubbed his nose. 'Wonder how he's doing? You know, Jimbo and' – he paused, looked around in mock terror and whispered – 'his dad?'

'Oh, Jeez,' cried Chico, pounding the bed. 'All alone in the desert with Crazy Chief!'

Jeroo slung the racket over his shoulder and strutted around the room. 'Bet he's got him on a route march under the burning sun. Carrying one sixty pounds and no water.'

Lester crawled painfully over towards the salsa dish and collapsed. 'They'll find the bones,' he croaked, 'picked over by vultures.'

The boys contemplated Jamie's awful fate for a while and Chico shuddered. They all burst out laughing.

They parked the Subaru by a trailhead, and pitched the small tent. Next to a primitive latrine, a faded map was trapped behind a pane of dusty glass, and a dotted line indicated the 'Hidden Palm Trail'. Some printed copies were stored in a box underneath. Jamie took a sheet and sighed. Does Dad really believe in this? he wondered.

His father applied sunscreen liberally over his face and arms and they loaded up the packs. They set out on the broad track, but it quickly narrowed into a steep and obscure path that wound between immense boulders. Here and there sprouted the spiky, twisted Joshua trees that were only to be found in this high desert area which gave the park its name. Jamie remembered that U2 had an album called *Joshua Tree* and made a mental note to download it when he got back. He wished he had some music now, but there was only the sound of his own laboured breathing, and the hiss of wind through the canyon scrub.

The sun was strong in an intense blue sky and they stopped frequently to sip water from their packs. Few words were exchanged. Jamie's dad drew gradually ahead, instinctively taking the lead as they emerged onto a broad rocky slope leading to a distant ridge. He was in pretty good shape, Jamie had to admit. But then he worked at it: the careful diet that drove Marcia mad, the punishing sessions at the gym. He'd even come in the top ten in the tough Iron Man triathlon at Camp Pendleton.

Jamie stopped, wiped his brow with his sleeve and looked around. His father continued to climb with steady strides. Jamie fished out the map from his shirt pocket and consulted it. He shook his head.

'Hey, Dad,' he yelled.

His father continued to climb upwards.

'Dad! Wait up.' Jamie waved the map.

His father stopped and turned. He indicated the high ridge and made to move on.

Jamie pointed to a distant cluster of huge boulders far away to his left. 'I think it's this way,' he shouted.

His dad shook his head vigorously. 'No, must be up here.'

There was a stalemate; both pointing in different directions, neither willing to budge. Finally his father turned and plodded back. They pored over Jamie's map.

'Look, son, it's perfectly clear. We're around here.' He

jabbed a finger at the map. 'So we have to head up there towards the ridge . . .'

'No way, Dad. We are *here*, and it ain't a ridge we're heading for, it's those boulders. The track goes left across that slope.' Jamie shaded his eyes. 'Fact, I think I can see a waymark.'

'That's never a waymark. It's a dead tree.'

'Bull, Dad.'

His father sighed. 'OK, have it your own way. But I think you'll find you're mistaken.'

Jamie now led on a transverse path, picking his way through the rough scree. The tree *was* a waymark and it pointed towards the giant boulders. His dad muttered occasionally in dissent but Jamie, consulting his map, headed for a narrow fissure in the rock ahead. He squeezed through.

The palm oasis, cradled deep within the nest of boulders, suddenly revealed itself. Jamie's eyes widened in delight. 'Wow!'

His father, breathing heavily, swung his pack to the ground and rubbed the back of his neck. He looked up at the towering palms. 'Dear Lord,' he gasped. Then he added, 'Funny. Could have sworn it was over that ridge. Maybe . . . ?' He caught Jamie's eye and smiled ruefully. 'Oops, guess I goofed. No Brownie points there.'

Jamie turned away to hide his smile of satisfaction. So Dad wasn't always right; the great chieftain *could* lead his men in the wrong direction.

They settled beside a green pool, where iridescent dragonflies darted over the still water and an unseen toad croaked. They ate their sandwiches greedily.

When he had finished, Jamie leaned back against the trunk of a palm and closed his eyes. 'It's so quiet. You can hear the silence.'

The air erupted as a jet fighter suddenly roared low overhead and banked away to the south. Jamie flinched at the unexpected intrusion.

'Jeez. What was that?'

His dad, shading his eyes, checked the plane with interest. 'Navy. We test down here too. There's a corridor from Mohave.'

'Was that it – the new model?'

'Eh? Oh.' He shook his head. 'No.'

Jamie persevered. 'So how's it going?'

'The X-Twenty? Oh, fine. Just fine.' There was a long pause until his father sensed that maybe more in the way of conversation was expected. He cleared his throat. 'Well, it's not a piece of cake. We're nearly there, but before they'll give us its airworthiness certificate, they put it through all the hoops. There's so many checks and double checks, then all the testing they demand, the documentation.' He chuckled grimly. 'Drives you mad.'

Jamie clasped his knees. 'Guess they have to be safe. I mean, anything new . . .'

'Oh aye. That's true enough.' His father examined his nails.

'Is it – is *she* . . . neat?' Jamie ventured.

'Neat?' His dad tasted the word. He caught Jamie's gaze and held it. 'No, son. She is *beautiful.* You know, like a free spirit? Like something you haven't built, just released. Like ... Oh, I don't know ...' He looked away, embarrassed.

'A bird?'

'Eh?' His father swung round. Then he nodded vigorously. 'Just so. That's it exactly. A fine, wild bird.'

They spent some time by the pool, watching the water beetles skipping across the surface and trying, unsuccessfully, to locate the toad. By the time they returned to their camp and lit a fire, a vast and spectacular sunset was fading in the sky. Bats darted among the boulders and in the distance coyotes howled. Later, Jamie retrieved a couple of blackened potatoes and juggled them from hand to hand. He gave one to his dad, who blew on it. They settled back against the SUV and began to eat.

'Was this Mom's idea?'

His father was taken aback. 'What? No! I just ...' He glanced at Jamie and nodded ruefully. 'Well ... I suppose so. She's so good at these things. What does she tell her clients? Building relationships. That's it.' He wiped his nose with the back of his hand. 'I'm lousy at it. But then I ... er ... I never had much practice. Leaving home and suchlike ...'

'How old were you?'

''Bout eighteen when I went to college, and then there was the scholarship and I never really went back.'

Jamie was intrigued. 'What did your parents say?'

His dad swallowed a mouthful. 'Oh, Father was OK. No, it was my mother. Eleanor.'

'She wasn't pleased?'

'*Pleased?* She took to her bed – for a month. Couldn't believe that her son and heir would not stay in Doran and tend the sheep. She just didn't get it. Or understand that I wanted another life, a career.'

Jamie went to the fire and brought back two scorched chicken drumsticks.

'Real dump of a place, huh?'

His father shook his head vigorously as he reached for the meat. 'Oh no, Jamie. The island of Doran is the most beautiful place I know. My mother, quite understandably, thought I was crazy to want to leave.'

'She bawl you out?'

His dad threw back his head and his laughter echoed around the rocks. Jamie thought that he hadn't heard him laugh for a long while.

'No. Bawling is not her style. Eleanor – your grandmother – is . . .' He searched for a suitable adjective. 'She is . . . the Return of the Ice Age! The Big Freeze. She didn't speak to me, wouldn't answer letters. I was deleted from her life. She even told people that her son was dead.'

Jamie was shocked. 'That is so sick! But when you became chief . . . ?'

'Of course, when Father died they tracked me down. They had to. But not her. Whenever I've been back, she hardly appears. She's never asked anything, never been interested to know about—'

''Bout us?'

Jamie's dad discarded a piece of burned chicken skin. 'No. Nothing.'

33

'So why do you still bother? All the work you put in for the clan? All that yelling on the phone? Mom says they're driving you crazy.'

His father laughed again. He munched at the drumstick, the grease glistening on his lips and chin.

'The Scottish clans go back to medieval times and are the backbone of the nation. There's a huge weight of history there, son, which you can't just opt out of. I am Clan Chieftain and that means I have the responsibility – even from afar. I have to know what's going on.'

'So is everyone on the island a clan member?'

His father shook his head. 'Not all of them, no. And that's part of the problem. You've got the pure-blooded clan descendants, the MacDorans, who can trace their family line back for centuries. Then there are many islanders who have looser connections, and others who came from the mainland to make their home there. They view things differently. And of course, some of the young people see no future on Doran and can't wait to leave. As I couldn't. Things are changing, and not always for the better.' He gave a sigh. 'There is a lot of trouble brewing and I will have to go over soon and bang some heads together to make them see sense.'

Jamie tried to suppress a grin.

His dad looked at him sharply. 'What? Oh, yeah. I suppose you think I was a bit heavy-handed – with your pals.'

'No, you were right, it was a dumb thing—'

'Jamie, it's hard to explain, but although I left Doran all those years ago, it is still with me. In my eyes, in my mind, in my heart. Every day. Course I care for Mum and I care for you, although you can't always tell – but I also care for Doran and the clan.'

He wiped his fingers on his jeans and struggled to his feet. For a moment he stood and stared at the fire, then gave it a kick with his boot.

'Did you know, Jamie, the Gaelic word for "clan" also means "children" or "family"? And, like many children and families, they don't always get on. A lot of bickering and fighting.' He looked back over his shoulder with a mischievous glint in his eye. 'But, as you can see, they're stuck with each other.'

5

Winning and Losing

The school band was swinging their version of *Only Got Eyes for You*, to which the Uni-Versals were performing their synchronized baton routine. As Jamie went through his warm-up exercises, he noticed Carol Masters in fishnets and sequins among the majorettes – fiercely counting the beats and twirling her baton. Jamie wondered if they might be able to hook up after the game. If he was going to get anywhere, he would have to make a move on her soon.

The Martin Luther King Sports Hall was filling rapidly. The Inter-school Basketball Championship always drew a big crowd, and the rivalry between

University High and Martin Luther was long-standing and intense. Jamie and his team kept themselves to one side of the hall, and the Martin Luther boys the other. Despite a feigned nonchalance, both were keenly checking out the opposition.

Jeroo was retying his laces for the fifth time. He gave a giant belch.

Jamie grimaced. 'Thanks for sharing that.'

Jeroo nodded. 'I know. I wish I hadn't eaten those chicken nuggets, but I was starving . . . It's gotta be the stress.'

The band and the Uni-Versals ended their number with a flourish. There was sparse applause and as the majorettes came hurrying by, Carol Masters gave Jamie a shy wave. 'Good luck,' she whispered.

Jamie stripped off his fleece and rubbed his arms vigorously. He looked up and saw his mother picking her way across a row of seats. She spotted him and waved. Too far away for conversation, she mouthed, 'Have you seen Dad yet?'

Jamie shook his head and mouthed back, 'Not with you?'

His mom shook her head and sat, putting her bag on the next chair to save Jamie's dad a seat.

Jamie gave her a thumbs-up.

Jeroo grabbed Jamie's arm and pointed across the court. 'Ain't that Rob Lewis? He the one you gotta beat.' He gave Jamie an anxious glance. 'You OK, Jimbo?'

'No, really freaked out, man.'

Jeroo held him by the shoulders. There was panic in

his eyes. 'Oh no. Please don't say that. Go, go, Jimbo. You the man.'

It was a tough match. The University High team cruised to a ten-point lead in the first quarter and maintained their stranglehold on the game by going into the end of the first half 44 to 19 up. In the locker room Coach Adams praised their defence. 'You guys kept a real tenacious pressure on the ball with good man-to-man defence. Jeroo, you were really in there, man.'

In the second half, Martin Luther upped the pressure, bringing the score almost level. The final quarter saw Jamie get into his stride, initiating a series of breaks and scoring a string of baskets. With seconds on the clock, Jeroo snuck an amazing pass to Jamie, who leaped high against Rob Lewis to pop in an impossible basket, clinching a tight but indisputable victory.

The Uni supporters went wild, and Jeroo bounded across the court to Jamie. They high-fived and the team ran a circuit of honour, holding the trophy aloft. Jamie searched for his parents, and saw his mom applauding wildly. Her bag was still beside her on the empty seat.

By the time the players had showered and changed, there was a small crowd waiting for them outside the sports hall. They came out to a cheer and a smattering of applause.

One of the parents shouted, 'Good job, guys. Nice game, Jamie.'

Carol Masters was with a group of the girls, whispering together. Della Reeves broke away and confronted Jamie.

'Hail the conquering hero,' she said, and planted a sloppy wet kiss. 'Oops. I'm so sorry, Carol. I clear forgot you had him tagged.'

Jamie smiled and wiped his face with his sleeve. 'Hi, Carol. Did you watch the game?' He groaned inwardly. What a stupid question.

Carol looked down. 'Sure, I watched it. You done good, Jamie.'

Jeroo jumped in. 'Course it was teamwork. That's the secret. Eh, Jamie? Planning, strategy, backup and . . .' The sudden chatter of a helicopter, circling low, drowned the rest of his words. Jeroo shook a fist at the sky and yelled. 'Will you ged-outa-here?'

They all left together, the guys on the team, some of the cheerleaders, and Jamie with Carol at his side. It seemed like a real beginning.

Jamie came in the door, flung his sports bag on the chair and switched on the TV in the lounge.

He yelled, 'Mom? You back?'

There was no reply so he walked through to the kitchen, grabbing an apple from the dish. He munched it as he picked up a newspaper and flicked through the sports pages.

The TV was talking to itself in the lounge.

'. . . *on the freeway. Six vehicles were involved and the emergency services have been working nonstop to reach the victims. Heavy cutting apparatus has been brought in . . .*'

Jamie gradually locked onto the news item. He squinted through the serving hatch and walked slowly

39

back into the lounge, nibbling round the apple core as he approached the TV.

'*Engines from five districts have mobilized, and paramedics are tending to those still trapped . . .*'

On the screen, above a flashing banner proclaiming 'Breaking News', was a helicopter view of a multiple freeway pile-up, with an assortment of vehicles in a heap of smoking wreckage. The camera zoomed in on a sliced Chevy, a blackened pickup – and a wrecked white Subaru SUV with a green and purple pennant.

The front door flew open and Jamie's mom stumbled in, carrying a bag of groceries and a pile of papers. She had the house keys clamped in her mouth.

'Hi, Champ! I tell you, the traffic out there is an absolute nightmare. I don't know what's going on.' She dumped her things on the table and pocketed the keys. 'Did Dad call? I tried him, but there was no answer. I guess he . . .'

She trailed off as she caught Jamie's expression.

'What?' She stared at the screen, uncomprehendingly. '*Jamie?*'

The doctors tried their best to save James MacDoran, but Jamie's father died on the operating table. Jamie wasn't sure if he wanted to see the body, and his mom said that whatever he decided would be OK.

He finally went in and spent a few moments alone beside the sheeted figure and the pale, exposed face. They hadn't been able to disguise the jagged wounds completely, but his eyes were closed and peaceful. Jamie thought somehow it wasn't much like his dad. He reached out and uncovered his father's hand, noticing pale bands where his wedding ring and watch had been removed.

His mom spent much longer in the room, and Jamie could hear her sobbing and talking softly. When she came out, they clung to one another, not knowing what to say.

A nurse finally approached. She carried a battered briefcase and a plastic folder with his father's ring, watch, credit cards, a few dollars, his BlackBerry, Moleskine diary and two pens. She placed a comforting hand on each of their shoulders and asked Marcia to sign for the items. She asked if there was anything she could do, if there was anything they needed. Jamie took the folder and shook his head.

They stood together, dazed and frozen in the busy reception area, with streams of people flowing past them in a noisy torrent of life.

Jamie heard the insistent ring tone first. There were other phones on the main desk calling in shrill harmony, but the distinctive strains of *Scotland the Brave* were unmistakable. He tore open the folder and answered his father's cell. The voice was distant and sounded aggrieved.

'James? Look, I'm awful sorry, and I hope it's not inconvenient. Did you no' get my messages?'

Jamie tried to collect his thoughts. 'Er . . . look, excuse me, but—'

'Well, never mind. You see, things are bad. Will

you be able to come as you promised? You're needed urgently.'

His mom was looking at him questioningly. Jamie put his hand over the mouthpiece. 'It's them, I think. The clan.'

'Are you there? James?'

His mother shook her head angrily. 'Tell them . . . no, I'll do it . . .'

She snatched the phone. 'This is Mrs MacDoran. This isn't . . . I'm afraid . . . I have to tell you my husband has just been . . . in an accident . . .'

'James? Oh my God. Is he all right . . . ?'

She took a deep breath. 'I'm afraid not. James is dead, Mr . . . Mr . . . ?'

'Angus, this is Angus MacDoran. I, er, I am so shocked. Oh, dear Lord, I don't know what to say . . .'

'Yes, and I'm sure you'll understand I can't speak now, Angus. I will call you, after, you know, after the cremation and—'

The Scottish voice was suddenly strong and decisive. 'Oh no. There can be no question o' *that*. The funeral will be here.'

She passed a hand over her eyes. 'Excuse me?'

'He is the chieftain. He must be buried here . . . laid to rest with his kith and kin . . . his own people.'

6

Land of the Brave

Jamie curled up on a purple seat in the transit lounge and punched his cellphone. He heard the ringing tone, then Jeroo's voice: '*Hi, friends and foes. This is Jeroo – the Big J that ends in an "oooh". Can't talk now 'cos I'm doin' something much more important, but you can leave a message or a text. Or money.*'

Jamie pulled a face. 'This is Jamie, dumbhead. I wish you'd change that stupid message. I guess you're getting your beauty sleep – which I have to tell you sure ain't working! I can't quite figure out the time difference – eight hours or something – or who's ahead of who. Anyhow, I'm in London, England, can you believe it?

Well, the airport anyway, which I guess is pretty far out, 'cos I don't see any old buildings. In fact, couldn't see *nothin'* as we came in – just a load of cloud and then . . . hang on, my mom is talkin' to me.'

Marcia was gesticulating and whispering, 'Do you know what international calls cost?' and Jamie put his hand over the cell.

'I know, Mom, I'm just leaving a message. I'm nearly done.' He turned away. 'Sorry 'bout that, she's pretty nervy, makin' this trip an' all, and now we gotta change planes and fly up to Scotland. Hey, Land of the Brave! Hope you're OK, and thanks for the nice things you said about my dad. Appreciate it. Tell the rest "hi". I'll keep in touch.' He punched out.

It was raining as the 737 touched down on the tarmac of Glasgow airport. Through the streaming cabin window Jamie glimpsed housing estates and dark surrounding hills shrouded in mist. Marcia's grey suit and Jamie's dark zip-jacket and khaki chinos were appropriate in LA, but now they both shivered as they stood in the bus taking them to the terminal.

They had gone through immigration in London, so there was no delay in spilling out with the other passengers into the arrivals hall. Jamie pushed the trolley loaded with their bags – and the skateboard he had insisted on bringing along. (His mom had tried to dissuade him: 'It's not suitable for a funeral, and anyhow we won't be there long enough for you to use it.') They scanned the expectant line of people, some holding up name cards, who were meeting the flight.

There was a large crowd of rugby supporters with flags; there were families, cab drivers and a separate group of three – an old man with flowing white hair and beard, a small dark man in a greasy raincoat and a teenage girl, clutching a set of bagpipes. The three watched the arriving passengers intently.

Jamie and his mom came to the end of the line and stopped. Marcia checked her watch. 'So where are they?'

Jamie shook his head. 'Maybe they got delayed. What do we do?'

'What *can* we do? Wait, I suppose.' She dragged one of the cases off the trolley and sat down on it.

The last passengers, mostly businessmen, filed into the hall and were collected by their drivers. The rugby team came through noisily. There were some cheers and flag-waving and flashes as photos were taken. The old man and his companions continued to scan each new arrival but eventually there were no more. Only Jamie, his mom and the small group remained.

There was brief eye-contact and some urgent whispering between the three. Marcia gave a tentative smile and mouthed, 'MacDoran?'

The group stared at them in silence. They seemed to have been struck dumb. Finally the bearded old man gave the girl a dig with his elbow and muttered something under his breath. The girl placed the reed of the bagpipes between her lips and blew hard. A terrible strangled sound escaped from the pipes. She looked mortified, but gradually a recognizably doleful tune

45

emerged. The two groups approached each other warily.

The old man extended a bony hand. 'I . . . er . . . ?'

Jamie's mother ventured, 'Angus?' His hand looked pale against her dark skin.

'Aye. And you'll be . . . ?'

'Marcia. And this is my boy. Jamie MacDoran.'

The reed dropped from the girl's mouth. The pipes deflated with a terrifying noise like an expiring chicken.

Jamie attempted a wave and his biggest drop-'em-dead grin. 'Hi, guys.'

Angus pressed a monocle into one bloodshot eye, which, grossly magnified, skittered around in panic.

'Oh my G—' He collected himself with an immense effort. 'My goodness. I cannae imagine how we missed ye. Well, er, here we are then. I am Angus, er, MacDoran and this lassie is my great-niece Hazel, and this, er . . . where the devil is he?'

The small man in the greasy raincoat darted forward from behind the pair. He attempted a small bow. 'I am Murdo McMurdo. An islander. At your service.' He fished into a raincoat pocket for an equally grubby cap, which he rammed on his head. 'Allow me to take your luggage.' He took hold of the two suitcases and eyed Jamie's skateboard with suspicion before tucking it under his arm. 'Is this all . . . ?'

Marcia nodded and then understood. 'Oh, well . . . No, of course, there is . . .' She indicated vaguely.

Angus looked relieved. 'Oh, yes. Himself. Murdo will see to it. We have the, um, necessary transportation. Now, if you'll just come with me . . .'

Jamie smiled at Hazel, but she was anxiously trying to gather up the bagpipes.

Jamie had never been in such an old car. 'Wolseley' it read on the battered and much re-sprayed hood. When they settled inside it creaked like an ancient bed. Marcia sat in front. She had tried to enter through the right-hand door but was surprised to find the steering wheel there. With a sudden pang she remembered James telling her that Britain was one of the few countries that still drove on the left side of the road.

Jamie and Hazel shared the back seat, the bagpipes placed firmly between them. Angus positioned himself behind the wheel.

If the Wolseley was old, the ancient Rolls-Royce carrying the draped coffin of James MacDoran looked as though it was on loan from a museum. It would only agree to start after repeated attempts, much pedal-pumping from Murdo and thunderous explosions from the exhaust.

The curious procession nosed its way through the airport traffic and headed north. Before long the neat suburban townhouses dropped away and they were on a road that wound between brooding mountains.

In the Wolseley they travelled in silence. Angus drove with intense concentration, swerving each time another car passed him. He changed gear frequently and gratingly as he muttered under his breath. He obviously didn't drive very often.

Marcia peered out of the window. The weather had

closed in again and there was rain in the air. 'Well, it's certainly very . . . er . . .' A suitable word did not immediately present itself. 'Wild?' she ended lamely.

'Eh?' Angus took his eye off the road and the car swerved dangerously. 'What? Wild? Oh aye. You could say that.'

He crashed the gears noisily and there was silence for a few more miles. Then, with much throat-clearing and muttering, Angus asked, 'Your journey. Was it verra long?'

Marcia nodded. 'Oh, it was. But I guess the worst thing is the change in the time zones, don't you agree?'

Angus shot her a bemused glance, and the car swerved again. 'Aye. Fancy.'

Jamie stole a look at Hazel, who was staring moodily out of her window. The bagpipes lay between them like a barrier. She was a clear-eyed, tomboyish girl of about fourteen with tangled auburn hair and a swarm of light freckles across her nose. She wore a T-shirt with '*BLUR: The European Tour*' on it, but the worn jacket and jeans had seen better days.

A sheep with two small lambs skittered away in fright as they passed and Jamie pointed them out, leaning over and laughing. 'They are so cute.'

Hazel turned to him, unsmiling. 'Will you mind the pipes, by the way?'

'What? Oh, yeah.' Jamie patted the bagpipes affectionately. 'Sorry, fellas.' He looked up at Hazel. 'Are these critters dead, or just playing possum?'

Hazel stared witheringly at him and once more gazed out of her window.

As they climbed higher, the mist and rain swept across the road, obscuring the view.

The Rolls-Royce, carrying the draped coffin and emitting occasional explosive reports from its rear, laboured to keep up. At its wheel, Murdo was talking animatedly with frequent glances into the rear-view mirror. 'She'll have a fit. You know what she's like at the best of times. A right Bessie. Or mebbe you've forgot, Chief? It's been that long since you were here. And why were you *no'* here?' he added accusingly. 'And why must you be returning like this . . . just when we needed you so bad? Just when we're in our darkest hour . . . and you, who could have saved us . . .' Tears welled in his eyes and he stared into the mirror. 'I tell you, James, it's no' right . . .'

Jamie became aware of a car horn blaring insistently from behind.

Angus gave a little cry: 'What the devil . . . ?' and tried to look behind him. The car veered towards the side of the road. 'Is it that wretched Murdo?' he shouted.

Jamie squinted out of the back window. 'No, I think some other guy is trying to pass. He's sure in some big hurry.'

Angus fought with the wheel, muttering, 'No respect. No respect.'

Murdo had wound down his window and was yelling into the wind, 'Will ye haud your wheesht? Och, you'll have us all in the mire.'

But the driver of the yellow Porsche, a fair-haired,

thin-lipped man in his late twenties, took no notice. Wearing Oakley sunglasses and gripping the wheel with one gloved hand, he was talking animatedly into a cellphone. He drew alongside the Rolls, forcing it to scrape the low bushes at the side of the road. With a burst of power, he forced his way past the two vehicles. The Porsche roared away into the gloom.

Jamie was impressed. 'Who was that?'

Angus and Hazel exchanged glances. 'A road hog,' she said.

Jamie whistled. 'Those are some pretty fancy wheels he's got there. I didn't think . . .' He paused.

Hazel faced him coolly. 'What? That folk round here could afford one of them?' She nodded and turned away. 'Aye, you're right – we cannae.'

Murdo continued his one-sided conversation in the mirror. He waved his arms agitatedly. 'Well, there y'are! Did you see that? That is what you're up against. Mister Duncan high-and-mighty Wylie. He's no friend o' Doran, do y' ken? He'll as soon slip the knife between your shoulder blades as shake your hand. You'll need to keep a sharp eye on that one . . .'

Jamie felt suddenly tired and his eyes were closing. The car hit a pothole in the road, Angus swore and Jamie jerked awake. He peered through the window. Through gaps in the clouds he could see vast sheets of water gleaming far beneath them.

'Gee, a lot of lakes . . .'

Hazel sighed. 'Lochs.'

'Excuse me?'

'They're called lochs.'

'You don't say? Well, a loch of lochs then!' No response. He crooked two fingers. 'A joke?'

Hazel looked at him pityingly.

Jamie settled back in his seat. 'Well, I guess we should be getting close.'

'You'll know when you're there,' she said.

7

Doran

Jamie was walking through a vast, hot desert, looking for something. A huge bird flew by, and his dad was sitting astride it, wearing an antique leather aviator's cap and steering it skilfully with his knees. He looked down at Jamie, and smiled and waved. Jamie wanted so badly to tell him something, only the bird flew on before the words would come. He was thirsty and his lips were parched and a fierce sun beat down on him ...

There was a jolt. Jamie opened his eyes, shielding them with his hand from the glare. He sat bolt upright and looked around. 'Hey!' he said as he pulled open the car door and leaped out onto the quay.

The weather had changed dramatically, and before him in all its splendour lay the Kyle of Doran, a magnificent sweep of open blue ocean sparkling in the bright sunlight. A fish jumped high into the air with a flash of silver. Jamie ran to the water's edge and stood there, speechless. Gulls wheeled and cried before him, and in the far distance he could just make out the rugged outline of a distant island.

'Are you away in a dwalm?'

Hazel was looking at him quizzically, with Angus and Marcia waiting behind. Murdo had parked the Rolls and was wiping his face with an oily rag. Beside it was the yellow Porsche, and to one side the coffin was resting on the quay, draped in the cloth that bore the emblem of the Clan MacDoran – a pair of clasped hands. His dad's words suddenly came back to Jamie, like a blow.

'*Although I left Doran all those years ago, it is still with me. In my eyes, in my mind, in my heart . . . I will have to go over soon and bang some heads together . . .*'

And this was his return. The final return. In a box.

'We need to board.' Hazel indicated a small ferryboat tied up at the quayside. It looked old and decidedly unseaworthy. On deck a couple of island lads wearing knitted jerseys stared at the group.

Murdo removed his driver's cap and put on another, more nautical, piece of headgear. He was obviously the ferry captain too. He tried another little bow. 'If you'll come this way, we'll see to the loading.'

The sudden roar of a powerful engine drowned his words, and a sleek yellow speedboat arced across the water, creating a huge, creamy wake. Suspended above the stern was a miniature submarine in the same canary colour. As it approached the jetty, the engine was cut and the bow settled back into the water. The blond, thin-lipped driver from the Porsche appeared and tossed a rope to the lads. He jumped nimbly onto the quay and swept off the sunglasses. His eyes were startlingly blue.

'My apologies for not meeting you at the airport. I was absolutely devastated to have just missed you.' He gave the coffin a quick glance. 'And, of course, my sincerest condolences. A terrible shock and a grievous loss . . . to us all.'

Marcia held out her hand. 'Thank you. I am Marcia and this is Jamie.'

'Oh my goodness, how rude you must think me. I am Duncan, Duncan Wylie of Doran.' Duncan pumped her hand vigorously. 'How good of you to be with us when all looks so . . . black . . .' There was an exchange of glances. 'Er . . . bleak, I might say.'

She withdrew her hand. 'I think we should probably get on board.'

'Of course, you must be exhausted. But I can't possibly allow you to cross in that leaky old tub.'

Murdo bristled, and was about to say something when Duncan took Jamie and Marcia by the arm. 'No, please allow me to transport you in some comfort. The others will follow with your things.'

They looked at Angus, who shrugged. 'Aye. Ye may as well.'

Duncan beamed and turned to Jamie. 'Now, young

man. I imagine you know a thing or two about marine craft . . . ?'

Jamie nodded. 'Well, sure . . . I live near the ocean. I do a load of surfing . . .'

Duncan raised an eyebrow. 'Indeed? I am impressed. Do you know, that is one thing I've always longed to try . . .'

The ferry slowly chugged its way across the water towards the Isle of Doran. Around the ferry, like a herding sheepdog, Duncan's speedboat roared in wide circles, casting impressive arcs of spray. Jamie watched in admiration as Duncan expertly handled the controls; Marcia, huddled in the rear, made vague noises of protest.

'Neat boat,' Jamie shouted against the wind. Duncan nodded. Jamie pointed to the miniature sub. 'Say, is that for real?'

Duncan grinned. 'Naturally. Made to my own design, and she'll dive to three hundred feet. Only room for one, I'm afraid.' He throttled back and let the engine idle. He looked at Jamie. 'Feel like having a go?'

Jamie hesitated. He could see the draped coffin on the ferry's deck, and he suddenly felt disloyal not to be accompanying it, standing watch over his father on his last slow journey to the island. And yet . . .

'Sure. What do I have to do?'

He positioned himself behind the wheel and Duncan explained the controls. 'Nothing to it,' he said. 'Only try not to bump into Angus. He gets upset so easily.'

Jamie gently eased the boat forward, feeling the power surging from the engine. He placed the ferry ahead and to his left and made a test run, parallel to it. Duncan nodded approvingly.

'Good. Very good indeed. I can see you're a natural.'

'And to throttle back?'

'Here.'

'Ah. This is so cool.'

His mother's voice came faintly from behind. 'Jamie. Could you maybe . . . ?'

'Sure thing, Mom.' He turned to Duncan and lowered his voice. 'How fast can she go?'

Duncan shook his head and whispered, 'I have no idea. Shall we find out?'

The speedboat leaped forward, its bow smacking the waves and then rising clear from the water. Jamie swung the wheel and raced across the bows of the ferry.

Murdo, his cap dripping with spray, wrestled with the wheel as the speedboat wake rocked the vessel. Angus and Hazel were thrown to one side.

'Oaf!' yelled Murdo, shaking his fist at Duncan. 'Thundering egregious bauchle!'

Jamie reduced speed and the bows settled back into the ocean. 'That was a-ma-zing. I reckon we were doing fifty . . . sixty?'

Duncan nodded. 'Mmm. Quite possibly.'

Intent on mastering the controls, Jamie had not noticed that they were fast approaching the island. A rugged shoreline with small sandy coves now presented itself. In the interior rose large hills, and behind them, a range of dark, distant mountains. At first it seemed un-inhabited, but as they neared the coast, Jamie could make out small dwellings, built from the same grey stone as the surroundings. Duncan took the wheel and they passed parallel to the shore.

Jamie suddenly pointed. 'Hey! Is that the castle?' He indicated an elegant stone building with its own jetty and small harbour. A satellite dish and various antennae sprouted from the roof.

Duncan peered ahead. 'Where? Oh, no.' He gave a modest smile. 'Actually, that's my pad. My family, Jamie, have been on Doran for centuries, and I've recently done the place up. The castle is . . . well . . . a little more *worn*. Look, over there.'

As they rounded the next headland, a harbour came into view overlooked by a large, turreted stone building. About its buttressed walls nestled a sprawling village running down to the water, with low houses built out of the same stone. Duncan nosed the yellow craft towards the jetty, at which a few old and rusted fishing boats were moored.

Jamie gazed up at the castle, which on closer inspection seemed in urgent need of repair. 'So that is where the chief hangs out?'

Duncan smiled. 'Welcome to Doran,' he said.

It took a while for the ferry to dock, and the sun was already dipping behind the mountains by the time they were all assembled on the quay to watch the lads carry the coffin gently onto land. By now a large group of islanders had formed and were watching from a respectful distance. Their faces were impassive, and some clutched babies or faded baseball caps.

Duncan fetched a couple of bags from his boat and approached Marcia. His eyes searched her face. 'I am sorry that your first visit to Doran has to be in such sad circumstances, but I assure you that you are both very welcome. Your husband was a fine man and a good friend to me, and to the island, and he will be sorely missed.'

'Thank you, Mr Wylie.'

'Meanwhile, I hope you will excuse me. I have some urgent business to attend to. I will see you tomorrow.' He turned to Jamie. 'Oh, and anytime you feel like taking my little boat out again for a spin . . .'

Jamie nodded. He liked this man. 'Sure thing, Duncan. Thanks.'

Angus watched his retreating figure with a scowl. 'Aye. It's time we were at the castle. Lady Eleanor will want to greet ye, I'm certain. But I should warn ye, she's no' been too well.'

8

The Castle

A long weed-infested drive led up to the castle, whose walls were stained with moss and hung with creepers. It seemed completely deserted, but once, out of the corner of his eye, Jamie thought he saw a curtain twitch in a high window. A small stone church had been constructed alongside the main building, sturdy and simple.

Angus led them up a short flight of steps to two massive riveted wooden doors. He grasped one of the handles and it swung inwards, revealing a high, gloomy hall, lit only by dim yellow panes. Dull varnished portraits hung on the panelled walls between tall bookcases crammed with bound leather volumes. At the far end was a large stone staircase. There was also a giant hearth, but no fire lit. A few threadbare rugs were thrown on the cold flagstones. Murdo deposited their bags on the floor. 'I'll just go an'—' He broke off as the sound of footsteps echoed on stone and a figure appeared, framed in the arch at the top of the staircase. Jamie could just make out a large-boned, stately woman of well over seventy. She stood very upright, dressed in dusty black.

'The Lady Eleanor,' muttered Angus. Murdo took off his cap.

Eleanor stared at Jamie and Marcia in undisguised amazement and hostility, then slowly began to descend the stairs, gripping onto the rail with one gnarled hand. At the foot she paused and looked up challengingly.

Angus hopped forward. 'M'lady, this is, er . . .'

Eleanor dismissed him curtly. 'I am well aware who they are. I had no inkling *what* they were.' She took a step towards Marcia and unashamedly looked her up and down. 'So?'

Marcia returned her cold stare and arched an eyebrow. 'So?'

There was silence.

Eleanor shook her head impatiently. 'It is hard. We are both bereft. A son taken.'

'And a husband . . . and father,' returned Marcia.

'Yes. Well.' There was a long pause, then Eleanor indicated Jamie with a casual wave of her hand. 'How is the boy?'

'He has a name. Jamie.'

Eleanor cut back, 'Yes. His father's and his grand-father's name.'

But Marcia continued, giving Jamie a nudge, 'And a voice.'

Jamie stepped forward. He wasn't sure whether to bow or to kiss his grandmother. He did neither. 'Thanks, ma'am. Everything's cool. Y'know, Dad told me a whole heap of stuff about . . .'

Eleanor didn't look at him. 'Is that so? A pity then that he decided to forsake his place and his people. This is where he belonged.' She shook her head grimly. 'I cannot fathom what kept him away.'

Marcia replied evenly, 'Perhaps it had something to do with the fact that you have no local aircraft industry?'

Eleanor's gaze was unflinching. 'He was weak and led astray. Not strong enough to resist the lure of . . . other things.'

Marcia was stung. 'He was strong and bright and loving. And we have made a long and difficult journey to honour him. And we will only stay here long enough to see him buried – at your insistence – in this . . . this place.'

The women's eyes locked in combat.

Jamie opened his case and put his cellphone and comics on the table by his bed. He dumped a few clothes on the floor, as there seemed to be no other furniture.

He walked up the flagged corridor and sat down on

his mother's bed, looking around at the high but gloomy room. She was peering out of a large window constructed of tiny leaded panes of antique glass. Apart from a basin with a couple of brass taps, and the bedstead, there was little in the way of decoration. At the far end, the ceiling slanted to a narrow slit window, as though part of some exterior tower. Across it, a family of spiders had thrown an intricate span of webs in which their victims hung suspended. The thinly whitewashed walls were heavily stained with patches of damp, and a pail had been strategically positioned in a corner.

'My room's the same,' Jamie said, 'only you've got a better view.'

Marcia grimaced. 'Well, it might be if they had a window-cleaner.'

'Mom. I'm starving. Why'd you have to say we'd already eaten?'

Marcia sat down beside him and sighed. 'I know. It's that . . . *woman*. She just makes me so mad. I don't want to be indebted to her for anything.'

'Do you reckon there's a McDonald's?'

Marcia reached for her bag and opened it. 'No problem. We are self-sufficient. I bought some sandwiches, some Cokes and' – she rooted in the bag – 'some Hershey bars in the airport.' She rummaged again. 'And an apple.'

'Good job, Mom.' Jamie grabbed a sandwich. 'Just in time. Or there might have been two funerals!' He saw Marcia wince. Him and his big mouth. He touched her arm. 'Sorry . . .'

Marcia shook her head. 'No, it's OK. We can't creep around this thing. We have to come to terms with it.' She took Jamie's hand and patted it. 'And we are. Dad would have been real proud of us.' She suddenly smiled sadly. 'If he could see us now.'

Maybe he can, thought Jamie. Maybe he's looking down on us. He tried to picture his dad, feel his presence. But it didn't work. 'Yeah. In draughty old Doran castle. Surrounded by a load of . . . complete weirdos.'

Marcia giggled, and put a hand over her mouth. 'Oh don't,' she gasped. 'After all, they are . . .'

Jamie tried to keep a straight face. 'Family?' he enquired.

They laughed uncontrollably. It was a necessary release and they could as easily have been weeping. Every word triggered a fresh bout of hilarity and the sound of their hysterics echoed down the stone corridors to where Eleanor lay grim-faced on her bed.

9

Last Rites

The weather had turned windy and cool by the following afternoon; in the stone church the old glass panes rattled and the candles guttered in their tall holders. The funeral service was short, and the church packed to the rafters with islanders. Eleanor and Angus sat in their private pews, and Marcia and Jamie occasionally glanced at them across the coffin, which was still draped with the clan banner showing the clasped hands.

Throughout the morning everything had seemed dreamlike to Jamie; he was walking and talking but somehow outside it all, watching. They had ventured into the village and found a deserted café with a grim-faced, silent woman who served them scones and tea. Jamie felt . . . he didn't know *what* he felt. He wasn't sure he felt *anything*. Sort of numb. He wanted to be strong for his mom, because he knew this was hard for her. They were trying to pretend this wasn't happening, but it *was*, and in this really spooky place.

He looked at her. She was staring fixedly at the coffin and seemed terribly lost and alone. We should have our family around us, Jamie thought bitterly, but this isn't our family. I am all she's got. And I am not enough.

A tall piper dressed in full clan regalia began a lament, an ancient wailing melody on the bagpipes that seemed to issue from the very earth itself and fill the building. Six sturdy pallbearers surrounded James's coffin and carried it lightly on their shoulders out into the open air. Jamie, Marcia and Eleanor, and then the entire congregation, followed behind and approached the simple grave that was opened in the hard earth.

A wind whipped their clothes as the shroud was removed and the bare coffin was lowered gently on ropes into the ground. The pipes ceased and there was silence.

Angus leaned over to Jamie and whispered, 'It's for you, laddie – to put in the first, y'know . . .' He indicated a spade at the graveside and nodded towards the pile of turned soil. Jamie took the spade, heaped it with earth and held it poised for a moment above the grave.

Many eyes stared at him. Then he tilted the spade and the first heavy clods rattled on the coffin lid. Jamie was unable to stifle a sudden cry that seemed to come from deep inside him and then the tears began to flow. They were for good times that had been, and for times that would never now be had; for words spoken and for words that would never be said; for a life cut short and a relationship unfulfilled. He dug back into the pile, furiously shovelling the soil into the grave until Angus restrained him.

'No, laddie. It's symbolic. You dinna have to fill it all in yoursel'. Pass it on.'

Through a blur of tears Jamie looked to his mom. But as she moved to take the spade, it was snatched by one of the pallbearers, a tall young man with broad shoulders and a long mane of chestnut hair.

'No,' he said coldly. 'This is clan business.'

The spade bit viciously into the mound and the man carried it, brimming, to the grave. His grey eyes held Marcia's as he tossed the earth roughly into the void.

'Well, things are really jumping now,' said Jamie, surveying the scene. It was evening and the castle hall was lit by dim bare bulbs and the flickering light from tall candles. On a table were platters of leftover sandwiches, a few jugs of cloudy lemonade and several bottles of unlabelled liquor. There were knots of islanders huddled together and a low drone of conversation. Hazel was handing round a depleted bowl of peanuts. She offered it to Marcia. 'I fear there's no' many left,' she said apologetically.

'That's OK, Hazel. I'm not really very hungry.'

Hazel motioned to the tables. ''Fraid the sarnies are

looking a bit dreary as well. But I could make you some fresh.'

Marcia smiled. 'No, really, we're fine.'

Eleanor stood centrally in a small group, still dressed in her sombre clothes. By the staircase, Duncan was deep in conversation with a couple of men.

Jamie and Marcia stood to one side, not so much ignored as uninvited into the gathering. Jamie glanced at his mom. 'You OK?'

She gave a tight smile. 'Oh, yeah. I'm fine. How about you?'

'Good. But it is kinda weird . . .'

'*Weird?* It's like something from *The Addams Family*. I knew it. We should never have come.'

'C'mon, Mom. Dad would have wanted . . .'

Marcia bit her lip. Her voice rose. 'Dad would never have wanted us to be . . . *humiliated* like this. I just hate the idea of leaving him here.' She fumbled in her bag. Eyes turned towards her and the buzz of conversation stopped.

'Mom . . .'

Marcia blinked back the tears and dug around in her purse for a tissue. 'Yes, I know,' she whispered. 'I'm being stupid and emotional and doing all the things I swore I wouldn't. But it's this place. It gives me the heebie-jeebies. I tell you, Jamie, we are out of here tomorrow, just as soon as they can fire that old tub up . . .'

Jamie glanced over her shoulder. He whispered back, 'Hey, don't look now, but I think Deep Freeze is kinda driftin' over.'

Eleanor stood before them and gave her usual challenging stare. 'I am afraid you big-city folk can't find our small gathering much fun.'

Marcia's eyes widened. '*Fun?* This is a funeral.'

There was silence.

'I suppose you will want to be away quite soon?'

'Yes. We'd hate to outstay our welcome.'

Eleanor nodded. 'In that case, I think a private word?' She indicated a couple of high-backed chairs.

Marcia looked at Jamie. 'Hon, just for a minute?'

Jamie took the cue. 'No problem. I'm gonna get a breath of fresh air . . .'

The two women settled into the chairs and Eleanor sat erect, her bony hands clasped in her lap.

'Let us make this as painless as possible. I am sure that it is as embarrassing for you as it is for us.'

'Excuse me?'

Eleanor's eyes glinted. 'I think you understand me perfectly. James has been returned to his rightful place and laid to rest according to ancient custom. I thank you for that. You see, we knew nothing of his life in . . . in America, and naturally were not informed of his liaisons . . .'

Marcia fought to control her voice. '*Liaisons?*' she hissed. 'I am his *wife*.' The word fell between them like a stone.

Eleanor continued undeterred, '. . . nor had we any notion that there was . . . an offspring. Of course, in the circumstances, one can see why he might have wished to keep it . . . dark.'

Marcia rose to her feet. 'If you are trying to be offensive . . . ?'

Eleanor looked up at her, her chin tilted defiantly. 'I don't like you either, my dear. Nor do I want you or your child in my life – which has been bitter enough as it is. As soon as the formalities have been completed, I am sure neither of us will wish to prolong this farce.'

'Formalities?'

'James was, although absent, the chieftain of this clan.' Eleanor's tone was icy. 'On his death, certain rights could pass to his heir. Not, of course, that it would be applicable or appropriate in this case. The boy can sign a few documents in the morning, and then you can both be on your way.'

Eleanor turned away and fixed her gaze on one of the bookcases. Obviously the audience was at an end, and Marcia was dismissed.

She walked quickly away towards a corner of the hall. Despite trying to compose herself, she was shaking. Duncan Wylie broke away from his group and approached her. She forced a smile.

Duncan returned it and murmured, 'Don't let the old battle-axe get to you.'

'Excuse me?'

Duncan nodded towards Eleanor. 'She's a shark, and if she smells blood she'll go for the kill.'

Marcia gave a bitter laugh. 'Thanks for the warning. But I didn't expect to find myself in quite such hostile waters.'

Duncan's blue eyes held hers. 'This must be very

difficult for you,' he said, 'and James would have been very proud of you and your fine lad.'

Jamie was sitting on the front step outside the hall, staring in frustration at his cellphone. He jabbed repeatedly at the recall button as Angus burst out of the hall. He was dressed in a pair of tartan trousers gathered together at the waist with a huge safety pin, a shrunken knitted island sweater and an open stained topcoat that had lost its buttons. His brown boots were scuffed, and the laces had broken and been retied many times. His long white hair flew in the breeze as he tried unsuccessfully to light his pipe. Spent matches rained onto the ground as he sucked vigorously at the stem.

'Damn and blast. Ah!' He spotted Jamie and waved the pipe. 'You're oot here?' He wandered over and gently lowered himself onto the step. 'Well, I cannae blame you. Can't stand all that din and chatter meself.' Angus indicated the cellphone. 'That's a pretty flashy contraption you have there.'

Jamie scowled. 'Top of the range, but it don't seem to work here.'

'Ah yes, you'll find we're not very well served in the communications department.' Angus made several more attempts at lighting the pipe. 'I seem . . . to spend more time getting . . . this . . . blessed thing alight than smoking it. Ah, there.' He sucked vigorously, emitting a pall of smoke. 'I think we have . . . ignition, as they say.' He looked up at the sky. 'So. Is it not a braw nicht?'

Jamie made a face. 'A *what*?'

'Well, it proves it's not always throwin' auld wives and pike staves.'

'Er . . . I guess.'

Angus looked keenly at Jamie. 'I see your mother and Eleanor are getting on like a house on fire.'

Jamie's jaw dropped. 'You are *kidding*!'

Angus pointed his pipe stem at Jamie. 'I mean, they're talking. Which is something, I suppose. Drat, I think it's quenched.' He puffed furiously. 'No, there's life in it yet. She's a hard woman . . . Eleanor.'

Jamie tried to dodge the clouds of smoke. 'My mom's no slouch. It's just tough for her right now.'

Angus nodded. 'Oh aye. Of course it is. Terrible hard. And for you too.' Again the keen look. 'You'd have bin verra close, I suppose? To your father?'

'Oh, sure. Real close.' Jamie felt the eyes burning into him. He looked away. 'Well, I mean, how close is close? Dad always worked hard. At the air-base or in his den, dealing with all his Scottish stuff.'

Angus chuckled. 'Oh aye. Clan business. He was excellent at that, your father. A good chief. He'll be sore missed.'

'Yeah.' Jamie paused. 'Tell me, Angus, what were the problems?'

'Sorry?'

'Dad told me there was trouble brewing.'

'Trouble?' It was Angus now who looked away and fiddled with the pipe. 'Oh, well now, I dinna ken any *trouble*. Anyway, nothing that cannae be fixed, if we have a mind to. And nothing that you need bother your head about.'

Jamie persisted. 'But who'll take over?'

'Eh?'

'From Dad? Who'll be chieftain now?'

Angus heaved a great sigh and stared sadly at the mountains. He suddenly seemed very old. 'Aye, lad. Well, you've put your finger on it there. Now, that *is* a problem.'

10

A Change of Heart

Dappled sunlight played across Jamie's face as he woke with a dreamy smile. Surf would be up and he'd soon be down at Point Dume with the buds. He listened for the sounds of his dad: the methodical snap as he sealed his lunch into a plastic container; the clink of keys dropping into his pocket; the zip as he closed his attaché case; the low rumble of the opening garage door; and the throaty purr of the SUV as it nosed out of the drive. The ritual was always the same, timed to the second and always unobserved by Marcia and Jamie, who would nevertheless use it to kick-start their own mornings. But today there were no familiar sounds. Jamie cursed. He must have overslept.

He stretched and reached over sleepily to turn on the bedside radio. Instead his hand connected with a tall pitcher of water, which almost toppled over. Jamie sat upright, shivering in the cold morning air. A weak sun filtered through the shutters, throwing shifting patterns on the flagstone floor. His stomach felt empty and, with a rush, images and memories flooded into his head. He was thousands of miles from Vego Park, from the ocean, from his friends. Dad was lying in the cold earth outside; there would be no more familiar waking sounds, no more morning routine, no more . . . His heart raced.

Jamie shook his head. Get a grip, he told himself. His mom needed him to be strong, to be the man, to support her. The previous night's gathering had finally broken up and Jamie and Marcia had retreated to their rooms to finish off the last of their Hershey bars. Jamie had sensed his mom was exhausted, so they had turned in early and he had fallen into an immediate and deep sleep.

He swiftly pulled on a pair of jeans, some trainers and his basketball team sweatshirt. His room also had a large fluted basin and a faucet on one wall, with two ugly chrome taps. He turned the tap marked 'H', which had worked reasonably well the previous day but now gave a series of giant shudders before producing a few drops of brown water. There were more violent convulsions somewhere in the wall, so Jamie hurriedly turned it off.

The other tap produced an intermittent stream of icy water, which Jamie sprinkled over his face. The shock brought him fully awake, and finding there was no towel, he dried himself on the bedspread.

His mom's door was closed, so he carried on down the staircase to the hall, where one of the large oak tables had been laid for breakfast. Eleanor, still dressed in black, was seated at one end and Hazel was struggling with something bony on her plate. In the centre of the table were several silver dishes.

Jamie took a deep breath, ran down the staircase and gave a wave. 'Yo, y'all. How ya' doin?'

Eleanor and Hazel stared at him.

'Anyone seen Mom?'

They both shook their heads.

Jamie took a deep breath. 'What do you put in the air round here? I tell you, I am starving. I could eat a Scottish donkey . . .'

Eleanor wiped her mouth with her napkin. 'I am afraid that is not presently on the menu,' she said dryly. 'But you may help yourself . . .' She indicated the silver dishes.

Jamie pulled up a chair opposite Hazel and reached for a cover. 'Only kidding. Cereal, waffles and juice will be just fine . . .' He lifted it, revealing a pulsating grey mass. 'Hey, what do we have here?'

'Porridge,' said Hazel, still fiddling with her bones.

'Excuse me?'

Hazel looked up. 'Porridge,' she explained patiently. 'You eat it. For breakfast.'

Jamie scooped a big dollop onto a plate. 'Yeah, I think I heard of this. Smothered in jelly, maple syrup . . .'

'With salt,' said Hazel, sliding the salt cellar across the table.

Jamie's jaw dropped. '*Salt?* You are kidding! No jelly? Syrup?'

Hazel looked at him coolly. 'Salt.'

Jamie shook a few grains of salt on the porridge and guided a spoonful to his lips. He gave a shriek and seized a glass of water, gulping it down. 'Hot. Real hot. Maybe I'll just . . .' He gingerly lifted the cover of the next dish. A mound of deep brown fishes stared back at him. There was a strong smell of smoke and oil.

'Kippers,' said Hazel, indicating the graveyard on her own plate, where she was poking at a fish head. 'Dig in.'

Jamie swiftly replaced the lid. With sinking heart, he opened the lid of the last dish.

Hazel again was a mine of information. 'Finnan haddies,' she explained. 'Haddock that's been cured in peat smoke.'

Jamie sat back. 'Really? Hmm . . . that's really neat . . .' His stomach rumbled.

Eleanor indicated a pot. 'Tea?'

'Coffee, thanks.' He looked around. Coffee evidently was not on offer. He lifted his glass. 'Oh well. I guess water will be just fine.'

Eleanor rose to her feet. 'I will arrange for Murdo to bring the car round.' She moved towards one of the large doors between the bookshelves and then turned. 'Oh, before you leave, there is a little business to attend to. When you have finished your breakfast, perhaps you might care to join us in the library?' Without waiting for an answer, she swept through the door.

Hazel continued to struggle with her fish. The head was almost detached.

Jamie watched it, fascinated. 'Reckon' he's givin' you the eye.'

Hazel ignored this.

'You live here, huh?' Jamie persevered.

'Eh?'

'In the castle?'

Hazel shook her head. 'Close by. With my mother. She and ma dad split up when I was small. I just help out here.' She put down her knife. 'Which is needed.' There was another long pause. 'So you're away then?' she enquired casually, not looking at him.

'Yep. Back to God's Own Country. Californ-i-ay. Jeez, I can't wait. School's out and . . .' He crooked two fingers and sang, '"*It's Va-ca-tion Time.*"' He gave a shout of laughter, but there was no response from Hazel and his fingers curled back into his palm. He struggled on. 'You know, weeks of surfing, catching up on movies, *partying . . .*?'

Hazel flicked him a glance. 'Fancy,' she said, but no more.

Jamie tried again. 'How 'bout you?'

'Oh aye, we're on our school holidays as well. Great craic. Harvest, milking cows, feedin' the chickens.'

Jamie took another taste of the porridge, but quickly spat it out. 'So tell me, where do you guys hang out?'

'Sorry?'

'You and the other dudes? Where's the action? You go down the mall, the multiplex or clubbing?'

Hazel nodded slowly. 'Oh aye. Always awa' on the ran-dan.'

Jamie slipped his cell from his pocket and switched it on. His face fell.

'You'll find that's no use here,' Hazel volunteered. 'We've all tried, but none of them work.'

'You mean there's no phones?'

'Oh, sure there are. They laid a cable from the mainland yonks ago. So you can make a call from the police station or the Community Centre, and of course Eleanor had to have a line here at the castle. It's awful expensive to get connected and anyways you have to go through a stupid operator on the mainland, so it's hardly worth the while. And who would I phone anyhow?'

Jamie shook his head in disbelief. 'But how do you keep in touch with your buds?'

Hazel frowned. '*Buds?*'

'Your friends, the other kids . . . ?'

'Oh, we know how to find each other. We've a pretty good network on Doran. It's no' a problem.'

Jamie stared at his dead cellphone. 'My whole life is in here,' he said. 'I'm not sure I could exist without it. Facebook, Twitter, eBay, TV.' He looked up in alarm. 'You *do* have TV?'

'Oh, sure.'

Jamie smiled and leaned back. 'So when you're in your room, you can keep up with *American Idol*, *The Wire* . . .'

Hazel looked at the fireplace. 'There's a receiver in the Community Centre,' she said, 'and we watch all we want. Except when the lads have taken drink and only want the footie on.'

'And movies? You have a movie theatre?'

Hazel stifled a laugh. 'No, we've none. But' – she reached for her bag and rummaged furiously inside – 'I do have *this*!' She proudly held up a small Panasonic DVD player. 'Is it no' a beezer? All the kids have them. And the local hire shop does a gey trade.' She replaced the player in her bag and for the first time looked directly at him. 'So they're paying you off then?'

Jamie didn't follow. 'Excuse me?'

Hazel nodded towards the library. 'Them'ens. Getting you to sign away?'

Jamie laughed. 'Look, I don't get—'

Hazel shot to her feet, planted her hands squarely on the table and glared at him. 'Away you go, Jamie! Are you glaikit or something? Your father was our chief. D'you no' think that you might have some small interest, some little say . . . ?'

'Say?' Jamie was taken aback. 'In what?'

Hazel's eyes seemed to flash. She mimicked him. '*In what?* Oh, nothing important, like Facebook or partying. Just our future, by the way. That's what. Life and death. Silly little things like that. Only I daresay you wouldnae be interested in *them*.'

Jamie was shocked by her sudden fury and couldn't think of a reply. Hazel shook her head, and began noisily to clear away the dishes.

Jamie watched her. 'Hey, girl, I didn't mean to make you mad . . .'

Hazel put down the plates, and again there was the intense look, as if she were wrestling with conflicting emotions.

'Jamie?' she said urgently.

'Yeah?'

The fire suddenly left her eyes. 'Oh, go boil your head,' she spat, snatching up the dishes and rushing from the room.

Alone in the vast hall, Jamie threw out his hands and addressed the empty table. 'Tell me – what did I say?'

He peered into the last dish again but hastily replaced the lid. Then he walked slowly towards the library door, put his hand on the handle and, after a pause, walked through.

The library was even dustier and more run-down than the rest of the castle. From floor to ceiling, bookshelves crammed with ancient hand-bound leather volumes lined the walls. Between them, framed portraits of past chieftains, many of them in full regalia, gazed fiercely down.

Beside the window, at a large oak table, sat Angus, Duncan and the young pallbearer who had seized the spade by the grave. There were also a few elderly men who Jamie recognized from the previous evening. Before them was a pile of parchment documents covered in spidery writing. Eleanor sat apart, in a high-backed chair at the head of the table. The men were deep in a heated discussion, which stopped abruptly when Jamie entered.

Duncan smiled welcomingly. 'Ah, Jamie. We were just . . . just talking about *you*, strangely enough.'

Jamie approached the table. 'No kidding.'

Duncan dragged back a chair. 'Come and take a pew.'

'Sure thing.' Jamie sat down and looked at them expectantly. There was an awkward silence.

Eleanor cleared her throat. 'This won't take long.' She nodded curtly at Duncan, who took the cue.

'No, no time at all. Just a few loose ends to be tied up . . . all very boring. Now, we just need your signature on a few things concerning your late father . . . tying up loose ends, you know? All legal gobbledegook . . . but while we have you' – he opened a plastic file and slid some papers across the table – 'we can get it all done and dusted.' He jabbed a finger at the sheets. 'Now, if you just sign here and here, and another one here. Use my pen . . .'

Jamie took the elegant gold fountain pen and was about to sign his name when he looked up. 'What is it?'

Duncan smiled again, patiently. 'What is what?'

'What am I signing?'

'As I said, boring old legal . . .'

Jamie put down the pen and grinned back at Duncan. 'You know something? Dad always told me you should never sign anything in a hurry. Ain't that right, Angus?'

Angus looked wildly at Eleanor, and tugged at his beard. 'Aye. Aye. I heard him say that once or twice right enough.'

Duncan glared at him, and Eleanor leaned forward.

'Jamie, you don't have much time. You have an aeroplane to catch.'

Duncan wagged a finger. 'No, Jamie is quite correct. He has every right to know what these documents are.' He turned back to Jamie. 'When a chieftain dies, another has to be elected to lead the clan. Do you understand?'

'Loud and clear.'

'In olden times, being a chieftain was a big responsibility.' Duncan waved a hand. 'These gentlemen whose portraits you see around the walls had to fight hard for the clan's survival – and sometimes they even died for it. But in this modern age the job has become, well . . . outmoded. A chore.' He leaned in conspiratorially. 'A bit of a joke.' He smiled, but then his face took on a more solemn expression. 'Your dear father, as I am sure you are aware, was extremely conscientious and had far too much of his precious time taken up with our trifling little problems. And now he is gone, we certainly wouldn't want to inflict them on *you*. You have your own life and future across the water . . . and I'm sure you'll want to forget all about us just as soon as you board that plane.'

Jamie nodded. 'I see.'

'Good lad. I knew you would. So, just here and here and—' Duncan smiled again and his finger jabbed once more at the papers.

'So what will happen?'

The men exchanged glances and once again Eleanor spoke.

'The situation is unusual. Angus is trying to identify the correct procedure.'

Jamie persisted. 'No, what I mean is . . . who will be chieftain?'

'Ah.' There was a trace of irritation in Duncan's voice, but the smile did not leave his face. 'The position is open to all clansmen and islanders, and no doubt there will be various candidates put forward . . . in due course.'

'Like who?'

Angus muttered grimly, 'Well now, Duncan here would reckon he is a strong contender . . .'

'And what about you, Angus?' Duncan fired back. 'Don't pretend you have no interest.'

Angus pointed a bony finger at Duncan and growled, 'I have no interest for *myself*, I can tell you. And I was well content to live out my remaining days as archivist to the clan. But now, to stop you, against all my inclinations, aye, I would stand.'

'And who will be the true voice of the islanders? Tell me that.' The young pallbearer spoke up. His look was intense, his voice low but strong.

Duncan snarled at him, 'Of course, Alistair, we all know your credentials.'

Jamie watched, fascinated, as voices were raised and tempers became heated. He leaned back in his chair.

It was Eleanor, striking her hand on the table, who finally brought silence. 'Enough!' Her eyes flashed and she looked keenly at each man. 'I am sure all this is extremely uninteresting for the boy. Now, let us finish this business in an ordered and calm manner.'

Jamie suddenly jumped to his feet. There was a strange light in his eyes. 'Will you excuse me a moment?'

He ran to the door, leaving the group staring after him.

His mother was standing in the hall, handing her suitcases to Murdo. He was dressed in his driver's uniform once more. Marcia spotted Jamie and straightened. She was clearly stressed. 'There you are. Where are your bags?'

Jamie touched her arm. 'Mom. Listen.'

She looked alarmed. 'What? What's wrong now?'

'Nothing. It's just . . . Look, Mom, don't go blow a fuse. It's just that I want . . . well, I think maybe I'd *like* to hang around here for a while.'

Murdo froze and stared at Jamie. His mother looked wildly around the hall and laughed bitterly. '*Hang around?* Are you *kidding*? After the way they've behaved? Nothing would make me stay a second longer than I have to in this madhouse.' She pointed imperiously at the floor. 'Could you get your stuff down here right now?'

Jamie looked meaningfully at Murdo. 'Hey, would you mind? Just for a minute?'

Murdo jumped. 'What? Oh aye, aye, I'll go and load these in the car.'

When they were alone, Jamie led his mom to the table and they sat facing each other. Her eyes filled with tears and he reached out and took her hand.

'Mom. Listen to me. I know how tough this has been for you.'

'So, *why*?'

Jamie chewed his lip. 'I dunno. It's real hard to explain. But I've been thinking about how Dad cared so much for this place, spent so much time worrying himself nuts about these guys. It was real important to him. He told me that himself. I can't just leave him here in the ground and run away, without ever knowing why.'

Marcia shook her head angrily. 'There is no way I'm getting on the plane alone, leaving you here with these ... with that *woman*,' she said. 'She never forgave your dad for leaving and she thinks we're to blame. You see the way she looks at us, looks down on us. I know that look, hon. She's probably never met a black person before and she most certainly doesn't want us around her. We're getting out of here, Jamie. Just get your things and let's go.' And then a teardrop ran down his mother's cheek and dropped onto the oak table. 'I can't leave you here too. You are all I have left now.'

'Look, Mom. I guess you've noticed I'm not great on the emotional stuff. But you know I love you, even if I don't tell you too often.' Marcia nodded and gripped his hand tightly. Jamie looked down. 'Dad too, only I didn't know him too well. I thought there would be time. But I'd like to ...'

'Love him?'

'*Know* him, Mom. And maybe now I have the chance, and if I don't take it ...' There was a long silence. His mother's eyes searched his face and Jamie held her gaze. 'Mom, what do you tell your patients when something terrible has happened to them, when they have lost something or someone real important?'

She dabbed at her eyes. 'I ... er ... I guess I try to

explain that they mustn't try to bottle it up inside. That they must face up to their grief and give themselves time to grieve – in their own way.'

Jamie nodded. 'And you know I'm always gonna be there for you. But just now maybe that's what we need to do – grieve in our own way.'

His mother sighed deeply. 'Well, hon, since I am always encouraging my clients to take control of their lives, I guess I can't complain if my son follows my advice.' She smiled sadly at Jamie.

'Hey, Mom. Remember what you said last night? 'Bout Dad looking down on us and being proud? I'd want him to be proud of me, and I'm pretty sure that chickening out ain't the way to do it. And you know something? I ain't a bit scared of Grandma. I reckon she's more scared of *me*.'

Marcia blinked away her tears. 'All right. But be practical. You gotta have money . . .'

'I've got money.'

She looked around wildly. 'But how will I know you're all right? You might be sick or hungry.'

'I'll keep in touch. Mom, I'm not out in the middle of the jungle.'

She snorted. 'I'm not convinced of that.' She gave a final dab to her eyes. 'This is madness and I know I am going to regret it, but OK. Don't take any nonsense from them, right? Make sure you call me every day . . .'

'I'll be fine. It's vacation time, so just think of this as' – Jamie paused a moment, then grinned – 'as a vacation . . . with the family?'

His mother rose slowly to her feet as Murdo re-appeared at the door, glancing anxiously at his watch. She called to him, 'I'll be right there.'

Jamie picked up her handbag. 'I'll come see you off.'

She shook her head. 'No need.' She took back the bag and gave Jamie a long hug. 'You take care, d'you hear?' She turned and, after one final look back, followed Murdo out of the door.

Jamie took a deep breath and headed back towards the library. As he stepped through the door they were all silent, gazing at him expectantly. He sat down slowly in his chair and smiled apologetically.

'Gee, guys, I'm real sorry about that.' He spread his hands on the table. 'Now, where were we?'

'You were signing these papers,' said Eleanor dryly.

'Oh, yeah.' Jamie looked around at the faces before him. 'That's right. Except, as I recall, I think I was *not* signing them.'

There was a sharp intake of breath.

'Not signing?' Duncan echoed lamely.

'Nope. Not just yet. You see, I've had this real neat idea. I thought maybe I'd cool my heels around here a while . . .'

Eleanor shook her head impatiently. 'That is entirely out of the question. Your mother—'

'Oh, don't worry,' Jamie broke in. 'That's all fixed. I just sent Mom home. She would have liked to stay and hang out with you too, but she's got all her patients to see to. They really depend on her. Say' – he leaned forward conspiratorially – 'has anyone told you she is a real hot-shot therapist? Uh-*huh*. Helpin' people pick themselves up and get on with their lives. So she's got no problem, knowing I'll be welcome here.' He looked earnestly at Eleanor. 'With my grandmom – an' all the MacDorans.' He beamed around the table. 'We can get real intimate. And you know something? Maybe I'll even get the hang of that porridge stuff!'

11

King of the Road

The morning was glorious, with a warm sun, clear air and the distant mountains framing a deep blue sky. It felt good to be back in a worn T-shirt and his favourite pair of baggy jeans with his iPod clipped to his belt. Jamie jumped onto his skateboard and rolled smoothly down the castle drive. Trainers planted firmly on the grip tape and knees bent, he made a couple of wide curves, gliding expertly towards the village below. He mouthed the words to a Drillers track on the iPod as he passed the first cottages. Many were boarded up and a few had FOR SALE signs tacked to their gates.

As he hit Main Street, his Birdhouse Falcon wheels

clattered noisily across the cobbles, sending a cat racing for cover. The village was small, with a depressed air. It boasted a grocer, a hardware store, and a deeply unfashionable clothes shop with woollens and stout shoes arranged in a random display. The café was as empty as before. Further along, there were some shops with CLOSING DOWN scrawled on their windows, and dented, rusting cars were parked haphazardly in the road. Doran Video, by contrast, had a small queue outside, clutching DVDs for return. As Jamie sped past, some shoppers turned to stare at him. He waved at them but they did not respond. At the crossroads, he cut in front of a horse drawing a wooden cart loaded with firewood. It whinnied in alarm and the driver reined it in.

Jamie called to him, 'Hi, how ya doing?'

The driver muttered something, and spoke softly to his horse to comfort it. A few regulars holding pint glasses were sitting in the sunshine outside the Doran Arms pub.

'Have a nice day,' called Jamie.

Their eyes panned left to right as he passed. Two old ladies with shopping baskets put their heads together and whispered.

At the far end of the village was a green and scummy duck pond. A group of boys dressed in scruffy jeans and sweaters were idly skimming stones on the stagnant water. One of them, a puny, freckled youth with bright red hair, spotted Jamie and darted into the road holding out his hand.

'Halt!' he cried loudly. The other boys ran to join

him, forming a ragged line. One of them shouted, 'Aye, you cannae pass.'

Jamie crouched low and bore down upon them. The boys dived for cover. Only the redhead stood his ground, hand still outstretched and eyes screwed shut. Jamie swooped round him and tailed his board.

'Hey, dude. You nuts or something? I coulda taken you out there.'

The boy opened his eyes and looked at Jamie indignantly. 'Did you nae hear me? I told yer t' halt.'

Jamie smiled. 'Guess I was into the music. What's your name?'

The boy thought a moment. 'They call me Wee Malkie.'

'I'm Jamie.'

'Oh aye.'

Jamie took out his earphones and offered them. 'You dig this stuff?'

Wee Malkie viewed them with suspicion and gave them a thorough polish with his sleeve. The other boys approached warily as he pressed them into his ears, wincing at the volume. He listened impassively.

Jamie looked at him expectantly. 'Hot stuff, huh? The Drillers. It's from their new album. Much better than *Blood in Your Eyes*. I reckon this track is really awesome.'

Wee Malkie removed the earpieces and handed them back. 'It's pants,' he said. He gave a sudden cough and spat some phlegm into the road.

Jamie shrugged. 'OK, so you're not into music.'

'Me? I love music. But that's rubbish.'

'OK. So who do you dig then?'

Wee Malkie thought a moment. 'Dougal Ross is excellent.' The other boys nodded in agreement.

'I've never heard of him. What band's he with?'

'Oh, he's no' with any *band*. He lives over yon.' Wee Malkie gestured with his arm. 'I saw a band once,' he announced. 'Oasis. They were playing in Oban. Big crowd, stage, flashin' lights an' all.'

Jamie nodded. 'Yeah, they came to LA too. I heard they were great!'

Wee Malkie wiped his nose with his sleeve. 'They were pants,' he said.

Jamie shook his head in disbelief and screwed the 'phones back into his ears. Wee Malkie motioned to the other boys, and they returned to the duck pond, pretending not to watch Jamie as he sped away.

Outside the village, the road deteriorated and was pitted with holes and stones that Jamie had to slalom around. In the fields, huge horned Highland cattle stood almost motionless, munching grass as they watched him pass. As he rounded a bend he saw a figure furiously pedalling an ancient woman's bike with a wicker basket mounted in front. It took him a moment to realize that it was Hazel, dressed in an old sweatshirt with a pink hood over her hair. She was lost in thought and didn't hear Jamie as he cruised alongside on the board. She suddenly saw him, snatched off the hood and wobbled alarmingly.

'Get away! Dinna play the loun!' she cried.

Jamie laughed, and swung in front of her. 'Have wheels, will travel.'

Hazel desperately tried to brake and keep her balance. 'You muckle sumph! You'll kill us both.'

Jamie held his hands aloft and declared, 'I am Jamie – King of the Road.' He didn't see the large pothole, which pitched him spectacularly onto a boggy patch of turf. The board performed a lazy somersault in the air and ended on its back, wheels spinning.

Hazel dismounted and approached warily. She gave a curtsey.

'Oh aye, your majesty. Very impressive.' She watched him as he lay sprawled and winded in the mud. 'Will you live?' A sudden thought struck her. 'Anyhow, what on earth do you think you're doin'? You're meant to be crossing with Murdo.'

Jamie sat up and rubbed his head. 'You don't say.'

'You *know* you are. He'll be doin' his pieces, 'cos it's a long drive an' . . .' She frowned. 'Where's your mam?'

Jamie checked his watch. 'I guess, just about approaching Glasgow airport.'

Hazel narrowed her eyes. 'So why are you no' with her?'

'She's always forgetting things.' Jamie laughed and Hazel pulled a face. 'No, I thought I might mosey around here a while.'

'What fer?'

'See the sights. Learn to speak with a Scotch accent.'

'Scots.'

'Scots accent.' He got slowly to his feet. 'Och. Aye.'

Hazel watched him witheringly. 'You're a bletherin' skite.'

'Come again?'

Hazel pointed a finger at her head. 'You're daft. Gone in the heed.'

Jamie nodded. 'Yeah, everyone tells me that.' He wiped down his baggies, adding casually, 'Thought you might be different.'

Hazel remounted her bike. 'Sorry ta disappoint you.' She looked at him for a moment, then added flatly, 'Go home, Jamie. There's nothing for you here. You're only wasting your time.'

The car horn surprised them both, and they turned to see Duncan sitting in a sleek silver Hummer. He looked at Jamie's muddied clothes and the up-ended board and gave his usual tight smile. 'No bones broken, I hope?'

'No way. Just trying out some off-piste turns.'

Duncan removed his sunglasses. 'I'm afraid the roads here are in pretty bad shape. Even the holes have holes. I chair the Highways committee but, well, as always it's money, money, money.'

Hazel suddenly swung the front of the bike round. 'I must be away. I've to do some messages for my mother,' she said and pedalled off hurriedly.

Duncan watched her go. He smiled again. 'Er, Jamie. Actually I'm glad I ran into you. Felt a bit bad about this morning and I'd like to make it up to you. Will you hop in?'

Jamie indicated the board. 'It's OK, Duncan. I got my own wheels.'

'Pity. Thought you might fancy a Coke? A burger, perhaps? At my place?'

Jamie hesitated. He felt his stomach rumble. 'No, I'm fine.'

'And fries?' Duncan looked disappointed. 'Oh well, if you're absolutely sure.'

He put the car into gear and drew away. Jamie grabbed the board and yelled, 'Hey, Duncan!'

The Hummer stopped abruptly, allowing Jamie to run up alongside. He held up the skateboard.

'I – er, I think I may have cracked it.'

Duncan leaned over and opened the door. 'Of course you have,' he said.

12

Duncan

The Hummer roared off with a scream of scorched rubber, causing the cattle nearby to shy away in fright.

Jamie whistled in admiration at the chrome dash and the interior finish. 'What's the model?' he asked Duncan.

'Oh, this is just my little island run-around. It's a limited edition – H Two Silver Ice. Does the job.'

Jamie had to admit that Duncan was an expert driver. Using the gears and economic flicks of the steering wheel, he negotiated the twisting, decaying road at extraordinary speeds. Sometimes he took off-road short cuts, bouncing across the springy turf, and within minutes they were at the quayside and the high gates that guarded Duncan's place. As they approached, the gates slid open to allow the car to pass through, then silently shut behind them.

Duncan applied the handbrake and took off his gloves. 'Home sweet home,' he said with a smile.

The contrast between Duncan's house and the rest of Doran was striking. The ancient waterside building had been expensively refurbished with the finest materials. It was obviously very hi-tech. The front door of the house swung open, and music filled the air.

Duncan led the way into a huge glass atrium which looked out onto the ocean. There was a heated outdoor swimming pool, and the still blue water of the pool and the distant ocean seemed to merge together.

'Make yourself at home,' Duncan said. There were deep leather couches, low tables, and a huge hearth piled with logs, which burst instantly into flame at the press of a button. A tennis match was relayed on a giant plasma TV screen and its hidden surround speakers.

'Cool pad,' Jamie said.

Duncan indicated the fitted kitchen area. 'Now then, are you hungry?'

'Hungry?' echoed Jamie, his face breaking into a huge grin. 'No, man, I am *starving*.'

The burgers were just the way Jamie liked them, slightly pink inside and smothered in ketchup and mustard, and the fries were thin and crisp and golden. Duncan didn't eat, but sat across the table, sipping a mineral water and listening intently to Jamie with an amused smile.

'. . . and this guy, Jeroo, well actually he's one of my best buds, he gives me this pass, you know, from real low down, and I catch it and swing round . . .'

Jamie felt relaxed with Duncan. Unlike the castle, everything was easy here. He took a gulp of Coke and belched roundly. 'Excuse me!'

Duncan shook his head, 'No, it's good to see a hearty appetite.'

Jamie speared some more fries. 'Man, you have no idea how good this tastes.'

Duncan nodded. 'Yes, the local fare can be a little – limited.'

Jamie spoke through a mouthful. 'So . . . how'd you get all this . . .' He waved a free hand. 'All this gear?'

Duncan sipped his water gently. 'Well, no one *gave* it to me, that's for sure. You have to work for things in life, Jamie. Go hard for what you want.' He smiled. 'I am sure you've found that.'

Jamie nodded. 'Oh, sure, sure.' Actually he had found that many of the best things in his life had come along accidentally, with little effort or planning on his part.

'Money has become a dirty word, I can't imagine why. It seems an excellent thing to me, if it enables you to have the things you want.' Duncan warmed to his theme. 'Most people just muddle along in their old ways. Can't see the future. No vision.' He put his glass on the table and looked intently at Jamie. 'But you're smart. I can see that. Like your father. Clever man . . .'

'Yeah. He was really bright. He—'

Duncan's gaze was unblinking. 'Your father knew that Doran was in serious trouble, Jamie.'

'Yeah, he told me that he—'

'He would have sorted things out. I am certain of that. Given time . . . but' – Duncan heaved a sigh – 'unfortunately time was not on his side.'

Jamie put down his fork. 'No.'

Duncan stood and leaned on the table. 'We were a good team. So now I have to try to follow his lead, his example, and try to finish his work.'

Jamie looked up at him. He brightened. 'Really?'

'Yes, Jamie. Which is what I was trying, however ineptly, to tell you this morning. I need a mandate to help me turn this place around. No one else here has any idea what to do. You've seen it for yourself: a crumbling old castle, a dozy town and roads full of potholes going nowhere. No real jobs, apart from a bit of fishing and raising sheep or cattle.'

Jamie laughed. 'Yeah, but it is kinda cute . . .'

'Cute?' Duncan spat the word disdainfully. 'Well, perhaps it may seem so to you. But, believe me, Doran is dying on its feet. In a decade there will only be the sheep and the heather and the fish. Mark my words.'

Jamie wiped his mouth with the crisp napkin. 'So what do you have in mind?'

'In mind?' Again Duncan echoed his words. 'No, not just in *mind*, Jamie.' He placed a hand on Jamie's shoulder and looked deeply into his eyes. He seemed to have come to a decision. 'Can I trust you?'

'Er . . . I guess.'

'Good. Then let me show you something.' Duncan led Jamie away from the table towards a darkened alcove. He disappeared, and Jamie peered into the pitch darkness. He gave a start as a brilliant picture of the Isle of Doran suddenly flashed onto a screen.

He could just make out Duncan in the gloom, holding a small handset. Duncan pressed a couple more keys and the image zoomed in to the harbour, the castle and in even tighter to include the very house in which they were standing.

Jamie whistled. 'Cool.'

Duncan's eyes gleamed in the reflected brilliance. 'No, Jamie. That is the past. But this, *this* will be truly amazing.'

Duncan tapped another key and the scene morphed into an artist's impression of the island. The old village was transformed into a futuristic, high-rise business centre. The castle was restored and gleaming, enclosed in a glass plexi-dome, and a vast yacht-filled marina replaced the harbour. On the hills sprouted forests of wind-powered turbines and nests of oil rigs surfaced in the sea beyond the headlands. It occurred to Jamie that maybe there weren't too many homes.

'This is what your father would have wanted for Doran and his people,' breathed Duncan. 'And I will realize that dream.' He snapped off the display and led the way back into the atrium. They sat facing each other in the deep armchairs, and Duncan studied Jamie over touching fingertips. 'So. Will you help him? Will you help me?'

Jamie swallowed. 'Gee. Well, it sure seems to make sense. But what the heck can *I* do?'

'Stay a short while, as you have rightly decided. Then, when we know each other better, give me your endorsement, help me with my campaign and entrust me with your vote, handed down from your father. Then you can go home with a contented mind.'

'I have a vote then?'

'Indeed you have. And your father would be proud that you used it wisely.'

Jamie walked up the castle drive carrying his battered skateboard. Swallows swooped against the glowing sunset sky, and the crumbling turrets and battlements dimly reflected the brilliant colours. Weeds sprouted where bricks had split or become dislodged and flowered against blackened, cracked windowpanes. Jamie could not help comparing the beautiful vision of Duncan's plan with this sad, lingering ruin.

He opened the great wooden door and felt his way into the dim hall, crashing against furniture. It was very dark here, lit only by a few guttering candles. Jamie banged his shin on a wooden bench.

He swore into the gloom.

Eleanor's voice floated bleakly out of the darkness. 'You may be a guest, but this is *not* an hotel.'

Jamie jumped. 'You sure scared me. Didn't see you sitting there.' Indeed, he could barely make out her form now, huddled in a chair by the unlit hearth.

'It would have been courteous to inform me that you

would not return for your tea. It is entirely spoiled.' Eleanor indicated the silver dishes on the table.

Jamie remembered the smoked fish and porridge and felt his stomach heave. 'Oh no, I couldn't. I mean, I've already eaten.'

'Indeed?'

Jamie could imagine, but not see, the arched eyebrow.

'Yeah. I had this big spread at Dunca— I mean, er, a Dunkin' Donuts kind of place. So I guess I'll just mosey up to bed.'

'Sit down.' Eleanor pointed to a chair opposite.

Jamie sat. He was getting really tired of her regal manner. He reckoned the Queen would be friendlier.

'You have decided to stay on, in my home. Un-invited.'

Jamie shrugged.

Eleanor spoke slowly and coldly. 'It is not my wish, but I cannot stop you. You are, however inconceivably, kith and kin. But as long as you are under my roof there are general rules that you will obey. There is no luxury here. We do not have the benefit of servants or labour-saving devices, and the place does not run itself. While you remain, there will be certain duties that you will be required to perform.'

'No problem, ma'am. Just point me in the right direction.'

Eleanor sniffed. 'The cow sheds are behind the main building. The animals are accustomed to being milked at seven a.m.'

13

Back to Basics

Jamie shivered inside his tracksuit as he picked his way across the yard, shielding his face from the fine drizzle that was driven against the cobblestones.

The redbrick cow sheds were screened from view by an ancient mossy wall. The unfamiliar animal smell hit him as he walked inside, and several large cows in the stalls eyed him expectantly.

Jamie rubbed his hands. 'Morning, guys. I mean, gals. Gee, it's cold enough to freeze your—' He noticed the full udders that swung slowly. 'Well, guess we had better get down to business.'

He looked around and noticed an aluminium pail.

He picked it up and approached the first cow, extending a tentative hand towards the udder. The cow shifted uneasily, emitting a low groaning sound.

Jamie smiled encouragingly. 'Whoa there, baby. Hold steady now.' He touched the taut skin, feeling the liquid within. 'Could you give me a hand?'

'You'll never do it standing up.'

Jamie jumped and dropped the pail. Hazel was sitting on a small stool in a separate stall, hidden by the bulk of the cow she was milking.

'Like I told you,' she said. 'Great holiday craik. Look.'

She brought over her stool and, leaning against the udder, pulled expertly at the cow's teats, squirting the steaming milk into the empty pail. The white frothy milk gave off a slightly sour smell.

Jamie pulled a face. 'That is gross.'

'Oh, did you think they put it in bottles themselves then?'

Jamie gave a little shudder. 'I can't do that.'

Hazel tossed her hair. 'Fine. Tell Eleanor.'

Jamie warily replaced Hazel on the stool and she drew his hand onto the teat.

'You're supposed to squeeze it, not wave it.'

The cow gave a mournful groan.

'It doesn't like me.'

'Well, how would you like someone—?' Hazel stopped, suddenly embarrassed. 'Oh, dear God, look ... like this.' She took the teat, and again the warm milk shot satisfyingly into the pail.

Jamie nodded. 'OK. I get it. Yeah.' He lunged again at

the udder and a few miserable drops pattered into the pail.

Hazel looked at him. 'You are totally pathetic, d'you know that?'

During the morning the drizzle turned into a hard rain that slanted across the village and hurled itself against the ancient stones. Jamie, huddled in the castle doorway, watched as the distant mountains were swallowed in the grey mist rolling in from the ocean. Through it, Murdo emerged, pedalling a woman's bicycle. A sack was slung across his shoulders and he wore a flat cap with a faded badge. He stopped at the door and a shower of water ran off the peak. Delivering mail was obviously another of his duties.

He nodded at Jamie. 'Fine day.'

'Awesome.'

Murdo fumbled in the sack. 'There's just the one. Ah ...' He extracted a damp advertising flyer and thrust it in Jamie's hand. 'For Angus. Special Delivery. Can't dally.' He touched his cap, replaced the sack and wobbled back down the drive.

Jamie took one more look at the rain-swept scene, sighed and headed back indoors. He got to the top of the stone stairway and, facing a solid old oak door, was about to knock when he heard shouting coming from within.

'Damn you to hellfire, you great heaving lump of stupidity!' It was Angus. There was a squeak and a thump. 'Take that ... and that ... Now what have you to say for yerself? WHAT! I have done no such thing. Illegal, am I? You take that back this instant, or I'll—'

Jamie pulled open the door and rushed inside, fists already half raised. He stopped in amazement.

The crooked turret room was piled high with columns of books and stacks of yellowing paper. A wooden filing cabinet spewed out a stream of fluttering files. Angus, perched at a desk by the window, was about to assault an antique computer.

'Hey, Angus! Are you OK?'

Angus, red in the face and white hair flying, snarled, 'Absolutely not! This dratted machine will be the death of me. Look.' He glared at the dusty screen. '*You have performed an illegal operation.* The barefaced cheek of it!'

Jamie approached, glanced briefly at the screen and tapped a few keys. 'You're OK now, Uncle Angus.'

'Eh?' Angus peered again at the screen. 'What? Oh, so I am.' He ran a hand through his wild hair. 'Well, fancy that.' He gave a sigh. 'Most of the time we can't get a telephone connection to the mainland, and when we do manage it, I'm fighting with this infernal machine.' He took off his glasses and smiled ruefully at Jamie. 'I fear, laddie, I'm a wee bitty computer illiterate. Many thanks.'

'No problem. Look.' Jamie held out the flyer. 'Special Delivery.'

'Ta.' Angus crumpled the paper without looking at it and flung it out of the open window. 'Take a seat,' he ordered.

Jamie looked around. There were no other chairs. Angus fixed him with a fierce and watery eye. 'There is so little time. And so much needed to be done. I fear I will not be equal to the task.' He struck his forehead with his palm. 'If only I understood . . .'

'Understood?'

'Aye.' Angus waved vaguely at the piles of books. 'It is all there, if only I could fathom it. Staring me in the face, and yet I cannae seem to make head nor tail of it.'

Jamie brightened. 'No problem. Any time you need help with Word or Windows, I'm your man. It's real easy once you get the hang of it.'

Angus jabbed a gnarled forefinger at him. 'You showed some spunk. I'll give you that.'

'Excuse me?'

'Standing up to us. That was plenty plucky.' His rheumy eyes swivelled erratically, then focused again on Jamie. 'You must think this is an utter madhouse.'

Right on, thought Jamie, but he kept his mouth shut.

'No, it is. You should have left while the going was good. Why did you no'?'

Jamie scratched his head. 'Dunno. Guess I like to make my own decisions.'

Angus smacked the table with his hand, raising a puff of dust. 'Excellent. So you'll not have taken everything Duncan tells you as gospel then?'

'Duncan?'

Angus laid a finger against his nose and chuckled. 'Oh aye. The Doran grapevine, Jamie. Your little lunch party? "At Home" with Duncan? Nothing is secret here. Our local version of the Worldwide Web. Eh?'

Angus convulsed with laughter, his beard shaking as he held onto the table for support. Various books and papers crashed to the floor. Jamie shook his head. It seemed that just about everyone on Doran was completely crazy.

14

Wee Malkie

The cold, wet weather departed just as swiftly as it had arrived. The low mist fled, revealing a watery sun that brought out the brilliant summer colours. Jamie breathed in the rain-scented air and decided to explore. He walked down to the harbour, then struck out across country towards the headland, but soon found himself without a clear path. As he climbed, the ground became uneven and heavily overgrown and he had to beat down large clumps of bracken until he glimpsed the ocean ahead. He was sweating as he began to descend but he finally broke through onto a deserted and boulder-strewn cove. The sand was coarse but very clean and dotted with starfish and brilliant white shells. Small waves lapped the shore and retreated with a hiss.

Jamie looked around, then ducked behind the largest boulder. He swiftly stripped off and leaped into the water. The shock took his breath away. He let out a cry. 'Aieeee. It's freezin' . . . But so *good.*'

Carried by a powerful current, Jamie was immediately out of his depth, but he was a strong swimmer and was soon powering across the water. He switched easily from crawl to butterfly to backstroke as he carved a wide arc back towards the shore. His skin glowed as he regained his footing and flung the water from his eyes.

Wee Malkie was leaning nonchalantly against the boulder, his arms folded.

'Swank,' he said.

Jamie, standing waist-high in the water, tilted his head to clear his ears. 'What?'

Wee Malkie watched him steadily. 'I can swim too, y'know? I'm no' bad as well.' He gave a violent cough.

'OK, OK. Now, do you mind, I'm having a quiet swim . . .'

Malkie looked around him. 'Oh aye. Spey Cove's now your private beach, is it?'

'And now I'd like to get out, because I'm freezing to death.'

Wee Malkie shrugged. 'Fine. What's stopping you?'

'My stuff is on . . .'

'Oh, if you're gonna stand there like a stookie.' Wee Malkie threw Jamie his shirt and watched him brazenly as he came out of the water holding it in front of him. 'So do they not wear dookers then? In Africa?'

Jamie fastened his shirt and pulled on his jeans. 'In *America*, pal, we respect other people's privacy.'

Wee Malkie considered this. 'What you come here for then?' he asked.

Jamie hopped on one foot, trying to brush off the clinging sand. 'Hey, dude, don't you have anything better to do than bug me with dumb-ass questions?'

Wee Malkie sniffed. 'Fancy yourself for chieftain, do you?' he said.

Jamie straightened. 'What? Me? Do I look like a chieftain?'

Wee Malkie shook his head. 'No, you dinnae. But I reckon you might have as much claim as that puddock Wylie.'

'Puddock?'

Wee Malkie pointed a forefinger to his head. 'Aye. Bampot. An' a crook to boot.'

Jamie was stung. 'Oh, come on. I'd say Duncan cares a lot for this place.'

A hint of a smile hovered around Wee Malkie's mouth. 'Oh aye? You know that for a fact, do you? Well, since you're so smitten, I reckon we'd better throw in the towel straight away.' He ran a hand through his spiky red hair and turned to leave.

Jamie followed. 'Who says he's a crook?'

Wee Malkie turned and spat out, 'Anyone that has had anything to do wi' him. Like my father, who lost his job because of him. Like half the islanders who he cheated outa their land.'

'So why don't you put up your own man?'

'Oh, we have. Alistair MacDoran. He's a good man, but he's nae got funds. No power. No friends in high places. Not like your pal Duncan.'

Jamie spread his hands in a calming gesture. 'Look, friend, I ain't involved.'

Wee Malkie faced him, his small face tight with disdain. 'No? More's the pity. You just came to swank about with your daft accent and your poncy clothes and fancy strokes. You're no more a MacDoran than . . . than *Jamie Foxx*.'

15

Family Affairs

The flames leaped in the great hearth, and Angus and Eleanor sat close in their big chairs, staring at them gloomily. Even on a summer night there was always a winter chill in the hall.

Eleanor sighed. 'My son had the last laugh. Inflicting a hoodlum on me.'

Angus glanced at her. 'Aw, dinna be sair on the lad.'

'He is an absurd embarrassment. And just at a time when all our energies are needed to fight Duncan.'

Angus gazed dreamily at the licking flames. 'Aye. I wish I could see clearly what was meant to be.'

Eleanor shook her head irritably. 'Oh, for goodness'

sake, man, don't start all that mystic nonsense again.'

'It's no' nonsense, Eleanor,' Angus retorted, tugging his beard. 'It is what is written – the destiny of a proud and ancient clan.'

'Wake up, Angus. This is the twenty-first century. We have to make our own destiny. I don't pretend things have turned out as I would have wished. Indeed, my life has been full of disappointments.' She looked sharply at him. 'Not least of which has been *you*.'

Angus's wild eyes widened and turned towards her. 'I never asked to put myself forward. I was perfectly content as the clan archivist.'

Eleanor rearranged the rug over her legs. 'Yes. Well, sadly we have no choice. And we cannot delay much longer. Duncan has money and power – he can buy support. We have only history and loyalty on our side. And we will have to make do with you.'

Angus rose unsteadily to his feet and looked down at Eleanor, rocking slightly. 'The islanders need a leader. No' a scheming pretender like Wylie.'

'They have Alistair.'

Angus shook his head. 'He's a fine lad, but he's no match for Wylie, who'll promise them the earth, then sell their birthright from under them. There must be some way. If only there were more time . . .'

High above them in his bare, bleak room, Jamie lay on his bed. He held his cellphone in one hand. He tapped some keys, waiting. Nothing happened. He brought the display closer and jeered.

'Guess what – *no network connection.*' He pressed the phone hard against his cheek. 'Yeah, Mom, everything is fine. I told you'd it'd work out. I'm having a real fun time and I think they are getting used to me.' He flung the phone down on the bed and crawled under the blankets, ''Night, Mom,' he muttered into the pillow. 'Love ya.'

Over the next week or so, the cow-shed chores got easier and Jamie's morning milk pails filled ever more rapidly. Even the cows seemed to sense that they were in good hands as he sat, pressed against them, directing the white frothy flow from alternate teats. Occasionally they turned a heavy head and gazed at him with their deep, moist eyes. The heat, the smell of animal and sour milk and the repetitive motion lulled him into a trance. He glanced down at the pail and saw the milk slopping over. He cursed.

'Why the torn face?'

Hazel stood accusingly before him. She was dressed in ragged jeans and a shapeless woollen sweater of indeterminate colour. Wheat stalks were impaled all over her clothes and sprouted from her tousled hair.

Jamie squinted at her. 'Come again?'

Hazel shook her head impatiently. 'Wha' stole yer scone?'

Jamie got to his feet, and picked up the full pail of milk. 'Excuse me. I'll just run and fetch a dictionary.'

Hazel did not move but looked at him challengingly. 'I thought you was learnin' tae speak Scots.'

Jamie lowered the pail. 'Oh, I *dig*. You just like comin'

on with the Scots hooey to mess with my vibe? Well, I guess two can play at that.' He kicked away the stool, removed a woollen hat from the back pocket of his jeans and pulled it down low over his eyes. He snatched the ladle from the pail and brought it to his lips like a hand mike:

'*It's another day, and I guess it's OK,*' he growled.
If you like to milk the cows, and if Eleanor allows
you might even feed the sheep, without sleep,
Guess I'm here to serve my time, why whine (don't whine)
You could be in the surf, 'stead of cuttin' friggin' turf.'

He executed a neat spin, tossed the ladle high, caught it at the last moment and brought it back to his mouth:

'*It's another day, can't have hassle in the castle,*
Guess I'm here to serve my time. An' that's fine,
just fine – with me.'

Jamie made some beat-box sounds and the animals shifted uneasily in their stalls. He threw the ladle one more time and caught it above his head in the brimming pail.

Hazel stared open-mouthed at Jamie. He put the pail down, bowed deeply, acknowledging ecstatic imaginary applause. Then she scowled. 'Huh,' she said. 'Anyways, I only came to remind you that you agreed to make breakfast today. In case you'd forgotten.'

There was an ominous silence in the hall. Hazel and Angus were seated facing each other across the great oak table. Eleanor, back stiff as a ramrod, had just taken her place at the head. The gleaming silver dishes were placed as usual on the table, but stood open, and empty.

Eleanor fixed Angus with an accusing eye. 'No porridge?'

Angus dabbed his mouth with a napkin and muttered, 'Er, no, there doesnae seem to be . . .'

Eleanor turned threateningly to Hazel. 'And, pray, where are the kippers?'

Hazel shrugged and examined her spoon. She felt Eleanor's eyes boring into her like a gimlet.

'We always have kippers. Is this some sort of a joke?' Eleanor's nostrils twitched. She sniffed the air. 'What is that unpleasant smell?'

Hazel and Angus hung their heads. The kitchen door flew open with a crash and Jamie hurtled into the hall. A white apron was wrapped around his jeans and he carried a tray on which were set a large silver teapot and four plates, heaped with burgers, bacon, hash browns and fried eggs.

Jamie planted the tray on the table with a flourish. 'Sorry to keep you folks waiting, but I had to run and fetch a few things from the store.' Taking a cloth from his shoulder, he delicately placed one of the plates before Eleanor. 'There you go. The Big MacDoran and all the trimmings. I would have fixed grits, but I guess they were clean out of them. The juice is comin' right up, folks.' Jamie served Angus and Hazel and stood back, beaming proudly. 'Now, *enjoy!*'

Eleanor gazed at her plate in horror. 'What is this?' she finally managed to splutter.

'This, Grandma, is breakfast – Californian style. Now, I done your eggs sunny side up, but if you'd prefer easy over . . .'

'I prefer' – Eleanor's voice took on an edge of steel that could have sliced the food before her – 'porridge, in my house. I prefer kippers or Finnan haddock, in my house. If I take an egg, which is rarely, I take it hard-boiled.' Jamie looked winded. Eleanor waved at the plate, averting her head. 'Fetch it away. The smell is turning my stomach. I'll just take a cup of tea – I trust you can have done nothing to ruin that?'

'Sure.' Jamie poured from the large teapot into her cup. 'Point of fact, you'll find that it's . . . er . . . coffee.' He glanced briefly at Eleanor, and went on hurriedly, 'But I swear, I make real good coffee.'

Angus had a sudden fit of coughing and Hazel tried to mask her smile with her napkin.

Eleanor rose to her feet and fixed Hazel with a steely glare. 'I am going to my room,' she announced. 'If the boy has not totally depleted our provisions, you may salvage something edible and bring it to me there.' She flung her napkin on the table and hobbled painfully towards the staircase.

16

Games

Jamie walked disconsolately through the village. Life either went too fast when you were having a good time, he reflected, or slowed to a crawl when you weren't. Certainly it had moved at a snail's pace the last few days, and his thoughts turned enviously to what he was missing back home. The surf would be up at the beaches, and he could be hanging lazily on his board in the rolling swell with Jeroo and Chico, waiting to catch the big one. Lester, who hated water, would sit by their clothes on the sand. Or they'd all sit beside the creek with their rods, trying and failing to hook an elusive salmon. Maybe he'd wander along to The Dime Diner, have a soda and, who knows, maybe even Carol Masters might drop by. The thought made him smile. What had Jeroo said? *The number one fan in the Jamie MacD Appreciation Society?* He grinned as he pictured her shy smile, the downcast eyes. Carol was suddenly replaced by a vision of Hazel, with her freckles and wild hair, and that superior smirk. Jamie scowled.

'Ah, hello there.' It was Murdo, standing on a chair, tacking a sign to a post. Jamie had almost walked straight into him.

'Oh, hi,' he responded glumly.

'You seem a wee bit doon-moued?' Murdo tapped the sign with his hammer. 'Well, this'll show your mettle. Are you up for it?'

'What is this?'

Murdo seemed astonished. 'D'you no' ken? It's the Big Day. The Games.'

Jamie shook his head. 'Games?' he echoed.

'Aye. The Doran Games. Saturday fortnight, in yonder glen.' He waved his hammer vaguely towards the hills.

Jamie looked at him suspiciously. 'What kinda games?'

Murdo gave the sign a final tap and dismounted. 'Athletic games,' he pronounced grandly. He gave Jamie a broad wink. 'No' a bad opportunity to prove yourself in front of the wee lassies. They'll all be chasin' the winners. You could find yourself a bonnie click.'

'Click?'

Murdo explained patiently, 'A girl. *Friend?*'

Jamie brightened. 'Oh? That's cool. I may just do that. You know, back home, I'm on the school team.'

Murdo gathered his chair and hammer. 'Well, there you go then, you'll have nae problem at all. I'll enter your name for the main events.'

Yes, thought Jamie, his mood lightening instantly. That's exactly what I need. A challenge. Suddenly life seemed to jerk forward into fast motion. He began to jog back towards the castle. He'd show them. Get in shape. A bit of training. A regime. He could already hear the cheers and the chant: 'Jamie. Jamie. JAMIE.' The US versus the UK. 'Jamie MacDoran heads the US team . . . steps up to the podium to receive the gold medal. They play "The Star-spangled Banner" as the flag is raised . . .' He punched the air.

He kept at it too. Over the next days he rose early with the sun and, before beginning his milking chores, struggled into his tracksuit and running shoes and loped along the deserted roads. Occasionally he would pass Murdo in his postman's cap, wobbling on his bicycle. 'That's it,' Murdo would cry. 'Don't let them catch you.'

Jamie soon became a familiar sight as he raced through the village, and some of the locals now smiled and waved in recognition. One afternoon, Duncan coasted alongside in his Hummer. 'What's all this?' he enquired.

'Training,' Jamie panted, 'for the Games.'

Duncan raised his sunglasses. 'That's terrific news,' he said, 'but I can see I'm going to have some serious competition.' He grinned, and then a thought crossed his mind. 'I meant to ask,' he said. 'How is your mother? Fine woman. Missing you, I'll bet.'

Jamie felt a pang of guilt. 'Well, I haven't spoken with her. I've been meaning to write . . .' He hung his head.

Duncan checked his watch and fished in the dashboard. 'I know how it is,' he said, passing him a cellphone. 'Why don't you give her a call?'

Jamie laughed. 'C'mon. They don't work here.'

Duncan indicated the large aerial on the rear of the car. 'Mine do. Satellite.'

Jamie took the phone and punched in the numbers. 'Are you sure?' he whispered.

Marcia's voice came in loud and clear. 'The MacDoran residence.'

Jamie grinned. 'Mom, it's me.'

There was a stunned pause before Marcia let out a wail of delight. 'Honey, I was just thinking about you, not two minutes ago. Oh, it's so good to hear your voice. How are you?'

'I'm fine, Mom. Everything is going great. I've been milking cows . . .'

'You are kidding me! *You?* Milking cows?'

'You'd better believe it. The cows think I'm pretty good. And I'm in training too.'

'Training? For what?'

'There's these big island Games coming up soon and I'm gonna compete. I'm getting real fit.'

'My, you sound pretty busy. But tell me, how's it working out with . . . with the family?'

'No problem, Mom. Everyone's been real good to

me. 'Specially Duncan. It's his satellite phone I'm using, so I can't speak too long.'

'Well, please thank him from me.'

'Will do. And Mom, how 'bout you? Are you OK?'

'Yeah, I guess so. I'm getting there. It's hard, but I'm working on it. Keeping busy too.' Her voice caught. 'Just call when you're ready to come home. Miss you, hon.'

'Me too.' Jamie closed down the call and handed the phone back to Duncan. 'Appreciate it.'

'My pleasure.' Duncan slipped his sunglasses back down. 'Keep on running,' he said as he accelerated away.

Jamie discovered an old rubber football in one of the cow sheds, fixed up a makeshift basketball hoop on one of the barn doors, and spent hours perfecting his approach and his throws. He collected heavy stones and practised lifting them slowly with outstretched arms. His already muscular frame became even more taut and defined. Even Hazel, he noted with satisfaction, was aware of his intense regime and increasing fitness. Several times he had caught her looking at him from a window or a doorway.

He was focused and enthralled. Life sped past.

The Saturday of the Games dawned with a clear blue sky, a warm sun and just the hint of a breeze. By ten o'clock it seemed as though the whole of Doran was making its way to the glen.

Jamie got his kit together, threw a bottle of water and a towel into his sports bag and set off down the drive at a trot. As he turned out of the gates, he almost ran into a figure dawdling down the road. It took a moment for Jamie to recognize Hazel. Her unruly hair had been partly tamed and was scraped into a tight bun behind her head and she was dressed in a tartan kilt, a short plum velvet jacket, white blouse and laced shoes. Jamie stared at her in amazement. Hazel blushed and looked away.

'Oh aye,' she said, 'you can scoff if you like. I feel a right prat.'

'No, I think you look . . .' Jamie searched for an appropriate adjective. What did she look? Different, certainly, and not at all like Hazel. 'Er, neat,' he said lamely.

Hazel pulled a face. 'Neat? Now there's a word I don't hear too often.'

'What games are you in for?'

Hazel's chin went up and she tossed her head. 'I'm no' in the Games. I am dancing, if you must know.'

'Dancing? You mean . . .'

'Oh, none of your disco, hip-hop, and suchlike. No *dirty* dancing. They're into Highland jigs and reels and stuff round here.' She glared at him challengingly. 'Is that OK with you?'

The roar of a tractor made them jump, and round the bend came Murdo perched on a rusted Fordson, pulling a trailer filled with crates and bales of straw. He waved cheerily. 'I'm taking stuff down to the glen. I'll give you a ride if you like. Hop in.'

Jamie threw in his bag and leaped on board. He

offered a hand to Hazel, who ignored it. She climbed in carefully, smoothing down her kilt, and sat on a crate, keeping her knees pressed firmly together. As they drove through the village, the throng of people making their way to the glen increased. Murdo sounded his horn and received insults in return. Others jumped up too, and by the time they reached the fields of the glen Jamie and Hazel were surrounded by many laughing townspeople.

Marquees had been erected, hung with fluttering bunting, and were already doing a brisk trade in teas and beers. On a wooden stage a pipe band was tuning up, and the echoing loudspeakers were being tested. A large good-humoured crowd was assembled, many wearing kilts or Highland dress, greeting each other and inspecting the pens of cattle that were also on show.

Hazel climbed down from the trailer and straightened her jacket. 'Well, I'll keep an eye out for you,' she said to Jamie.

'Sure. And I'll try and catch the dance routine.'

'Fine.' Hazel moved away.

Jamie shouldered his bag and pushed through the crowds. He felt a tug on his sleeve. It was Wee Malkie and his gang, who were trailing behind him. They had made no effort to improve their usual ragged appearance.

Malkie's thin face gazed up at him. 'What you doon fer, by the way?'

'You name it, boy, and I'm doin' it.'

Donald, a blond, floppy-haired member of the gang, piped up, 'I didnae ken you Yanks went in for the Games?'

Jamie turned to face them. 'You kiddin'? I guess

you're forgettin' that the US has won more Olympic medals than any other nation.' There was muttering among the lads. Jamie held out a hand. 'Now I'm not sayin' that I am an Olympic athlete, but . . . well, I guess I can hold my own.'

Wee Malkie stared at him, his thin lips pressed together.

Jamie caught sight of Murdo, who was now selling programmes. 'Hey, Murdo. Everything OK?'

'Aye. Fine and dandy. They're all expecting you.'

Jamie breathed in deeply and flexed his knees. He felt good. This was going to be his day.

The loudspeakers blared out the names of competitors as Murdo led Jamie over to one of the contest areas. A large rectangle of grass had been roped off, surrounded by an expectant crowd. Already a dozen or so giant islanders in kilts and singlets were limbering up and rubbing grit into the palms of their hands. They eyed Jamie curiously.

'What's this?' Jamie muttered to Murdo.

'Hammer throw, of course. You'll be used to that?'

Jamie nodded. 'Oh. Yeah. Sure.' He watched the other competitors, trying desperately to get the hang of what was required. Some were doing knee bends, or executing balletic turns. Others were getting the feel of the hammer, which was actually a solid iron ball attached to a wooden shaft by a chain.

The announcer entered his booth, picked up his microphone, and a list of names echoed round the grounds from the loudspeakers: '*Alistair MacDoran,*

Gordon Craigie, Duncan Wylie, and lastly a big Doran welcome for our visitor from over the seas, Jamie MacDoran.'

There was scattered applause. A group of young girls eyed Jamie approvingly and whispered, heads pressed together. The most brazen of them, a big girl in a micro skirt and outsize sweatshirt with JANET spelled out in large white letters, gave him a little wave. They all giggled. Jamie waved back.

Duncan, swathed in a scarlet silk dressing gown, strode into the area. He clapped Jamie on the back. 'Jamie! Good lad. Going to show us how it's done?'

Jamie gulped. 'Well, I guess I'm game for anything.'

'Grand. Grand.' Duncan performed some swift knee bends. 'I'm afraid I'm getting too old for this sort of thing.'

There was a roar from the crowd as the competition got underway. One after another the kilted giants seized the shaft of the heavy hammer. They wound themselves up into a spring, then spun like dervishes with arms outstretched before releasing it. Each time the ball flew in a graceful arc before dropping to the ground, where officials measured its distance.

The distorted voice of the announcer rippled round the glen: '*A fine throw there, Hamish. And next is number thirty-three, Duncan Wylie.'*

There were cheers and a few disguised boos from the crowd. Duncan beamed, punched the air and whipped off the dressing gown, revealing the kilt beneath. He looked incredibly fit, with a muscular chest encased in a tight-fitting cotton vest, and well-defined thighs. He rubbed grit on his hands and gripped the hammer shaft, feeling its weight and finding his balance. He twisted his body slowly. Then he began to turn, gathering speed until at the very last moment he released the shaft, sending the ball flying through the air and watching as it eventually bit into the lush turf. The officials ran over to examine the ground and then signalled to the announcer in his booth.

The metallic announcement blasted out of the speakers: '*And Duncan's throw equals that of Hamish.*' There was applause. '*But there is one more contestant to show his mettle. Wee Jamie MacDoran, a newcomer to these shores, and to these Games. Are you ready, Jamie?*'

All eyes were on Jamie, who nodded and took off his tracksuit to reveal his basketball shorts and University High vest. The group of girls responded with wolf whistles. Duncan, walking back to the enclosure, gave him a thumbs-up.

Jamie gritted his hands and grasped the wooden shaft. The metal ball, dangling on its chain, felt incredibly heavy. With great concentration he began to turn, the ball strung out before him. He spun faster and faster on the spot as the crowd watched spellbound. Jamie whirled like a top, drilling into the turf with his trainers until the hammer flew involuntarily from his grasp. The crowd ducked as it hurtled backwards towards them, and the announcer fled just before the ball crashed onto the roof of his booth. A howl of feedback echoed around the glen.

As Jamie straightened, he caught sight of Wee Malkie's pinched face gazing at him in horror.

Jamie did not redeem himself with the shot put either. He studied Alistair and Duncan and the other competitors as they glided or spun within the turf circle, pressing the shot against their neck before planting a foot on the mark and hurling the metal weight as if it were a mere basketball. But when his turn came, the heavy shot slipped from his hand and plopped miserably to the ground just a few centimetres outside the circle.

In the silence that followed, the girl with JANET across her chest called out, 'Hey, Jamie, I think you dropped something.' Her friends camply mimicked the action, and the crowd rocked with laughter. Hazel, standing nearby, looked stonily ahead.

Tossing the caber also came as something of a surprise to Jamie, who had never tossed anything heavier than a pancake. All the contestants were required to lift a young fir tree, around five metres long and weighing about forty kilos, and throw it so that it turned over with the smaller end facing away. The others, with immense exertion, mostly achieved this feat, but when Jamie's turn came, he found he could hardly lift the trunk off the ground. He felt his arms breaking as he staggered a few paces with the caber just clear of the turf. He glimpsed Eleanor in the crowd, her hand over her eyes, just before his legs buckled and the tree dug itself firmly into the ground. Jamie looked up in alarm as it wobbled, then raced away as it toppled, narrowly missing his fleeing heels.

*

The final event was obviously the most prestigious of the Games – a running race around three giant circuits of the glen. There was scarcely an empty space around the whole track and some fifty entrants were limbering up in the crowded enclosure. Jamie was sitting, dispirited and mud-spattered, on a barrel. He had been the object of much amusement during the day but now seemed to have become invisible, with everyone transferring their attention to the big race. He was aware of Angus standing over him.

'Oh dear. You look fair forfochten. Pay no mind to it. It's only a game.'

Jamie looked up at him wearily. 'Sure thing, Angus.'

Angus surveyed him and pulled at his beard. 'You'll take part in the running?'

'No way. I am pooped, man. I quit.'

'Is that it? You're going to let them get the better of you?'

Jamie spat angrily, 'Oh, c'mon, Angus. I *tried*.'

Angus grabbed Jamie's shoulder and brought his face down close to him. The watery eyes scanned Jamie's features. 'Then you'll have to try a wee bitty harder. The MacDoran way.'

Jamie shook his head and pulled away. 'No can do, Angus.'

Angus straightened. 'Aye. *Can do*.' He fumbled deep in his pocket. 'Here. Take this.' He held out a small blue stone with a circle of glass inserted in its centre.

Jamie laughed bitterly. 'What's this? The booby prize?'

Angus stared intently at Jamie and thrust the stone into his hand, closing his fingers around it. 'Hold it fast. This Stone of Doran was your father's. It has belonged to all the chieftains.'

The announcer's voice crackled out from the speakers: '. . . and let's have a big welcome yet again for the plucky visitor to our shores, Jamie MacDoran, who has entertained us all this afternoon.'

There were cheers from the good-humoured spectators, many now well fuelled with drink. The announcer broke in again: 'Oh, and Jamie . . . I'll try to keep out of your road this time.'

The crowd erupted in whistles and cheers.

Angus whispered urgently, 'Go on, lad.'

Jamie rose to his feet, bowed and clasped his hands above his head like a boxer. As he made his way to the starting line, he passed the group of girls. 'Janet' confronted him brazenly, hand on hip. 'Still standing, Jamie?' She gave him an oversized wink. 'Dinnae fret, love, you just hirple around after 'em.'

Her friend chimed in, 'Aye, better watch out for Wylie – he's been champion racer six times . . .'

And another added, 'An' Alistair is the fastest man in the west.'

Janet blew him a kiss. 'But we're rooting for you, Jamie.' The girls clutched each other and collapsed in hysterics.

At the line was a mêlée of runners. Some stretched, others bent double, touching the ground with their fingertips. Duncan was inhaling deeply and Jamie recognized Alistair, the young pallbearer, sitting on the grass massaging his calves. Jamie stretched his legs and arms, then shook his limbs to relax them. He could feel the stone in his hand and somehow it felt comforting.

The speakers barked back to life: '*Righto. Now we have the culmination of today's events. It's the triple circuit. Competitors, if you'll take your places, please.*'

The runners lined up on the grid and Jamie found himself penned into the middle of the group.

'*If you're ready? Get set.*'

A pistol shot rang out and the runners were away, quickly establishing space between themselves and the other competitors. Jamie hunched his shoulders and notched himself into the centre of the pack. Ahead he could see Alistair and Duncan pulling away from the field, but he settled for a steady, comfortable pace. He had plenty of time. The sun was already dipping towards the mountains, and the air was cooling noticeably. Faces passed in a blur as they shouted words of encouragement, but he concentrated on the thud of his feet on the springy turf and the rhythm of his pounding arms.

By the start of the second circuit, the field had thinned visibly. Runners had developed cramps and limped to the trackside, or were trailing, winded and breathing heavily. Jamie increased his pace and overtook the group immediately in front of him, pulling himself up into sixth position. He hung on there for a while and gradually moved up two places until he was fourth in the field. Ahead of him was a brawny lad in a kilt, then a sizeable gap before Duncan and Alistair, who were alternately taking the lead.

The brawny boy, red in the face and sweating profusely, turned to look back at Jamie, then tried to sprint away from him. Jamie concentrated on keeping the rhythm of his stride and heard the lad's breathing begin to rasp in his throat. Jamie gained on him steadily, positioning himself in his slipstream and feeling the boy's sweat land on his face. With a groan, the boy suddenly threw up his arms and veered into the crowd, where supporting hands caught him.

As Jamie rounded the far curve, he saw Duncan ease back into second position and Alistair still powerfully in the lead, his mane of hair flying in the wind. Nothing had changed by the beginning of the final circuit, but the three front-runners now lapped the stragglers. Jamie could feel the beginning of a stitch on his right side. He took deep breaths and it seemed to pass. He was surprised that his legs still felt supple and strong – and was glad he had kept to his training regime. On the long straight towards the mountains he could feel the breeze behind him, pushing him forward. The cries of the crowd beat in his ears and he realized he was gaining on Duncan.

Soon they were abreast of each other, almost touching. Duncan did not look at him, but Jamie knew that he was well aware of his presence, the older man's mind working like a computer, plotting his strategy. As they entered the last bend, Duncan suddenly swerved across Jamie's path. His arms were pumping and his elbow, shielded from the eyes of the crowd, caught Jamie viciously in the ribs. The crowd gasped as Jamie stumbled and almost fell to his knees. He recovered as best he could, but his rhythm had been broken and he was winded and he now trailed in third place. He clenched his hands in frustration and felt his right fist tighten around the Stone of Doran. As he pressed the smooth surface, he felt something surge from it, like a warm current flowing into his limbs. Suddenly he was flying, his legs leaping across the turf and the wind hammering his face. The crowd yelled as he swept into the final straight and, in overdrive, powered easily past Duncan – whose face was white and etched with exertion. Jamie could see the finishing line looming as he closed on Alistair, who snatched a glance back in alarm. At the tape, both runners thrust themselves forward and collapsed on the ground, chests heaving and eyes closed.

The crowd went wild. Even Eleanor put a hand to her mouth as Angus stared intently at Jamie's prone body. Wee Malkie and his gang danced in a frenzied circle.

The loudspeakers crackled back into life: '*Well, I never,*' gasped the announcer. '*That has to be . . . wait a minute. Can this be right? A dead heat? . . . Yes, not a hair's breadth between them. And . . . I believe I can announce . . . an all-time record for the Games.*'

Jamie opened his eyes as the cheering began and saw Alistair doubled up and gasping for breath. Their eyes met and Alistair straightened, flung back his hair and walked over to him. He extended a hand to haul Jamie roughly to his feet and embraced him warmly. 'Great race, Jamie,' he said.

Angus caught Eleanor's eye, but she looked away swiftly. Jamie saw Duncan, wrapping himself once more in his silk dressing gown. He walked over to him.

'Hey, dude. Seems we got ourselves into a tangle back there . . .' He held out his hand. 'No hard feelings, huh?'

Duncan wrapped a towel round his neck. 'No, of course not,' he said. He hesitated a moment, then seized Jamie's hand. 'Good lad. Your dad would have been proud of you.'

Hazel ran towards Jamie to congratulate him, but he was already being mobbed by an admiring crowd. Wee Malkie and his gang were plying him with questions and Janet and her girls jostled against him.

'You've a fine pair o' pins there,' said one, touching his leg. 'If they need a massage you've only tae ask!'

Hazel watched them, her smile fading. She bit her lip. The musicians suddenly struck up on the dais and the dance troupe leader yelled across: 'Hazel! Will you come *on*!'

Flustered, she ran late into formation, and with back erect and feet flying in the Highland reel, stared stonily ahead.

17

After Dark

Jamie enjoyed his moment of fame at the centre of an admiring crowd of young islanders. Finally, there had been whispered conversations and the group split up, darting away into the gathering dusk.

Jamie walked slowly away from the glen. When he reached the road, one of the lads was waiting. He was tall and dark-haired and wore a tracksuit. 'Would you consider joining us at a wee gathering?' he asked casually.

Jamie smiled. 'Sure. I got no other plans.'

The boy held out his hand. 'I'm Craig, by the way,' he said. 'You can come with me.'

Jamie hoisted his sports bag over his shoulder and Craig set off at a brisk pace up the road. 'Is it a party?' asked Jamie, feeling aches in his legs as he tried to keep up.

'Sort of,' replied Craig, 'but it's no big deal.' He was obviously not hot on conversation.

After a mile or so, Craig turned abruptly from the road and onto a rough path that led up the hillside through the bracken. They walked in silence until they reached a group of farm outbuildings. At the rear was a dilapidated black barn. There was no sign of life. Jamie looked enquiringly at Craig, who approached the barn and rapped three times on the door.

There were shouts from within and the door flew open, revealing a bright and crowded interior. Someone had hung a hand-painted sign that read AFTER DARK, with a picture of a boy and a girl gazing into each other's eyes. Oil lamps were slung from the rafters, and bales of hay lined up beside a battered trestle table on which were piled assorted plates and cutlery. Groups of youths were talking animatedly, and in one corner Wee Malkie and his gang were heaving logs onto a roaring fire that licked at an iron range above.

Janet spotted Jamie and let out a whoop, throwing open her arms. She had tied a large stained apron around her micro skirt and pressed him into it. 'There you are, ma little beezer.'

Jamie disengaged himself. 'Hi, Janet.'

Janet gave a squeal of delight. 'He knows my name!' She followed his gaze down to the huge letters across her chest and put a hand to her mouth. 'Oh, silly me!'

Jamie looked around in surprise. 'So this is where the action is?'

'Aye, welcome to the wicked world of Doran After Dark.' She took a step back and raised an eyebrow. 'Why? Did you think we sat around with the old 'uns scoffing haggis and cream teas?'

'Come on, Janet,' said Craig, 'can't you see he's famished? Get the man some grub.'

After a brief tussle, Janet wrenched a bowl of grubby crisps from the grasp of one of the lads. 'Stop hogging them, and give someone else a chance.' She glared around. 'Where's them Scotch eggs?'

'All gone,' came the chorus.

Janet ran a hand through her hair. 'Typical. They're just gannets,' she pronounced in disgust.

'I guess you must be the chef?' asked Jamie, indicating Janet's stained apron.

'Jings, you'd not want to touch a dish that I'd a hand in. Instant death. No, Gordon is our resident gastronomic wizard.'

A brawny boy in a kilt, stirring a large black pan on the range, turned and smiled. Jamie recognized him as the lad who had faltered in the final circuit of the race.

'Hi, dude. You OK? You took a nasty fall.'

'Nae problem. Peaked too soon.'

'Och, he's fine,' said Janet. 'Though he took a couple of rows of spectators down with him.' She whispered to Jamie, 'Gord is a genius at the cooking – known around these parts as Gordon Bleu. I swear he's better than any of the lassies. These ignoramuses don't appreciate good cooking – crisps, bangers and Scotch eggs is all they want – but if you want to try something amazing, grab yourself a seat.'

She led Jamie to the table, gave a plate a quick wipe on her sweater and handed him a knife and a bent fork. Gordon came over with a sizzling pan. Jamie perched on a bale and was gradually surrounded by the other kids, who watched him curiously as he tasted the stew.

Jamie waved his fork. 'Mmm, this is real good. What is it?'

Gordon gave the pan a stir. 'Whatever I could lay my hands on. Rabbit, grouse, herbs, some tatties, cream . . . I'm sure it's not a patch on what you're used to up at the castle.'

Jamie exploded. 'You are kidding! It's all porridge and finny this and kippered that, fish heads and bones.' He swallowed another forkful. 'This is *soul food*, man.'

Gordon flushed with pride.

Janet planted her hands on the table. 'I hope you realize this is a great honour, Jamie. We don't let any old visitors into our socials.'

A voice came from down the table. 'That's 'cos we don't *have* any visitors!'

There was general laughter.

'Well, soon as I get back home, I'll tell the gang.' Jamie smiled expansively around the table. 'They'll be down on the beach now, surfing. We throw some wild beach parties – plenty of fries and steaks and Cokes and great music.'

'Do you live in Hollywood then?' a thin girl in a tracksuit asked.

Jamie nodded. 'Close. Hollywood is a part of LA. It's mostly TV now, but it's where all the big film studios used to be.'

'Is it full of film stars?'

Jamie leaned back. 'You bet. Will Smith never stops calling me, and if I look out my window I can see Brad Pitt polishing his Lexus next door.' There was a silence. 'No, I'm just kidding,' Jamie added quickly. 'Though I think I did see Halle Berry once. Buying onions in the deli.'

'Do you go to school?' Andrew, a stocky member of Malkie's gang, put in.

'Sure do.'

'Our school had to close down three days last month. Two of the teachers left. They had to bring someone temporary over from the mainland.'

'I saw in the paper it's all gangs and drugs in LA,' said Donald, Wee Malkie's blond henchman. 'You cannae go out at night for fear of being murdered.'

'Aye,' said Janet. 'Just like here.'

Jamie wiped his mouth. 'Aw, you shouldn't believe everything you read or see in the movies. LA's a big place. Sure, there are some scary neighbourhoods, and a couple of my buds live in those, but it's pretty cool where my crib is.'

'Have you got a sweetheart?' the girl in the tracksuit asked out of the blue.

Jamie looked down, confused.

140

Janet cackled. 'Oh, Rhona, you shameless hussy. Of course he has, an' his poor heart is breakin' from the separation. Unless' – she wagged a finger and looked closely at Jamie – 'he's found a bit of local talent.'

Jamie feigned shock. 'You promised not to tell.'

Janet punched his shoulder. 'Oh, not *me*, you bampot. Though I could surely show you a few interesting Celtic moves.' There were some jeers from the table. 'No, I fancy that Little Miss Muffet has her eye on you.'

Jamie looked perplexed. 'Come again?'

'Oh, you know who I mean. High and Mighty Hazel. Thinks she's a cut above the rest of us. Snooty, like the rest of them up yonder.'

There was general discussion. Some thought that Hazel was the only sensible person at the castle, and that she often went out of her way to help the islanders.

'Hazel's OK, I guess,' Jamie said with a wry grin. 'Not that we exactly hit it off. Most times she ain't talking to me.'

Janet seized Jamie's hand and gazed into his eyes. 'Who needs words, when you have . . . *passion*?' There were more catcalls.

'So, have you come to see how the other half live? Jeer at the natives?' Something in the change of tone alerted Jamie, and he turned to see a thin-faced boy with cold eyes glowering at him.

Jamie shook his head. 'No, pal, I certainly—'

'Oh, we may be in the sticks, but we can read and tune in to the radio and we have heard all about America the Beautiful and how great it is. The big superpower, eh? Bringing democracy to the heathens – Iraq, Afghanistan. Just send in the troops and the tanks and the helicopters, and carry the casualties out in body bags. You must be reet chuffed now you got your own black fella running the show – the blessed Obama.' The boy stood up and leaned his hands on the table. 'So what advice would you give us poor bairns, stuck in this wee hole?'

Jamie shrugged. 'Look, dude, I ain't got no advice.'

The boy looked surprised. 'Is that so? What a pity. And here was I hoping you might be able to give us a few tips, the American way. Give us a leg up.'

'Oh, shut it, Calum,' said Craig. 'If you're so soured with this place, why don't you pack it in? Go across the water?'

'Do you think I wouldn't in a trice?' Calum spat back. 'But who'd have us? Where's the work? Where's the opportunities for the Scots? Oh, we may have a Scottish Parliament, but they're under the thumb of the English scumbags at Westminster. And they've sold out to your lot . . .' Calum looked directly at Jamie. 'No offence, pal.'

Jamie shook his head, but didn't rise to the bait.

'You muckle sumph. Go and ask your friend Duncan,' sneered Craig. 'I'm sure he's got room for you in his grand schemes.'

'A sight better than waiting for Alistair to pull us through,' Calum retorted. 'He's all talk and no trousers.'

There were loud shouts from the group: 'Alistair is OK.' 'His heart is in the right place.' And, 'He's one of us.'

Calum's face was white with fury. 'Oh, it's easy to

laugh at Duncan. But at least he *has* plans when no one else has come up with anything. And he only has the best pile on the island, some pricey motors and a hi-tech boat. So, tell me, who's got the last laugh?' There were some cheers.

Janet banged the table. 'Now shut it! We're meant to entertain our visitor, not bore him to death with our squabbling. Let's have some music.' She looked around the barn. 'Where's Dougal? Come over here, Dougal, this instant and give us some beauty.'

A sallow, black-haired youth was propelled to the top of the table, and Wee Malkie produced an acoustic guitar from a corner of the barn. There was a hush as Dougal settled himself opposite Jamie, and made a few adjustments to the tuning. Jamie noticed his unusually long and tapering fingers.

Dougal's song began instrumentally, with his fingers fluttering over the strings, not so much playing as coaxing them into melody. And then he shut his eyes, and a powerful voice emerged with words that rose and tumbled forth. Was it English? Or some ancient Celtic tongue? It didn't matter, because voice and instrument were entwined, at once strange and familiar. Jamie was entranced. He thought he had never heard anything so joyous and so sad. Dougal sat almost motionless, his face composed and drawn and only his fingers moving with extraordinary agility. He was not playing the guitar. It was playing *him*. When at last the music wound down and there was silence, Jamie was aware of Wee Malkie staring at him defiantly.

Janet cleared her throat. 'Aye, well, I'm glad someone could show our guest a bit of class. Now' – she rose to her feet – 'is anyone going to help me clear these pots?'

There was a sudden clatter of activity as the table was swept clean, and only Dougal remained seated, eyes closed, his hands resting on the guitar. Jamie touched him lightly on the shoulder. 'Hey, dude. That was incredible. I never heard anything like that.'

Dougal opened his eyes. They were light green and seemed to be lit from within. His voice was almost a whisper. 'Oh yes, Jamie. Course you have. You've heard it before, only you were not listening.'

Puzzled, Jamie shook his head. 'Yeah, but how?'

The green eyes seemed to mock him. 'In the blood, Jamie. *In the blood.*'

Jamie's jaw dropped and Dougal suddenly laughed loudly and swept the strings with his hand. 'Hey, did you hear this great wee tune from the new White Stripes album?' He hunched over the guitar and ground out a riff.

Jamie grinned delightedly. 'Man, you are something else.'

Angus was sitting at his desk, poring over a large and ancient leather volume. A couple of candles stuck in jam jars provided scant illumination as his finger traced the spidery writing on the yellowed pages. He stopped at a phrase and stared at it. ''*Til angels bring the key . . .* Angels? Hmm.'

The door creaked open and Jamie peered in. 'Angus.

Thought I heard you.' He looked around. 'Who nuked the power?'

Angus chuckled. 'Eleanor's economies. Says the leccy's too dear. Come in, come in. D'you fancy a wee dram?'

'A what?'

Angus pulled open a drawer and extracted a dusty, unlabelled bottle and a couple of small glasses. 'A dram. Aye. To celebrate a great victory.'

'I don't drink.'

'Me neither. But a wee taste?'

Jamie sat down on the desk. 'OK.'

Angus poured two small measures of a dark amber liquid into the glasses and handed one to Jamie. He touched them together. 'Hale jing bang.' Angus drained the liquid at one gulp and let out a deep sigh of content-ment. 'Ah. That's more like it.'

Jamie took a little sip and clutched his throat. '*Ahhhhh!* Jeez, Angus, what is it?'

Angus beamed at him. 'Nothing but the pure water of life. That'll put you back on your feet.'

'That reminds me.' Jamie fished in his pocket and pulled out the blue stone. 'Thanks for this. It sure brought me some luck today.' He held it out on his palm.

Angus shook his head. 'Luck has nothing tae do with it, laddie. That is the Stone of Doran, smoothed over the centuries by the hands of our chieftains. You see the glass here?'

Jamie tilted the stone. 'Yeah. It's sorta cloudy. From age, I guess. How'd it get in there?'

'It was put there, hundreds of years ago, by Kenneth, one of the Ancients, a verra wise man and a great seer—'

'Seer?'

'Aye, he was blinded in battle, but he could still picture things in his head, foretell the future, mebbe. Many of his sayings were written down here.'

Angus turned back to the desk and squinted at the leather volume.

'It seems to have a meaning, if only I could divine it.' He turned over a page. 'Listen. This is some of it:

'*Turn aside from Wrath and from the depths you shall find a way to the sanctuary of light.*'

'Sounds like the Bible. Wrath? As in anger?'

Angus stroked his beard thoughtfully. 'Mebbe. Or we have a Cape Wrath hereabouts. And what about this?

'*The Head shall venture from the Body and interpret from afar . . .*'

Jamie laughed. 'That is seriously weird. What's he getting at?'

Angus prodded the page with his forefinger. 'Aye. It's no' always easy to decipher. But you see, I fancy sometimes it just could refer to the clan.'

'The head?'

Angus looked up at him. 'Aye.'

'You mean . . . the chieftain?'

Angus nodded.

'From afar?' Jamie thought a moment. 'Like . . . Dad?'

Angus tapped the side of his nose. 'Could be, eh?'

'What else does it say?'

Angus shook his head and closed the book. 'Aw, not much as makes any sense.'

Jamie jumped to his feet. 'C'mon, Angus, fair deals. If this ancient guy was writing about my dad, I think I got a right to know.'

Angus gave a deep sigh. 'Aye, laddie. But I have been twisting it about in my head for months and I cannae make head nor tail of it.'

Jamie put out his hand decisively. 'Show.'

Angus reluctantly re-opened the volume and turned it towards Jamie. He closed his eyes and recited: '*While serpents shall entwine and multiply their kind, the Eye shall behold, though the Head not see, 'til angels bring the key to understanding.*'

Jamie examined the ancient script. 'Whew! Snakes and angels!'

Angus smiled grimly. 'What did I tell you?'

Jamie searched the page for the words. 'What was that about the Eye and the Head? If the Head is the chieftain, yeah, then what is the Eye?'

'I dinna ken. But . . .' Angus hesitated.

'Yes?'

'Ach, it's a daft nonsense, but there is an old myth from these parts that concerns "the Eye of Doran".'

'Who was he?'

Angus chuckled. 'Och no. Not a *person*, but 'twas meant to be a special spot on the island known only to the chieftain, from where he could see all that happened.'

Jamie looked up in delight. 'That's neat! Where is it?'

Angus sighed. 'No, laddie. It was a story, no' a real place. Though when we were wee bairns we often dreamed we'd discover it.'

'So Dad never found it?'

Angus shook his head. 'No. Nor his father, nor any of the chiefs in our times. 'Tis most likely just a tale.'

Jamie looked thoughtful. 'I see. What was it? *The Eye shall behold . . . ?*'

Angus nodded. '*Though the Head not see . . .*'

Jamie picked up the Stone of Doran and held it out. 'You're right, Angus. Don't seem to make any sense at all.'

Angus gently closed Jamie's fingers over the stone. 'Hold it tight, laddie, you may have more use for it yet.'

18

A Challenge

When Jamie woke the next morning, he sensed it was late even though the curtains were closed. His limbs felt like lead and there was a dull ache at the back of his head. He found his watch on the bedside table and sat up with a start. Ten thirty! He smiled to himself and leaned back against the pillow. He had shared victory with Alistair and won back his honour. He deserved a lie-in. When he finally stumbled downstairs, still yawning and rubbing his eyes, he found Hazel vigorously wiping the oak table.

Jamie grinned. 'Guess I overslept.'

Hazel did not look up. 'Uh-huh.'

'Sorry about the cows.'

'It's all done.'

'And breakfast.'

'No matter.' She dipped the cloth in a bowl of soapy water, wrung it out and attacked the table again.

Jamie moved in front of her. 'Hey. Something wrong?'

Hazel shifted her bowl and continued wiping. 'No. Should there be?'

Jamie allowed himself a small smile. 'Did you see the race?'

'Uh-huh.' Jamie looked expectantly at Hazel and she glanced back at him. 'Glad you didn't let Duncan spoil your chances,' she said.

Jamie pulled a face. 'Duncan? Oh, that was just an accident.'

Hazel chewed her lip and moved down the table. 'Oh aye,' she said flatly. 'Accidents always seem to happen when Duncan is around.' She gave the table a final wipe and flung the cloth in the bowl. She made as if to leave. 'Saw you with your fan club after,' she added lightly.

Jamie laughed. 'Yeah? Well, I guess the chicks here are OK once you break the ice. We all went to After Dark and partied a bit. You bin there?' Hazel didn't answer. 'Hey, you should have come along. We had a ball – and some great food and music. They seemed pretty interested in—'

Hazel banged the bowl back on the table, and some suds slopped onto the surface. She looked fiercely at

Jamie. 'Oh aye, the Doran chicks are easily impressed. But,' she added conspiratorially, 'you know what?'

'What's that?'

Hazel looked around and lowered her voice. 'If you *rea ly* want to make an impression hereabouts . . .'

'Yeah?'

Hazel dabbed at the spillage slowly, and then shook her head. 'Oh, no. You couldnae . . .' She picked up the bowl and turned away. 'Sorry.'

Jamie followed her, intrigued. 'What? Try me.'

Hazel continued walking. 'I shouldn't have mentioned it. It's too hard. You have to be very skilled . . .'

'Hazel. Stop. What are you *talkin'* about?'

She turned and looked at him. 'Oh, nothing. Just the Doran Challenge.'

'What is that when it's at home?'

Hazel came slowly towards him. 'Well, if I tell you, you'll have to do it.'

Jamie spread his hands. 'OK.'

'And not tell a soul?'

'Aw, c'mon. If no one knows, how they gonna be impressed?'

Hazel smiled mysteriously. 'They'll know.'

Eleanor and Angus walked slowly down the neglected orchard, leaning heavily on their canes. Both moved stiffly and with some effort. Their conversation was equally stilted.

'He showed real spunk. Why will you no' admit it?' said Angus after a long pause.

Eleanor sniffed. 'Well, something was required after his previous humiliating exhibition.'

'He beat Duncan.'

'Yes, well, I'll admit that did give me some small satisfaction.'

'So maybe he can do it again.'

Eleanor stopped and positioned her stick before her. 'Stop dreaming, Angus. The boy performed well in a race. And so he should. He's young and strong, and they say that his' – she hesitated – 'his *kind* are prone to athleticism. But that does not make him a leader.'

Angus stared at her defiantly. 'He had the Stone.'

Eleanor looked at him sharply. 'Who gave it to him?'

Angus's jaw was pushed forward. 'I did. And it worked. You saw how it worked.'

Eleanor began to walk as fast as she could. 'You are an irresponsible old fool,' she muttered. 'I will hear no more of this tomfoolery.'

Angus hobbled painfully after her. 'He has qualities, I tell you. He could help our cause. Why won't you give him a chance?'

'I gave him a chance,' Eleanor threw back at him. 'To go back to where he belongs. And the sooner he does so, the better. He has no place here.'

Angus halted, breathing heavily, and shouted, 'You'll see. He'll surprise us all. Make us proud. You mark my words. He will.' He shook his fist at Eleanor's retreating figure before a fit of coughing overcame him.

*

Jamie let a few days pass while he made his plans. He didn't want to appear too eager. But now a fine day dawned, a cock crowed and a blackbird gave a stuttering call in a faraway tree as Jamie gently opened the main door of the castle. He was dressed in jeans, sneakers and a light sweater and he carried a small backpack. He looked up at the tower and consulted his watch.

'Time to go.'

The cock crowed again and Jamie swung the pack onto his back. He walked swiftly to the base of the castle walls, grabbed hold of the creeper and began to climb. The growth was thick, offered good footholds and his progress was steady. When he was level with the first floor, he moved across to a drainpipe and levered himself upwards.

A curtain twitched at a window and Hazel watched him with a smile. Jamie hoisted himself onto the parapet and stood up. Without too much difficulty he inched around the roof of the hall towards the tower.

It took him longer than he expected, trying to avoid loose slates and picking his way over mounds of debris that had accumulated over the years. There were many broken bottles, a smashed clock, and reams of crumpled paper. Jamie wondered how much of it had been thrown out of Angus's window. By the time he reached the foot of the tower the sun had risen in the sky and it was already quite warm.

Jamie rested a moment and consulted a piece of paper. He felt in the pack, pulled out a tam-o'-shanter and put it on his head. He looked up again at the tower.

He could see some good hand- and footholds but from here the climb would be much more challenging. Nothing I can't deal with, he told himself. Just take it one step at a time and you'll be OK. He grasped the first jutting piece of stonework and hoisted himself up.

Hazel walked out onto the drive and, shielding her eyes from the sun, looked up at him. A couple of deliverymen paused to see what was going on and were soon joined by Murdo on his bicycle.

Jamie's progress was painfully slow as he moved carefully from each hold to the next. The sun was hot. He paused to wipe the sweat from his face and nearly lost his grip. Steady, he reminded himself. You ain't in no hurry.

A small crowd had assembled in the drive and were gazing upwards, pointing and gesticulating. Jamie ignored them and concentrated on finding accommodating crevices that could bear his weight. Much of the stonework was smooth but he found hand- and footholds where he could and he eventually scaled the first floor of the tower. His fingers closed on a window sash above him and he heaved himself up.

Inside, Angus was sitting at his desk, poring over his books, alternately scratching his head and scribbling on a sheet of paper.

Jamie tapped gently on the windowpane. 'Morning, Angus.'

Angus looked towards him and nodded. 'Hrmmph. Morning.' He turned back to his book and was about to write something when he gave a cry, dropped his pen and rushed to the window. 'Dear God, boy. Whatever do you think you are up to?'

Jamie adjusted his grip on the ledge. 'Just doin' the Challenge, Angus.'

Angus's eyes swivelled wildly. 'Challenge? What challenge? Wait, I'll fetch you in . . .'

'No. It's cool, Angus. I'm gonna make it.' Jamie attempted a thumbs-up and almost slipped. 'Whoa there,' he said. He tried to smile confidently at Angus. 'I'll be pitchin' in with the vocals when I'm a bit higher.'

Angus stepped back. 'Vocals?' he echoed faintly.

The Doran grapevine had done its work and the number of villagers in front of the castle had multiplied, watching open-mouthed as Jamie continued his climb. Wee Malkie and his gang were pointing and shouting, and Alistair and Duncan were struggling to unfold a large tarpaulin.

Eleanor, disturbed by the noise, emerged from the hall and signalled to Hazel. 'What is happening?' she snapped. Seeing everyone's upturned faces, she too looked upwards and gave a start. 'Has the boy lost his wits?' she cried.

Hazel shook her head.

Eleanor looked around. 'Where's Murdo? Ah, Murdo, get a ladder and fetch him down this instant.'

Murdo touched his cap. 'Yes, m'lady.' He made no move.

'Well, man, what is it?'

Murdo shifted uneasily. 'It's just that I dinnae have a ladder that can reach.'

'Well, fetch the fire services, then.'

Murdo saluted again. 'Aye, madam. Present for duty.'

The tarpaulin was unfolded, only to reveal a large hole in its centre. Alistair ran up to Eleanor. 'I'll try to get below him,' he said. He tore off his jacket and raced to the wall, and began to climb the creeper in pursuit. He was taller and heavier than Jamie and his progress was slow.

Fifteen minutes later, Jamie had almost reached the top of the tower. His arms ached from the effort of supporting his body, and occasional tremors shook his legs. He could see the crenulated battlement above him. The stone looked weather-beaten and was spotted with lichen. Colourful weeds sprouted vigorously from a deep crack. As Jamie's fingers explored it for a hold, a blue jay hurtled from within, chattering in alarm, its patterned wings fanning his face.

'Oh, Jeez!' Jamie cried out in alarm as he swung free on one arm, his legs suddenly dangling in empty air. His heart hammered in his chest and he felt a tide of panic sweep over him. I'm gonna die, he thought.

He closed his eyes, took a deep breath and reached again for the crevice with his free hand. He painfully hauled himself upward. One leg found a shallow foothold and with a huge stretch, he grabbed hold of the battlement above him.

A cheer came up from the crowd. Jamie gave a grim smile and carefully reached behind him with the other hand into his backpack. He extracted a sheet of paper, cleared his throat and began to sing.

'*You take the high road and I'll take the low road and I'll be in Scotland before you*— Ooooooh!'

The ancient masonry crumbled and a large chunk of battlement broke away and crashed down from the tower, bouncing off the slate roof beneath and showering Alistair, who was searching for footholds below. Jamie dropped down about a metre and his palms dug into the jagged brick and he just held on. He felt blood trickling down his wrists. The crowd scattered in alarm as fragments of stone rained onto the drive. The sheet of paper drifted away on the breeze.

Jamie looked down and swallowed hard. 'This ain't in the script,' he muttered. He was scared and tired. For a moment he had no idea what to do. But once again he managed to reach behind him with one bloodied hand to open the pack. He delicately fished out a piece of rope with a hook on the end. Sweat ran into his eyes as he looked upwards, and with an immense effort he threw the rope towards the remaining battlement. It clinked on the parapet but instantly fell back, dislodging more eroded stone fragments.

A groan rose up from the crowd. Jamie felt a numbness spreading into his fingers, but as he hung trembling, he was also aware of a strange warmth seeping from the old building and into his body. As if the castle itself was vibrating and he was tuned in to its frequency.

He gathered up the rope, grimacing in pain, and gave one final mighty throw. The hook sailed into the air, snagged on the weather vane and held. Jamie gave it a gentle tug, then a harder pull. It seemed secure. Gingerly he began to hoist his full weight towards the parapet.

The crowd had fallen silent, watching as, hand over hand, Jamie inched himself upward on the rope. There was a metallic twang, and the top of the weather vane began very gradually to bend.

Eleanor pressed a handkerchief to her mouth. 'I knew this would end in tears. Whatever has possessed the boy . . . ?'

Hazel bit her lip and tears welled in her eyes. 'It was only a joke,' she whispered.

Jamie fixed his eyes on the twisting metal. The letter 'N' vibrated and clattered to the ground and the arrow spun crazily around on its arm.

In the silence they heard Jamie's voice again. '*For me an' my true love will never meet again . . .*'

As the vane bent double, Jamie managed to heave himself over the battlement, which then disintegrated in a large cloud of dust. When it cleared, Jamie had disappeared entirely from view. Some of the islanders removed their caps and closed their eyes.

A moment later, however, his head bobbed up from amid the rubble. His face was covered in dust and streaked with tears of exhaustion. He gave a little wave. A huge cheer of relief exploded from the throats of the onlookers.

Jamie yelled tunelessly into the air, '*On those bonnie* – yeah – *them real mean bonnie banks of Loch* . . . er . . . *Loch* . . .' He scratched his head.

'*LOMOND!*' sang the crowd in exuberant harmony.

Jamie beamed down at them and bowed to the north,

south, east and west. From the backpack he unfurled the Stars and Stripes and tied it to the mangled vane, where it fluttered bravely. Jamie saluted and yelled, 'And I claim the Doran Challenge!'

A perplexed murmur arose from below. Eleanor muttered, 'What was that? The Doran Challenge? What challenge? Is the boy totally crazed?' She fixed Hazel with a steely eye. 'Do you know anything about this?'

Hazel fiercely wiped away a tear and hung her head.

'Have we not had enough deaths? Would you have me send you home in a box too?' Eleanor's harsh voice rang around the hall. She sat imperiously in her chair, grasping her stick as Angus hovered unhappily at her side.

Hazel and Jamie stood before her, caught in a stray shaft of sunlight that had managed to pierce the yellowing glass. They looked like prisoners in a dock – Hazel with her amber hair standing on end and Jamie with his hands heavily bandaged and his head still liberally coated with brick dust and birds' feathers.

Jamie motioned with his arm. 'See here, I wouldn't have—'

Eleanor broke in, her voice like thunder. '*I have not finished!*' She paused and continued in a softer but no less ominous tone, 'You have endangered yourself and risked the life of young Alistair, you have damaged the very fabric of our ancestral home, and you have made this family a laughing stock. Is this how you wish to repay my hospitality?'

Jamie willed the ground to open up so he could disappear.

'You may speak.'

Jamie gulped. 'Er, no, ma'am.'

'I do not hold you fully to blame since you are obviously unaccustomed to our ways.' Eleanor turned to look at Hazel. 'You, young lady, should have known better than to entice him into such foolishness.'

Jamie broke in. 'Oh, c'mon, Grandma. You can't pin it on her. I shouldn't have been so dumb to fall for that jackass stunt.'

Eleanor gazed above their heads, studying the flying golden motes in the sunbeam. 'This may be the way the MacDorans conduct themselves in *the United States*.' She made it sound like a region far beyond the boundaries of the civilized world. 'Where obviously they have little respect for decent behaviour or for the values we hold dear. You have imposed yourself upon me in the name of a kinship I find hard to recognize, and seem intent on conducting yourself like a wild beast. But here, in our society, *it is not acceptable*. Nor will it be repeated.' She banged her stick suddenly on the floor. 'Do I make myself clear?'

Jamie swallowed. 'As a bell, ma'am.'

19

Deeper In

Jamie lay on his hard bed and stared at the ceiling, where some of the ancient moulding was crumbling and stained with damp. He felt thoroughly depressed.

Earlier he had gone to apologize to Alistair, who was feeding baby goats in a field above his farm. Alistair obviously bore no grudge, welcoming Jamie, thumping him heartily on the back and declaring, 'There's nothin' to be sorry for. Gave us all a good laugh, and I tell you, we're in sore need o' that. Besides,' he added, pulling up his shirt and slapping his belly, 'you did me a favour.'

'I did?'

'Aye. Showed me I'm no' as fit as I thought I was. Too much booze and not enough exercise.' He eyed Jamie. 'So what made you decide to kick your heels around here a while?'

Jamie grinned ruefully. 'Maybe it wasn't such a bright idea.'

'Aw, no.' Alistair struggled to put the milk teat into the baby goat's mouth. 'It's good to have some new MacDoran blood around the place. I loved your father, by the way. He pulled me up, helped me get myself together. I dunno, but he always seemed to have time for you, had a way of understanding your problems. He treated me like a son. Oh.' Alistair blushed furiously. 'I'm sorry, that was pretty tactless.'

Jamie looked down. 'It's OK. He was very caring.' He felt a sudden pang of jealousy. Strange, he thought, how his dad had touched so many other lives – strangers who seemed to know him far better than he did.

Alistair gently put down the baby goat, which scampered away. 'Aye. And I thought, with him as chieftain, we could turn this place around.' He straightened and smiled at Jamie. 'I am sure it looks like the back of beyond to you, but Doran is a special place, as you may find out one day.'

Jamie liked this strong man with broad shoulders, long chestnut hair and clear grey eyes. Though he couldn't help feeling there was something sad about the eyes, even when they smiled. 'Many people seem to be pinning their hopes on you now,' he said, 'to become chieftain.'

Alistair looked away. 'Aye. It is a great burden, and I'm not sure I'm worthy. Your father was a fine and honourable man, and his shoes will be hard to fill.'

Jamie returned to the castle and stayed in his room, trying to make himself scarce. It wasn't just Eleanor's cold rage or the barely concealed laughter from people in the village. He had let himself down and squandered the brief respect he had earned at the Games. What would his dad have said? He would have gone ballistic. Just like Eleanor. Funny how alike they were.

His gaze settled on the suitcase lying half open in the corner. It was still full of his stuff, and at one end some plastic peeped out from behind a sweater. It was the folder containing his dad's personal belongings, which he had meant to give his mother before she left.

Jamie carried the folder to the bed and unzipped it. He felt a sudden stab of sadness as he touched the gold ring and diary. He fished out the watch, which was still running on US time, and pressed it against his cheek. Macbeth's lines from Mr Steadman's class came back to him:

'Tomorrow, and tomorrow, and tomorrow,
Creeps in this petty pace from day to day.'

He opened the Moleskine diary and thumbed back through the blank day pages.

'To the last syllable of recorded time—'

The familiar strokes of his father's strong handwriting suddenly shocked him.

27 June

The last day. The final words.

J ball game. Sports Hall MLK 3 p.m.

Not quite the last words. In a box below, in neat letters:

DORAN TRIP NOTES

Finalize dates.
Check out Wassets. Backers?
Ask A if any truth in James Malcolm Frazer hoard. Help solve finances!
More realistic - tourism? IT improvements.
Home industry/crafts.
Cost?
Key team players. A etc.

Jamie pored over the words. Much of it made no sense. What were 'Wassets'? Who was James Malcolm Frazer? And what was a hoard? Who were the key team? And was 'A' meant to stand for old Angus? Or Alistair?

He closed the diary and replaced it in the folder. His dad's last thoughts had been of his beloved Doran and his son had brought disgrace on his name. Jamie grabbed his skateboard and fled down the staircase, but even a fast run on the board along the drive did little to improve his mood. He tried a fancy turn as he left the village, but it didn't quite work out and he kicked the board hard in frustration.

There was a sudden crash and a scream. Jamie looked around to see where the noise had come from. There was another crash as a pane of glass in a run-down old cottage opposite shattered.

'Leave me alone! Haven't you done enough? I have nothing, I tell you, leave me alone!' There was a thud and another scream, and Jamie raced to the cottage door.

'Everything OK in there?' he yelled.

There was a silence. Then a low murmur.

Jamie turned the handle and half opened the door. Caught in the shaft of daylight was a terrified old woman, pressed against the wall by a youth with one hand over her mouth.

'What's going on in here?' he asked.

The youth turned. It was Calum, the thin-faced boy from the party.

'Nothin',' he said. 'It's my mother. Havin' one of her turns. She has them all the time.'

The woman's eyes darted frantically above his restraining hand.

Jamie moved into the shabby room, noting the few sticks of upturned furniture and the smashed crockery. The woman struggled feebly in Calum's firm grip.

'I don't think she can breathe,' said Jamie. 'Can you loosen up a bit?'

Calum slowly removed his hand from the mouth of the woman, who drew in a great gulp of air. His cold eyes fixed on Jamie. 'Dinna fash yersel', he said. 'She's all right. Aren't you, Ma?'

The woman looked imploringly at Jamie and then at Calum. She nodded her head. 'Aye. All right.'

'There,' said Calum. 'What did I tell you? Lucky I was here or she might have done herself an injury.'

Jamie righted a chair and gently eased the woman onto it. 'There you are, lady. Everything will be OK.' He glanced up at Calum. 'Has your mom seen a doctor?'

Calum shrugged. 'Oh aye. He says she's not right in the heed. Should be out of here, in a home. But she won't do as she's told. Stubborn as a mule. Ain't you, Mam?'

The woman dropped her head and gave a sob.

'There now,' said Calum, taking Jamie by the arm and propelling him to the door. 'She won't want you to see her upset. It was good of you to call. But I can handle it from here.'

Jamie hesitated. 'If you're sure there's nothing . . . ?'

Calum stood in the doorway, his arms folded. 'Aye. Positive.'

Jamie picked up his board and walked out of the village and along the crumbling road. The incident had unsettled him and his dark mood deepened.

Over the brow of the distant hill he caught sight of Hazel, pedalling towards him on her bike. He turned his back and occupied himself with tightening one of the wheel bearings with his penknife. He heard Hazel dismount.

'Look, I just want to say that—'

Jamie didn't turn. 'Don't bother.'

'No. I'm really—'

Jamie turned and faced her, his lips drawn back in a snarl. 'Yeah, Hazel, you're really *what*? You gonna tell me you're sorry for landing me deep in it with Eleanor? Huh? Well, I don't buy it.'

Hazel lifted her chin. 'Is that so?'

Jamie took a pace forward, eyes blazing. 'Look, girl, you been gunning for me ever since I landed. You and the whole gang. With your put-on Scottish talk, and your petty little ways. You know something? You really spook me.'

Hazel threw back at him, 'Right. And you would know, would you? Know about our ways?'

'Sure. I got eyes.'

Hazel flung down her bike and confronted him. 'Aye. You have eyes but you don't see. You have ears but you understand nothing. You come here all high and mighty, thinkin' you're God's gift to the island, lookin' down your nose at us and our backward little land.' She tossed her head and mimicked him. '*What? You don't have the latest cellphones? Oh my, there ain't no disco? You have to eat* porridge?' She punched his shoulder furiously. 'There's a bloody battle going on, and you're bang in the middle of it, but you think you're on your *holidays*. You're no' a real MacDoran, just a – a jumped-up playboy from LA.'

Jamie grabbed her arm and eyeballed her. 'Listen, girl, I am as much a MacDoran as my dad.'

Hazel pulled a face. 'Oh, is that so?'

'Yeah. I don't see *you* climbing up that tower.'

Hazel tossed her head. 'Pah, I could do it blindfold and not bring down the whole building in the process. And what's more . . .'

'Yeah?'

Hazel glared at him and spat out the words: 'I – *can – sing*.'

Faces almost touching, they stared furiously at each other until Hazel suddenly burst into laughter. She turned away, convulsed with hysterics.

Jamie was disconcerted. 'What? What's so funny? Huh?'

Tears poured down Hazel's face. She sang tunelessly, '*The bonnie, bonnie banks . . .*' before doubling up in howls of mirth.

Despite himself Jamie was forced to laugh. 'Oh, c'mon. It wasn't that bad.'

Hazel wiped her eyes. 'No. It was nae that bad. It was far, far *worse*.'

They collapsed onto the ground in fits of hilarity, holding their sides and fighting for breath. Eventually Jamie said, 'Will I ever be able to hold up my head round here again?'

Hazel shook her head. 'I don't think so.'

Jamie chuckled. 'Man, I really blew it big time.'

Hazel trumpeted noisily into a grubby handkerchief and then added casually, 'Well, mebbe they were a wee bit impressed.'

Jamie glanced at her. 'Really?'

'Uh-huh. Quite plucky, I suppose, in a kind of stupid, cack-handed way.'

Jamie looked at her suspiciously. 'Is that meant to be a compliment?'

'Heaven forfend,' said Hazel, picking up her bike. She looked down at Jamie. 'Aw, come on,' she said, holding out her hand.

The library table was heaped with books and papers, behind which Angus was urgently leafing through a particularly ancient and decaying volume. Murdo, Alistair and Duncan sat silently in their high-backed chairs, and Eleanor drummed her fingers impatiently.

'But what does it *tell* us, Angus?' she said after a long silence.

Angus looked up from his book. 'Eh? Oh well, the circumstances of course are somewhat unusual: the deceased not having stated in his will . . .'

Eleanor tossed her head. 'Yes, yes, we are all aware of the difficulties, but where is the remedy?'

Duncan rose to his feet. 'The remedy, Lady Eleanor, is quite clear . . .'

Eleanor waved a bony hand at him. 'Sit down, Duncan. You have waited for this day all your life. I'll thank you to wait a moment longer. Angus?'

Angus raised a large magnifying glass and pored over the text. He gave a little exclamation. 'Ah.' He began to read, very slowly: '*If there shall be no self-evident and willing successor, then according to the ancient lore of the Clan of Doran, handed down through the centuries from our illustrious—'*

Eleanor drummed her fingers again. 'Yes, you may dispense with all that waffle. What is the conclusion?'

Angus murmured under his breath, flipped over a page and stabbed at the book with his finger. '*... that after a period of time shall have elapsed since the death ...'*

'How long?'

Angus raced ahead, mumbling, '*Er ... shall not exceed ... er ...'* He looked up triumphantly. '*Two calendar months!'*

Eleanor raised her eyes to heaven. 'Yes? What shall happen?'

'*Er ... an open and free election of all representatives of*—'

Duncan jumped to his feet again and struck the table. 'Finally. You have it in writing. As I have said repeatedly, you cannot delay a proper vote any longer. I have already stated my intention to stand, and Alistair here has been nominated by the islanders. And either you produce a family candidate for chieftain' – he consulted the date on his watch – 'within one week—'

'But there is one.' Angus spoke quietly but intensely.

Duncan glared at him. 'What?'

Angus tapped the book. 'A self-evident successor.'

'Who? No! You can't mean ... ?' Duncan began to chuckle. 'Not *Jamie*? Our in-house mountaineer? He may be from the City of the Angels, but I reckon he's with the fairies!'

Angus was thunderstruck. He rose. 'What? What did you say?'

Duncan grinned at him. 'A phrase, Angus. Fairy, as in . . .' He flipped a limp wrist.

But Angus was muttering furiously to himself, ''*Til angels bring the key . . .*'

Eleanor tried to restore order. 'Out of the question. The boy has no place here, he has no inclination, and besides, he has already signed.'

Angus interrupted her. 'No, he signed nothing.'

'No matter. If our poor fortunes are to rest with that wild, misguided youth then we are indeed lost.' Eleanor rose stiffly to her feet and leaned on her stick. 'No, Duncan, we will fight you fairly and squarely. Angus here will represent the family and, as you say, Alistair will doubtless carry the nomination for the islanders. Both true MacDorans.'

Duncan stared at Alistair, who coloured and looked down at his hands. There was an awkward silence.

'I will take my chances,' Duncan said. Gathering his papers, he strode quickly from the room. His car was in the drive and he flipped open the satellite phone and punched a couple of buttons. When the connection was made he spoke softly. 'It's going to plan. Yes. Pretty much on schedule. But I need the other. Yes. As much as you can manage. There are hearts to be won, or should I say palms to be greased? The vote? Yes, there should be no problem. But time is short, and I need to make sure.'

*

Jamie was carrying his skateboard under one arm and Hazel pushed her bicycle as they climbed the steep hill.

'What did you mean? You know, about a battle?'

Hazel shrugged. 'You've seen Duncan, the way he lives.'

'Yeah. Pretty smart dude.'

'Aye, smart enough to have bought up a good part of the island,' Hazel returned heatedly. 'And he wants to buy more.'

'But that's cool, if it makes things better, more commercial.'

'Aye, but money doesn't always make things better. It makes things different, that's for sure. And there are many islanders who would pocket the money and hang the difference.'

Jamie shook his head. 'I dunno. People are always jealous of dudes who make their own way. Maybe you got it wrong. Perhaps Duncan just might be the guy to turn the place around, like he says he plans to.'

Hazel stopped and faced him. 'Aye, and pigs might fly. Whatever Duncan is planning, you can be sure it's for his own good and no' ours.'

'Where does he get it from?'

'What?'

'His cash. I've seen his place – it's like a movie-star pad, like something out of Bel Air. And then there's the Porsche, the Hummer, the speedboat and a *submarine*? Come on. That kind of money don't come from fishing. He's gotta have huge assets.'

As he said it, a light bulb flashed on in his head.

Assets. *Check out Wassets.* Is that was his dad was on to? Wylie's backers?

Hazel answered him, 'I think he's in business – investment or something. He's often over on the mainland. But he's certainly not investing in Doran.'

'OK. Tell me, what would you do?' asked Jamie.

'If I had the money? Well, you've probably noticed the place could certainly do with some improvements.' Hazel gave a humourless laugh, but then her expression hardened. 'No, more than that, we've got to give this island back its respect. Turn it into a place where people want to stay and bring up their bairns, instead of dreaming of going across the water. That means jobs, and that means a home industry. Yeah, we've got good land, and fine cattle and sheep, and we've got the fishing, but who's heard of Doran? Where's the PR, the hotels, the B & Bs, the restaurants? Where's the tourism? I don't mean *bad* tourism, swarms of trippers and theme parks. But a real classy heritage site – quality trade.' Hazel's eyes were shining, and she ran a hand through her wild hair. 'Och, I've a headful of wild schemes that could really put Doran on the map.'

Jamie smiled. 'You sound just like Duncan.'

Hazel spat contemptuously. 'Hah. I don't think it's our interests that Duncan has at heart. But I would give the power and the profit back to the islanders where it belongs.' She paused a moment and then added, 'Any road, he's no' really a MacDoran for a start.'

Jamie was surprised. 'But I thought . . . ?'

Hazel shook her head as she pushed her bike. 'Oh

173

aye, he ponces about as though he is. But he's descended through the bastard line, who were a wild band of reivers.'

Jamie looked puzzled.

'Raiders and cattle-rustlers on the Borders,' Hazel explained. 'They got hold of some boats and tried to seize power here, lang syne.'

'What happened?'

'They plundered the place, and failed, and had to flee back to England. They've been trying to get a foothold here ever since.'

Jamie nodded thoughtfully. 'So that's why Eleanor hates his guts. Gee, is she some tough lady!'

'Aye,' Hazel agreed, 'she can be a right targe. And she's awful ancient, like everything around her. Angus is loyal but daft as a brush, and there's a lot of other old folk who remember the past and want to hang onto it. But that's no' the way forward. That's why so many islanders began backing Alistair as a force for change. He's dead popular, got a lovely wife and wee bairns, and he got off to a great start, but lately, I don't know, he seems a mite troubled. Your father managed to keep the peace, but now . . .' She trailed off into silence.

'You think Duncan wants to be chieftain?'

Hazel hesitated for a moment. 'I think he wants the power. Yes. And to increase it. Maybe he also wants to settle some old scores.'

They reached the brow of the hill, which revealed a magnificent view of the village and castle below them and the glittering expanse of ocean beyond. Jamie took a deep breath and exhaled slowly.

'Dad used to say that Doran air was like wine. Never dug what he meant, but I guess he was right. You know something? This place kinda grows on you.' He gazed into the distance, shielding his eyes from the sun. 'I just wish he was here.'

Hazel looked at him thoughtfully. 'It still hurts?'

Jamie considered this. 'It kinda comes and goes. I mean, I never thought about him that much. He was always there – well, actually *not* there that much, I guess, but you know what I mean. Your mom and your dad, they're like trees, or school, or your house – you take them for granted, 'til suddenly they're gone. And when I saw him laid out in the hospital, I suddenly realized that there were a heap of things I'd not asked him, and now I never would. And I thought of all the stuff he knew – he was *seriously* bright – and how that had all gone too. All that knowledge. What a stupid waste.'

Hazel nodded. 'Aye.'

Jamie spoke passionately. These were feelings he'd never been fully aware of before. 'You know,' he said, 'I can sometimes sense him looking down at me and I'd really like to be the person he was. No,' he corrected himself, 'to be my *own* person, but someone he would have respected. And I guess that might be why I stayed here, 'cos it would have been too easy to slip back into what I was before. 'Stead of becoming who I could be.' He covered his face with his hands. 'Jeez, am I talking a load of garbage?'

Hazel smiled. 'I've heard worse rubbish from you before now.'

Jamie cleared his throat, and peered at her through his fingers. 'So, where's da Eye?'

Hazel looked puzzled. 'Come again?'

'The Eye? Of Doran?'

She looked away. 'Who told you about that?'

'Angus.'

'I told you, he's daft as a loon.' She paused, then added casually, 'So what did he say, by the way?'

Jamie tried to remember. 'Something about it being a place known only to chieftains. From where they could suss the whole island.'

Hazel began to push her cycle forward again. 'Fancy.'

Jamie followed her. 'You don't believe it?'

'I've no' seen it,' she replied.

Jamie poked a playful finger at her. ''Cos you ain't no chieftain.'

Hazel flung down the bicycle and faced him furiously. 'More's the pity! For if I were, I'd give that Duncan a bloody nose and a whack that would send him flying across the water. And I'd buy back the homes and the farms he has let go to ruin. An' I'd give this island a kick up the backside and tell it to get back its pride. And I'd make the name of Doran sound through this land.'

Jamie stared at her, open-mouthed. Hazel's face was flushed and her eyes flashed with fire. My Lord, he thought, this girl changes mood as often as the weather. She put her hands on her hips and glared at him scornfully.

'You might like to know that I too am directly

descended from the line of chieftains. Like you, Jamie, my great-great-grandfather was James Angus MacDoran, and his daughter Elizabeth was my great-grandmother. But, as you may have happened to notice, the job is no' open to us poor wee hens. Have you no' read the sign? "Females need not apply." Though there's not a man here that's worth a docken.' She gave him a look of withering disdain as she picked up her cycle and sped off down the hill.

20

Arion's Ride

Jamie sat on the hillside for some time, his mind in a whirl. Eventually, he began to walk slowly back to the village. Hazel always seemed to throw him off balance, unsettle him. Just when he was beginning to feel a connection to this place, she had shown him how little he knew of its history or problems. Of course, Hazel was right. He hadn't thought it through properly; unlike his dad, he had nothing to offer. He was, after all, just a visiting American kid, a tourist. He didn't belong here, and would never fit in no matter how hard he tried. He might as well pack his bags and get back to his buds, to make the most of the remaining vacation days in the surf.

Wee Malkie was sitting by the duck pond. He didn't look up as Jamie trudged by, but addressed the scummy water. 'So it's been decided.'

Jamie stopped. 'What?'

'Our fate.'

Jamie approached. 'Am I meant to fill in the missing blanks? Malk, what the heck are you talking about?'

Wee Malkie chewed his lip. 'Aye. It's been announced. The vote for chieftain is in a week. Up yonder.' He nodded towards the castle.

'So who's gonna win?'

'Hah! No contest. It'll be a shoo-in.'

'For Duncan?'

'Aye.' Wee Malkie spat a green blob into the water. He fumbled in his pocket and brought out a grubby envelope. 'This is for you.'

Jamie opened it. There was a handwritten note inside:

WE ARE WAITING AT 'AFTER DARK'. COME IMMEDIATELY IF YOU CAN. IT'S IMPORTANT.

Jamie turned the note over. 'Who's this from?'

Malkie shrugged. Then he slowly looked up at Jamie. 'So will you or no'?'

It took them some time to reach the barn, because Wee Malkie had to pause frequently to cough and hold his side. His face was waxen, and he fought for breath.

Jamie was concerned. 'Are you OK, dude?' he asked

after a particularly violent bout of coughing racked the boy. But Malkie only nodded and waved him on.

In a paddock behind the black barn, a group of horses were tethered to a rail and Jamie was surprised to spot Dougal grooming them.

Jamie whispered to Malkie, 'I thought Dougal was a musician.'

'Aye, the best,' Malkie panted, 'but he's also got a fine flair for breeding horses. He's sold a fair few over on the mainland.'

Dougal nodded as they approached. He looked smaller than the last time Jamie had seen him, his body compact, with the wiry physique of a jockey.

'Greedy beggers,' observed Dougal as the horses nuzzled in his pockets, hunting for carrots. In the neighbouring field a black horse with a long silky mane and a proud look watched them intently, pawing the ground.

'What's eating her?' asked Jamie.

Dougal gave a low whistle. 'Lord, don't let him hear you say that. That, my friend, is Arion, and he is no she.'

Arion pawed the ground again and neighed shrilly.

'Why isn't he with the rest?' asked Jamie.

Dougal laughed. 'Arion won't do *anything* with the rest. He considers himself a cut above – and maybe he's right. He is a direct descendant from a long line of Arabian stallions that have lived on Doran for centuries. Owned by the bigwigs in the clan and reserved in the old days for the chieftain himself.'

'He's your horse, huh?'

In answer, Dougal held out a carrot towards Arion,

who tossed his head and raced around the field, long mane streaming in the wind.

Dougal gave another peal of laughter. 'Look at him go. No, Jamie, he's no' mine, or anybody's. As a great favour, when he's in the mood, he lets me ride him. But he often won't allow anyone else near.' He flung down his brushes and pointed towards the barn. 'You're expected,' he said. 'I'll follow you in in a minute.' He picked up a saddle and turned back towards the horses.

Jamie dropped his skateboard outside and ducked under the lintel, looking around. It took a moment for his eyes to adjust to the dim interior, and then he saw that, as before, the place was filled with youngsters. But there was no party spirit now – only a tense atmosphere. The low buzz of conversation died as Jamie entered. He didn't notice Janet at first, sitting at an old treadle sewing machine. She jumped to her feet and broke the silence with her customary whoop.

'Aw, you beauty, you came.' She rushed towards him and gave him a big hug.

Jamie grinned. 'Well, the note said it was important.'

'Aye, it is.' She led him over to sit at the table, and immediately a group formed around him. He recognized familiar faces: Craig, Gordon, Rhona, the rest of Malkie's gang. There was no sign of Calum. Dougal ran in to join them.

'OK,' said Jamie. 'Shoot.'

Craig cleared his throat. 'You may have heard that the vote has just been called; the Clan Meet is now only a week hence.'

'Yeah. Malkie told me. I guessed it would be later.'

'So did we. Which is why we have to move quickly. Why we called you.'

Jamie shook his head. 'I don't get—'

Dougal broke in. 'We need to know where you stand.' There was a murmur of assent from the group.

Jamie looked surprised. 'Where *I* stand?' he repeated. 'I can't see that it makes any difference—'

'It makes *all* the difference.' Craig was gazing at him intently. 'You are our last chance.'

Jamie laughed. 'C'mon. Is this some sort of wind-up? I mean, I'd really like to help you guys any way I can, but what the heck do you want *me* to do?'

There was silence. He felt Dougal's green eyes staring at him.

'Stand for chieftain.' Dougal's words hung in the air, and then there was a roar of approval and pounding of fists on the table.

'What?' Jamie exploded. 'Me as chieftain? You must be kidding. You *are* kidding?' He looked in panic around the row of intent faces hanging on his words. 'Look, guys, I really wish you well but, hey, I'm going to be outa here any day. Maybe this week. I got a plane to catch. I ain't seen my mom in weeks, I got school and . . .' He trailed off and looked appealingly at Janet. 'Anyhow, you already got your candidates.'

'And a great bunch they are,' she replied heatedly. 'Angus, who's as old as the hills – and doesn't want the job. Duncan, who'd sell us out to the highest bidder . . .'

'What about Alistair? He seems a pretty sussed guy. I know my dad reckoned—'

Gordon interrupted. 'We *all* reckoned on Alistair. He was our great hope. But there's been a sore change in him of late. He's drinking more than is good for his health, and some say . . .' He paused, then added in a low voice, 'That he is already in Duncan's pay.'

Jamie shook his head impatiently. 'Yeah, I know, the Duncan Conspiracy Theory. Are you so sure he is the Big Bad Wolf that you make out? Maybe you should give the guy a bit of leeway, see what he is offering.'

'Oh, we know what he is offering.' Malkie spoke up. 'And some of us have already taken the shilling.'

'Yeah? Like who?'

'Like Calum, who now runs his errands.'

'I'd have thought Calum had enough on his plate, looking after his sick mom.'

Janet gave him an incredulous look. 'Jamie, whoever told you that? Calum has no mother. She died years ago.'

Craig rose to his feet and leaned on the table. 'Jamie, your dad was a great chieftain. Helped our families, helped all of us. Bought Janet her machine there so she could start her dressmaking, was helping Gordon to get enrolled to train as a chef, Dougal to expand his horse breeding. Things were looking up 'til Duncan appeared on the scene. Now your dad is gone, but you are his son and we have watched you. Seen how you act, what you have done.'

Jamie looked down, confused. 'Seems to me I done

nothing but screw up since I got here. I'll be honest with you. I really dig this place, and all of you too, and I am kinda touched that you'd even think I could help you.' He raised his head and met their gaze. 'But I am not my father, and I don't know how I could possibly be a candidate.'

Dougal banged his fist on the table. 'Bloody hell, man! You're next in line. You have a right.'

Janet put a hand on Jamie's arm. 'Look, you don't have to give an answer now. This is no' a wee thing and it needs a muckle o' thought. If you say no, we'd have a guid greet but we would understand. It would be a mighty undertaking and a heavy burden on your life. If you said yes, we'd be right with you, and I think we could count on many of the islanders joining us. You'd get the castle folk behind you for a start.'

Jamie was incredulous. 'Tell that to Eleanor! She hates my guts.'

'She hates Duncan more.' Janet looked at him imploringly. 'Just say you'll think it over? Please.'

Jamie nodded. 'OK. Will do, but I gotta tell you—'

He was silenced by Janet pressing a finger against his lips. 'Look,' she said, suddenly jumping up and running to the sewing machine. She snatched some scarlet material from its surface and, pressing the unfinished dress against her jeans, paraded around the barn as if on a catwalk. There was laughter and catcalls. 'Stuff it,' she yelled at them. 'Eat your heart out, Kate and Stella. You have nothing on the next *Janet* collection!' She flounced out of the door and the group followed in a noisy conga line, blinking in the bright sunlight. The horses turned their heads to look at them curiously.

Donald swept a hank of blond hair from his eyes. 'Do you ride?' he asked Jamie. 'Come out with us.'

'Course he rides,' said Craig. 'Our man's from the Wild West. He was born in the saddle.'

Jamie tried to remember if he had ever sat on a horse. He dimly recalled posing for a photo as a child atop an old nag in the Tucson Movie Museum.

'Would you like a go?' Dougal selected a docile chestnut mare and led her over to him. 'Jessie here will give you a guid ride. I'll just finish tacking her up.' He slipped a bridle over her head, whisking away the head collar, then efficiently buckled the straps and handed the reins to Jamie.

'Well, OK. If you'll come along and keep an eye on me,' replied Jamie.

Dougal whistled for Arion, who was grazing on the far side of the field. The stallion looked up and tossed his head.

'Come here, boy,' said Dougal, going through the gate and into the field and advancing towards the horse. Arion gave a snort and trotted away.

Jamie laughed. 'I can see who's boss.'

Arion dodged Dougal and approached the fence; he stopped abruptly and splayed his front legs. Dougal approached softly and fastened a head collar on the horse before leading him through the gate and over to the group.

'He is some beauty,' said Jamie admiringly. While

Janet took Jessie's reins from him, he picked up a carrot from the ground and slowly held out his hand. Arion straightened and pulled towards him. 'Attaboy,' said Jamie. Arion nuzzled his hand.

'Good grief,' said Dougal. 'I've never seen him do that before. I think he's taken to you.'

Jamie patted the horse's neck while Dougal gently fitted a saddle and bridle. 'Do you think he'd let me get up on him?'

Dougal shook his head. 'No way, pal. He tried to throw me yesterday. No, Jessie's your cuddy. Nothing fazes her.'

'Oh, c'mon. Just for a minute? See what it feels like?'

Dougal tightened the girth and turned to Jamie. 'Well, you can try. But just for a minute, mind. I'll hold him in case he gets frisky.' He gripped Arion's bridle.

Jamie put one foot in the stirrup and heaved himself into the saddle. He gathered up the reins and beamed down at the group. 'It feels good,' he said and stroked the silky mane. Arion turned his head to look at Jamie.

'Ride 'em, cowboy,' called Janet.

'Right,' said Dougal. 'That's it. I'll help you down.'

But as he released the horse's bridle, Arion gave a whinny and trotted off briskly through the gate and back across the field. Jamie clung on as best he could, trying to press his knees into Arion's flanks. 'Good boy,' he whispered.

Dougal ran after them, calling urgently to the horse, but Arion gathered speed, circled the field and began to canter towards the far fence.

'Oh God,' breathed Janet, 'he's going to get himself killed.'

With an easy jump, Arion sailed over the wooden rails. Jamie slid forward on the saddle but managed to hang onto the mane like grim death. 'Be gentle,' he whispered to the horse as he worked himself awkwardly back into the seat of the saddle.

Dougal leaped onto Jessie and wheeled in pursuit, with Craig, Donald and Janet following close behind on their own horses. Wee Malkie watched them go, his thin lips compressed.

Arion trotted out across the scrubby pastures, occasionally looking round and eventually breaking into a light gallop that Jamie found much easier to manage than the painful trot that jarred his butt against the hard saddle. Gradually he found a rhythm that synchronized his body with the motion of the horse, and he felt Arion relax beneath him. Jamie held the reins, but had no illusions that he steered their course. Arion knew exactly where he was going, gracefully leaping a small stream and heading out towards the distant hills. Jamie felt the wind in his face and the sun on his neck. He smelled the sweet scent of the heather beneath Arion's hooves. He was scared but exhilarated, and he finally felt confident enough to turn and wave at Dougal's posse, who were trying to keep up.

As the ground rose more steeply, Arion veered sharply to the left and Jamie was again almost pitched out of the saddle. As if sensing his discomfort, Arion slowed and Jamie was able to right himself. He dug his knees in firmly to try and grip the stallion. 'Have patience,' he murmured, 'and I'll get the hang of this.'

They passed a series of ever larger rocks, then deep fissures in the hillside as the terrain grew rougher. Small rills trickled across their path as Arion slowed to a walk and picked his way upwards, with Jamie leaning forward and clinging to his neck. 'Where are you taking me?' he breathed, and Arion's ears twitched in response. Jamie heard the distant sound of falling water, which grew steadily louder as they turned to enter a narrow gorge. The echo of Arion's splashing hooves bounced off the rocky walls, and the roar of water became deafening. Jamie closed his eyes.

Arion stopped and Jamie peered round his head. Before him, a foaming cataract fell from a rocky shelf into a shallow basin, the spray reflecting a brilliant rainbow that wavered in the damp air.

'That is awesome,' Jamie gasped. Arion neighed and moved forward. 'Whoa there,' cried Jamie in alarm. 'Just hold it.'

But Arion walked calmly towards the falling water. Jamie buried his head in the horse's mane as he felt the icy torrent drench his shirt and jeans. They passed through the falls and into a cave hollowed out of the hillside. Arion turned round to face the curtain of water and tossed his head. The noise from the cataract was incredible, but they were safe in a dry haven. Jamie let out a cry of delight.

'Fantastic,' he shouted and patted Arion's neck. The horse looked round again, then pinned back his ears and trotted out through the waterfall once more. They raced past the other riders, who had been gazing in horror at the foaming waters, and headed back out of the gorge.

'Where to now?' breathed Jamie and Arion, as if in answer, swerved to the right, making for a distant group of giant boulders that rose from the midst of extensive woodland. Before long they had entered the forest. Slender mossy trunks and light foliage dappled the air with a luminous green glow. Jamie, shivering in his wet clothes, was aware of Arion's muffled hoof beats on the damp turf and felt the leaves brush his hair. Then suddenly they emerged into a huge circular glade, a natural amphitheatre where no trace of tree or vegetation grew. Before them towered a vast rock, like an inverted triangle, pointing down into the earth. Its base was so slight, eroded by water over time, that Jamie wondered how it could possibly support the massive weight above. Arion reared suddenly, and this time Jamie was caught totally off guard and tumbled backwards out of the saddle, falling with a heavy thud onto the soft damp earth.

The other riders burst into the glade to see Jamie lying sprawled motionless on the ground and Arion gently licking his face. Dougal jumped lightly down from Jessie and ran over. He picked up Arion's trailing reins and knelt to cradle Jamie's wet head. 'Are you all right?' he asked anxiously. The others gathered around.

'Oh God,' Janet cried out. 'Shall I give him the kiss of life?'

Jamie slowly opened his eyes and saw the circle of

worried faces. He smiled dreamily. 'That was some roller coaster,' he said. He tried to focus on the giant rock above him. 'What is this place?' he asked.

Donald answered him. 'They call it "Bobantilter". It's an old word, meaning an icicle.' He nodded towards the rock. 'An' I suppose it looks a bit like one. It's always been a sacred place, but a bit spooky.'

Jamie sat up and wiped his face with a sleeve. 'And the water? What was that?'

'That is another very special place,' Craig replied. 'Mentioned in all the old writings as a magic spot. We thought we had lost you.'

Arion neighed impatiently. 'No,' Jamie said, struggling to his feet, 'Arion knew exactly where he was going, didn't you, boy?' The horse flicked his tail and pawed at the ground. 'Givin' me the grand tour, huh?'

Dougal was looking at him intently, the mocking smile playing once again around his eyes and lips.

Janet gave a shiver. 'Let's be going. This place gives me the creeps.'

Jamie moved towards Arion and reached out to take back the reins from Dougal.

'Don't push your luck.' said Dougal. 'You can ride back on Jessie. I'll take Arion.' He looped the reins back over the stallion's neck.

But Jamie patted Arion's nose. 'No way,' he said. 'He brought me here. He'll take me back.' He breathed deeply, grasped the reins and swung back up into the saddle. '*Vamos, amigos,*' he said.

They rode back in silence in the fast fading light.

Malkie and the others came running out of the barn to meet them. They watched as Jamie dismounted, removed the tack and, with a pat, sent Arion cantering away into the field.

Gordon asked Jamie if he wanted something to eat, but he shook his head. 'No thanks, I guess I'll head back. I'm really pooped.' He picked up his board and gave a weary wave. 'Thanks, guys, for everything.'

Dougal took his arm, his green eyes gleaming. 'Will you think on it?' he whispered urgently. 'What we asked of you?'

Jamie nodded and turned away into the dark.

21

Time and Tide

The night was a troubled one. Jamie had strange fevered dreams, alternating with sudden clear moments of panic when he sat bolt upright in bed, his face wet with sweat, shivering in the cool air. The events of the day had deeply unsettled him, and the heartfelt appeal from the young islanders weighed heavily on his mind. He was touched by their unexpected faith in him, but surely there was no way he could put himself forward to be the new chieftain? He would make an ass of himself, as he had done at the Games and when he scaled the castle. He would shame his dad's memory. Yet... the crazy ride on Arion, the magic and beauty of the place, seemed to awaken some deep echo in him that he could not deny.

Morning found him wide-eyed and restless, so he dressed quickly in jeans and T-shirt and decided to leave the castle without breakfast. He needed to clear his head, and when he spotted an old rod and tackle stuffed in a corridor cupboard, he reckoned a spot of fishing might just do the trick. He passed Angus, who was making his way slowly up the stone staircase. 'I'm gonna catch you something for supper,' he said, and waved the rod.

He did not notice Eleanor, who was sitting in her high-backed chair facing the hearth.

'I need a word with you.'

Jamie's heart sank. He shook an angry fist at the back of the chair, but moved reluctantly round to stand before her.

Eleanor gave him her steely glare. 'Have you seen to the animals?'

'It's Hazel's turn today.' He indicated the rod. 'I was going out.'

'Without your breakfast?'

'Yes. Do you have a problem with that?'

'Don't be insolent. And yes, since you ask, I do have a problem. With *you*.'

'Oh, really?'

'I need to know your intentions.'

'Excuse me?'

Eleanor shook her head impatiently. 'How much longer do you intend to impose yourself upon us? While I was prepared to allow you to spend a little time here, to recover after the funeral, I had not intended it as an open-ended invitation to settle. As you know, the clan has important business to attend to in the next days, which does not concern you and at which your presence might prove to be an embarrassment. I think it might be better for all concerned if you made arrangements for your immediate departure. Murdo will assist you.' She looked away. 'I think that is all.'

Jamie gave a low whistle and put down the rod. 'You really are something else, Grandma. I gotta hand it to you, you come right out with what's on your mind.'

'I think this conversation is terminated.'

'Really? Well, of course I'll go. I've an open ticket and I can leave tomorrow. I would hate to be an embarrassment. But don't you think it's kinda sad that a grandmom—'

'Stop calling me that.'

Jamie's eyes opened wide with surprise. 'Grandmom? But you are—'

Eleanor turned on him with fury. 'I have only your word for that. How do I know what tricks your mother played on my poor unsuspecting son?'

Jamie's eyes narrowed. 'What are you getting at? That Dad wasn't my father?'

Eleanor looked around wildly. 'How can I tell? He was raised in this culture, he knew his place and he would – in time – have presented me with a suitable family, and grandchildren, instead of . . . instead of . . .' Her voice faltered.

Jamie stood before her. 'Go on. Say it, Grandma, say what's really on your mind. *Instead of a black daughter-*

in-law and grandson. That's what you mean, ain't it? That's what you've been getting at ever since I landed here.'

Eleanor looked down, breathing heavily.

'Well, I got bad news for you, Grandma,' Jamie continued, angry now. 'I am the black son of my father, and it's taken this trip to make me realize what a great guy he was, and what he meant to this island and to me. But when he left, to follow his career, *you* erased *him* from your life. You can't blame me and my mom for that. You can't bear to think he had his own career, that he found someone to love. A real smart black woman who he loved. It happened, Grandma, whether you like it or not.' He took a step backwards. 'Before you go bawling others out, take a good look at yourself. You know what I see? A sad, lonely, bitter lady, who turned away her son, and now her grandson. I thought I might get through to you. I wanted to. I *tried* to. But I can see now, I was just wasting my time.' Jamie picked up his rod and tackle. 'And now, if you'll excuse me, I'm going fishing.'

Eleanor watched, open-mouthed, as Jamie made his way to the door.

'Have a nice day,' he said as he passed through.

As he headed down to the ocean, Jamie could feel his heart pounding in his chest. What had he done? Stood up to Eleanor, and about time too. Had he gone too far? What would Dad have said? Jamie smiled. Somehow he felt his father would have approved. But what the heck, he'd be out of there tomorrow, so what did it matter?

The float bobbed in the clear sea water, but Jamie doubted it would fool any self-respecting fish. He had fished a few times with his friends in a creek near his house, but they had never caught anything. He was not the world's greatest angler, but even he could tell that the ancient rod and reel were far from cutting-edge technology. Still, it felt pleasant enough to be perched on the giant boulder in Spey Cove, feeling the sun's warmth seep into his body.

Wee Malkie appeared below him. Of late, he seemed to be shadowing Jamie, materializing from nowhere and offering his commentary on the world.

'You'll catch nothin' there,' he volunteered now.

'Gee, thanks, Malkie. And how would you know?'

'I'm from here and you're no.' Wee Malkie hopped up onto the rock beside him and inspected the tin of wriggling worms.

'I see. So you're a really sussed dude, huh?'

'How's that?' said Wee Malkie absently.

Jamie tapped his forehead. 'Guess you got all the Doran info stashed in that little computer brain of yours.'

Wee Malkie nodded modestly. 'Aha.'

Jamie narrowed his eyes. 'OK then. Prove it. Tell me something. Where's the Eye of Doran?'

'Wha'?'

Jamie laughed. 'You must know that.'

Wee Malkie shrugged. 'There's no such place.'

Jamie prodded the boy's thin shoulders, feeling the bones through the frayed shirt. 'Sure there is. Only you don't know where it is. Fact is, Malkie, you don't know *nothin'*. So shut it.' He gave a flick to the line and the float bobbed merrily.

Wee Malkie chewed his lip unhappily. 'I do.'

Jamie ignored him and gazed out to sea.

Wee Malkie sneaked a look at him. He added, 'It's yonder. Only you cannae get there.'

Jamie shrugged contemptuously. 'Huh. You'll have to do better than that.'

Wee Malkie ran a hand through his spiky hair and looked at him in desperation. 'It's true. They say you'd have to climb up from Auchter Bay, but there's no way. We've all tried.'

Jamie relented. 'OK, dude,' he said, handing over the rod. 'You have a go.'

There was the sudden roar of a supercharged engine and a flash of yellow, and Duncan rounded the headland in his speedboat. He spotted the pair and cut the engine, coasting gently into the cove.

'Hey, you,' he shouted at Wee Malkie. 'Get out of here. I've told you before, no fishing.'

'My father always fishes here,' responded Wee Malkie defiantly.

Duncan surveyed him with contempt. 'Your father is a fool and a layabout. And he has already drunk away the generous money I paid him for his farm. So scram before I give you a good hiding.'

Wee Malkie snatched up a pebble and, with a great effort, hurled it at Duncan. It fell into the water, pitifully short.

'Right! You're for it now.' Duncan revved the engine and ran the boat up onto the beach. Wee Malkie threw the rod into the water, jumped down from the rock and took to his heels.

Duncan leaped lightly onto the sand and glared after him.

Jamie climbed down from the boulder. 'Wasn't that a bit tough on the kid?' he asked.

Duncan scowled. 'He's scum. Like his whole family. Wastrels. That's what's bringing Doran down.'

Jamie regarded the broken rod. 'Actually,' he said, 'it was me . . . fishing. I just lent him the rod.'

Duncan beamed at him. 'No problem, friend. Any time.' A thought struck him. 'But look, if you want to do some real fishing, then why don't you step aboard? You can ditch that old pole. I'll show you what the big boys use.'

They headed out almost a mile before Duncan stopped the boat and dropped the sea anchor. He showed Jamie how to strap himself into one of the sprung bucket seats behind the fixed rods, and how to bait and cast the line. He had all the latest technology on board and took great delight in demonstrating the newest features – sonar mapping, radar and a fully equipped kitchen.

As rock music blasted from twin speakers, Duncan's rod began to bend and he gave a yell. He expertly reeled in a large sea bass. Jamie watched in admiration as Duncan neatly removed the hook and flung the thrashing fish to join several others in a holding tank. 'How'd you do that? They just line up for your bait. Don't give me the time of day.'

Duncan smiled. 'Psychology, Jamie. You have to think like a fish, then you can catch him. This fellow is simple. It's the sharks and the marlins you really have to outwit. Your brain against theirs.'

Jamie stretched and breathed in deeply. 'You know, this is really cool.' Somehow, when he was with Duncan everything seemed easy. It was a lifestyle he could get used to. Surely Duncan wasn't as bad as people made out? Maybe they were just jealous. He was a bit high-handed, but at least Jamie could talk to him. Duncan seemed genuinely interested in what he had to say and treated him as an equal.

Duncan scanned the horizon. 'Yes, you can't beat it. I'll take you out properly one of these days. Go for the really big ones.'

Jamie grinned. 'Magic.' He indicated the miniature sub behind him, suspended in its cradle. 'So what do you use that for? Catching sharks?'

'No, that's just my little indulgence. Serves no real purpose. But when everything gets a bit stressed on the surface, I can sink down into another world where it's calm and peaceful. There are things on the sea bed you wouldn't believe. I'd love to show you but, as I said before, it's a single-seater.' His expression became more serious. He switched off the stereo. 'Jamie. Do you recall our little talk? 'Bout Doran and its future?'

Jamie nodded.

'Well, thing is, I need your help now. Time is getting short.'

'How's that?'

Duncan's eyes searched his face. 'You know we have to elect a new chieftain? It's already long overdue and I finally got Angus to admit that it must be done next week. Now, you know my plans for this place? This is your chance to let me make them a reality.'

'Like how?'

Duncan dropped his voice. 'Join with me. Come on the campaign trail these next few days and help me realize your father's dreams. We'd make a strong team.'

There was a pause and Jamie looked away, uncomfortable in Duncan's steady gaze. 'I'd sure like to help you, Duncan . . .'

Duncan clapped him heartily on the shoulder. 'There, I knew you would.'

'But . . . I'm not sure yet. I need a bit more time. Chew it over.' Jamie saw Duncan's lips compress, but he went on. 'See, I've gotten to talk to some folk, and well, it's, like, not all cut and dried. Some people seem to think . . .'

Duncan smiled at him. 'Jamie, I trust you've not been listening to tittle-tattle?'

'No.' Jamie struggled on, aware that every word dug him in deeper. 'I mean the people who have sold their homes and their—'

'Oh, they've been spreading their lies, have they? Painting me as the villain when I bailed them out of ruin?' Duncan gave a bitter laugh. 'Whatever happened to gratitude?'

'No, it's just that I think I owe it to my family—'

'Come on, boy, don't mess me around.' Duncan's eyes glittered with anger. Then he tapped his nose. 'Oh, I see your game. Very well then, name your price.'

Jamie frowned. 'Excuse me?'

'Well, that's what it's about, isn't it? What it all comes down to in the end?' Duncan threw back his head and barked with laughter. 'Smart lad! Good for you.'

Jamie looked bemused, but Duncan drew close and spoke earnestly.

'Listen, Jamie, and listen well. We don't have much time. I have this thing almost in my grasp. Eleanor and the other diehards are a spent force; don't waste your time with them. There is no real opposition.'

'What about Alistair? He seems a pretty popular guy with the islanders.'

'Yes, and he'll swing many votes behind him. Which is fine.'

Jamie frowned. 'Fine? I don't get it.'

Duncan spread his hands. 'Come on, Jamie, you're smarter than that. Don't you realize, Alistair is on *my* team? He has been, shall we say, very well looked after. And to show his gratitude he will transfer those islander votes to me.'

'Oh,' said Jamie, winded. So it's true, he thought, remembering the talk at the barn. *Taking Duncan's shilling.*

'Now, if you join our winning team you too will be very well looked after. I am offering you a stake, Jamie, a stake in the big time. And just for starters . . .' Duncan

201

reached behind him into his windcheater and drew out a thick leather wallet.

Jamie was shocked. 'Hey, hold on there. You got this all wrong. I ain't askin' you for nothing and I won't take nothing.' He waved away the proffered notes and unbuckled his harness. 'No, man, I really dig this place and I just want to do anythin' I can for the best. You know, for Doran.'

Duncan replaced the wallet slowly and when he turned back to Jamie the anger was gone. Indeed, all expression was gone and his face was a tight mask. 'Of course you do – we both do. That was just a little test – which, I must say, you passed with flying colours. Your father would approve.'

Jamie bit his lip. 'Look, man, I'm really grateful for . . .' He motioned around him. 'Well, for everything. But I gotta do my own thing, work it out for myself. That's something my dad did teach me.'

Duncan stared at him, then nodded. 'And that's why, in your own time, I hope you will want to give me your support.' His voice changed and he smiled broadly. The storm had passed. 'Now then, let's see if we can help you land something respectable.'

Jamie rose. 'Fact is, Duncan, I'm feeling a bit queasy. Haven't got my sea legs yet. Think I should maybe get back to dry land, if that's OK.'

Duncan unbuckled himself and moved towards the wheelhouse. 'Of course. I'll run you back to the harbour.'

Jamie looked back towards the shore. 'Know what? Think I'll explore a bit more.'

'Fine. Just tell me where to put you down.'

'D'you know Auchter Bay?'

Duncan arched his eyebrows in surprise. 'Auchter Bay? I'm sure I can find you somewhere more interesting.'

'No, Auchter Bay sounds neat to me.'

'Well, it's wild and there's not much to see there, and you can't . . .' Duncan looked down at the ocean, slapping under the bows of the boat. He shrugged. 'Well, if you really *insist*. Auchter Bay it is.'

The yellow speedboat roared into life and Duncan took it in a long curve towards land. For a while he ran parallel to the rocky foreshore, then, cutting the engine back to a dawdle, he nosed his boat round a rocky headland into the perfect crescent of a deserted bay. A wall of high chalk cliffs backed a fine golden sand beach, with only occasional outcrops of rock.

'Auchter Bay,' said Duncan. 'I told you it was pretty wild.'

Jamie jumped into the shallow water and waved. 'It'll do fine. Thanks a bundle, Duncan. Appreciate it. Catch you later.'

Duncan waved back from behind the wheel. The sunlight glinted off his dark glasses. 'Take it easy. You can always head back to town if you get bored. Take any track.' He indicated the beach. 'All roads lead to Rome.'

'No problem.'

Duncan consulted his watch. 'Anyway, I'll check back here in two hours. That'll be four fifteen exactly, and if you're feeling lazy, I'll run you home.' He gave another wave as he revved the engine and the powerful boat surged out to sea.

The Doran Arms had its usual afternoon complement of regulars sitting at its gnarled oak tables. A drone of conversation rose and fell like the wind.

Murdo and Alistair sat together with a couple of other men. One was a gaunt roof-thatcher called Lachlan and the other was Hamish, a red-faced fisherman who had filled some small glasses with whisky and was now adding water from a jug.

Murdo waved him away. 'Thanks, Hamish. Dinna droon the miller.' He took a gulp and smacked his lips appreciatively. He turned to Alistair, who was staring gloomily into his glass. 'So how's the campaign going?'

Alistair didn't look at him. 'Fine.'

Hamish sat down opposite Murdo. 'How's things up yon?'

Murdo grimaced. 'Bad. Verra bad. Never worse,' he added gloomily.

'She's putting up Angus?'

'She'd no choice. There's no one else.' Murdo gave a sigh. 'He's a good man.'

Hamish shook his head. 'He's twa bubbles aff the centre.'

Lachlan broke in, 'And she's a carnaptious Bessie.' He laughed loudly.

Murdo looked at him disapprovingly. 'Keep a calm sooch, Lackie. She's no' had an easy life.'

Alistair swirled the liquid in his glass. 'Easier for her than for some,' he muttered.

'Aye,' Murdo agreed, 'but she's gettin' on.'

Alistair looked up wildly. 'They have had their time. Things ha' got ta change. Or Doran will be for the birds and wee fishies.'

Murdo peered at him. 'Aye, and that's why plenty folk are putting their trust in *you*. I hope you're no' thinkin' o' sellin' out to that bauchle Duncan? Losh!' He shuddered. 'I'd rather cut my own throat.'

Alistair looked away. 'I didnae say that. The man is a scheming toad. But he's smart and he has plans.'

Hamish lowered his voice. 'And to cap it, he's got dosh.' He looked around. 'And the way things are goin', there's plenty folk around who'll take it.'

Murdo spat. 'More fool them.'

Lachlan rounded on him. 'Oh wisht, man. Easy for you to say. You have nae bairns to feed.'

'If we pulled together we could get this place back on its feet,' said Murdo, glaring at him. 'Good lord, Lackie, *you've* talked about it enough.'

Lachlan mocked him. 'Aye, talk is cheap.'

'And dithering is worthless!' returned Murdo heatedly. 'Help ma boab! Alistair, you are our last chance, man. You have to stand up to that devil and take the islanders with you. Or we are lost.'

Alistair mumbled and drained his whisky. 'Time I was away,' he said, and lurched unsteadily from the table.

22

Cliffhanger

The walk along Auchter Bay took longer than Jamie anticipated. Although the sand was fine and strewn with small shells, long fingers of rock acted as natural break-waters and he was forced to negotiate each of them. He was sweating as he reached the headland at the far end. He turned and looked upwards at the towering cliffs above him. Wee Malkie was right: there was no way to climb up. In fact, when he came to think of it, he couldn't remember seeing paths or inlets at all on his walk around the bay.

Jamie was surprised to see that the waves were almost lapping his feet. 'Oops,' he said. 'Time to head home.'

He began to run back along the foot of the cliffs, through the surf. The wind had picked up and the tide was coming in fast. By the time he reached the spot at the centre of the bay where Duncan had left him, he was wading through knee-high water. He stopped and peered ahead.

'All roads lead to Rome? OK. Only I don't see any road.'

A large wave knocked him flat and he floundered towards some rocks that formed a wide flat ledge at the base of the cliff. With an effort he hauled himself up onto the shelf.

'Jeez. Duncan never said nothin' about this,' he said aloud. He consulted his watch. 4.30 p.m. He peered out over the dazzling, empty ocean. 'So where are you, dude?'

He scrambled to his feet and looked along the bay. The sandy beach had all but disappeared and the tide was still rising fast. Already waves were breaking powerfully over the ledge. Jamie retreated towards the cliff face, looking desperately for some way of climbing higher. The cliff was composed of crumbly chalk and offered few hand- or footholds. Jamie searched in his pocket and brought out some sweet wrappers and the Stone of Doran. Another search produced his penknife, which he opened without quite knowing what to do with it. He was about to replace the stone in his pocket when something made him examine it more closely.

Jamie raised the blue stone to eye level and looked closely at the glass inserted into it like a lens. Something cloudy within seemed to move and swirl. He put the stone to his eye and squinted through it, first out to sea and then turning towards the cliff.

Through the lens he saw the cliff face appear through a clearing mist. Set in the cliff, a metre or so higher and to the right of the ledge, was a dark and distinct rectangular shape. Jamie took the stone away from his eye. The cliff showed no marking, just a vast expanse of white chalk. As the waves threatened to pull him from the rock, Jamie held the stone to his eye and moved towards the rectangle. He stretched up a hand but couldn't quite reach it. Frantically he built a small heap with some of the larger rocks nearby and climbed on top. Now he could reach the dark shape and he pressed it with his hand, then threw his full weight against it. There was a grinding sound and the leading edge of the rectangle swung inward, like a giant door. A wave crashed against Jamie, dragging him back. As he fell, he plunged the penknife into the chalk and clung to the cliff opening. Painfully, and with all his might, he hauled himself upwards.

The speedboat rocked in the waves, pulling urgently at its sea anchor. Duncan, seated at the controls, took a deep gulp from his chilled can of lager. He smacked his lips and reached for the powerful binoculars that hung from his neck. Adjusting the zoom, he brought distant Auchter Bay into clear focus. Panning swiftly across the base of the cliffs, he noted with some satisfaction the pounding surf and the total absence of any sign of life.

He consulted his watch.

'My goodness,' he murmured. 'Is it that late? Time and tide wait for no man.' With a smile he fired the ignition, retracted the anchor and with full revs headed the boat out to sea.

Jamie landed in a sodden heap in the cliff opening. There was no time to examine his unexpected surroundings as the waves were already splashing inside. He was vaguely aware of the cliff door gently closing behind him as he ran blindly forwards and upwards along a curving tunnel that was excavated from the chalk. The further he penetrated into the cliff, the dimmer the light became and the fainter the pounding of the sea. After a time, he tripped in the gloom, scraping the palms of his hands as he put them out to break his fall. The Stone of Doran clattered away into the darkness.

Jamie swore and sat on the floor, licking his bleeding hands. He looked around for the stone – the lucky talisman that had, once again, brought him good fortune. At first he could see very little, but as his eyes became more accustomed to the darkness he noticed a faint luminous shape less than a metre away. He moved slowly towards it – was it some sort of animal, a reflected eye perhaps, or a glowworm? It didn't move or blink. Maybe it was a discarded watch? But then who else could possibly have found their way into this passage? Cautiously he stretched out his fingers towards the luminous shape and found them closing around the cool surface of the Stone of Doran. The luminescence was coming from the glass at its centre. Once again, Jamie raised the stone to his eye and looked through. To his amazement the lens not only acted as a viewfinder, but also revealed the scene before him, clearly illuminated as if by a night-vision camera. Jamie whistled in astonishment, turning his head this way and that, taking in his new surroundings.

23

Sounds of Silence

Wee Malkie scraped listlessly at a greasy pan. There was no washing-up liquid and the cold water dribbling from the tap made little impression on the embedded traces of countless fried meals. There was a crash from behind a scuffed door, which burst open as his father stumbled into the room, hauling up his trousers and cursing. His hair stood on end, his shirt was buttoned incorrectly and he clutched an old magazine from which many pages had been torn. He looked wildly around the room as though unsure of his purpose, grunted and flung himself into the only armchair.

'Are you goin' out?'

'What?'

'You heard me. There's things need fetching.' His father waved a grubby piece of paper.

Wee Malkie sighed, and stood the pan upside down on the draining board.

Wee Malkie had always been called Wee Malkie. Not just because of his small and delicate appearance, but because his father was Malcolm too. He had no brothers or sisters, and his mother had fled to the mainland a few years after Malkie was born. She was not from Doran, but a city girl from Dumfries, and had never fully adjusted to island life. Wee Malkie barely remembered her. He kept a blurred photo of her in his drawer; it showed a thin, angular woman with mousy hair holding an outstretched bundle that was allegedly Wee Malkie in his swaddling clothes. Even in the photograph she seemed anxious to give him away.

His father had been a striking and popular man with fiery red hair, clear Doran eyes and bulging muscles. Wee Malkie remembered being hoisted effortlessly onto his shoulders when he was tiny and being carried at a reckless speed through the woods. Back then, they had picnics on the beach and exciting outings on the ocean, with his father laughing as he pulled powerfully at the oars. Malcolm owned a farm and ran his own construction business; at one time he had employed a dozen or so islanders to renovate the island's older buildings and erect new homes. But business had fallen away, and there had been a glut of homes for sale. No one had wanted to build new ones so he had reluctantly sold off parcels of his land, one by one – to the only buyer: Duncan Wylie. Now just the ramshackle barn remained, and the weekly benefits payment from the post office. And Wee Malkie. They moved around each other with a never-quite-expressed sense of resentment. There were no rows, but there was no laughter, and precious little talk either.

Wee Malkie always 'did the messages' – fetching the meagre groceries from Menzies' store, sometimes asking for them to be put on the slate, to be paid later when his father had the money. Recently the slate had got longer and the money shorter, until old Mr Menzies had taken the boy aside and said, 'Look, Wee Malkie, could you tell your father that while I welcome his custom, I'd welcome his cash even more.'

He had reported this back to his father, who at the time had been filling in his Lottery coupon in between swigs of ale. 'Menzies is a grasping leech,' he had snarled. 'I've a mind to take my business elsewhere.' The trouble was, there was nowhere else to take it. Menzies' Family Provisions had the monopoly on the grocery trade in Doran, but with a declining population and increasing transportation costs, there was little enough profit in it.

Wee Malkie now took a string shopping bag from its nail, threw in some empty soda bottles and snatched the list from his father. He fingered the few pound coins in his pocket. They would clear some of the debt, but he'd have to put the new items on the slate again. Mr Menzies would not be pleased.

He swung out of the barn and kicked aimlessly at the

ground as he made his way through the dense woodland that separated his home from the potholed road winding down to the village.

'Hey!' The hand shot out from behind a tree and suspended Wee Malkie in the air before he could even see to whom it belonged. His feet scrabbled to find the ground.

Duncan drew the boy towards him effortlessly and looked at him with distaste. 'What have we here?'

'Put me doun.' Wee Malkie's thin face was unusually flushed. He coughed.

Duncan arched his eyebrows. 'Oh, not so brave now, are we?'

'My dad'll kill you. I'm fetchin' his messages.'

'Kill me, will he?' echoed Duncan. 'I don't think so. He's far too busy drinking himself to death.' He lowered Wee Malkie to the ground but held him firmly at arm's length. 'Where's your pal?'

Wee Malkie glared at him. 'Who?'

'Our Yankee friend.'

'I dunno.'

Duncan grabbed his arm, and twisted it viciously behind him. 'Tell me.'

Wee Malkie yelled. 'Ow. I swear. With you?'

Duncan gave the arm another twist. 'With *me*?'

'Aye. On the beach. Ow. You're hurtin' me . . . When I buzzed off. I've no' seen him since.'

Another twist. 'Sure? What else did you see?'

'Ouch. Nothin', I swear it.'

'If you value your life, remember that. You saw

nothing.' Duncan pushed him away and Wee Malkie rubbed his arm vigorously.

'I think it's broke,' he said.

Duncan put his hands on his hips. 'Good. Now get out of my sight, or I'll break the other one too.'

Wee Malkie raised his fists and glared at Duncan, his face contorted with fury. Duncan moved towards him, and Wee Malkie fled, the string bag and its plastic bottles bouncing against his bony knees.

24

Hands

It was pitch dark, and without the aid of the stone Jamie would have seen nothing. The passage wound upwards, always rising, and the chalk gave way to rock, damp and slimy to the touch. It also opened out, as though he was passing through a series of caves rather than a constructed tunnel. Occasionally he would hear something scamper away from him, but he never saw anything. The air had become cooler, and now he was shivering in his wet jeans and T-shirt. He was also very thirsty. He hadn't drunk or eaten anything since he was on Duncan's boat, and then he'd had only a couple of Cokes and some pretzels. That was – how long ago? He looked at the luminous dial of his watch: 7.05. Could he really have been walking for two hours? His aching legs told him that he had, and he suddenly felt afraid. He had no idea where he was going, whether this path led anywhere, or maybe just petered out in the middle of the mountain. Even more alarmingly, he'd reached a fork in the path which led to two separate stone caverns. Both were equally dark and uninviting, like two eye sockets in a skull.

Suddenly his attention was caught by a small but distinct mark on the wall of the right-hand opening. He examined it closely through the stone. It was quite faint, and covered with a thin veneer of lichen, but the markings were not accidental. Someone had carefully carved two clasped hands – the symbol of the Clan MacDoran.

There was no sound in the hall except for the scraping of cutlery on plates, and the occasional spluttering of a log in the hearth. Angus and Hazel stared intently at their plates as they chewed. Eleanor was engaged in cutting her food minutely. She gave a sigh and stared at Jamie's empty chair.

'Perhaps he had a more pressing engagement,' she said. 'But it would have been kind to let us know.' She lifted the lid of one of the silver dishes and regarded the piece of dried meat. 'This will be inedible shortly.' She returned to prodding the food before her.

The meal had been inedible to begin with, thought Hazel. She had forgotten to put the chicken in the oven on time, and when she had remembered, she'd cooked it at far too high a temperature, blackening the skin and leaving the inside pink and raw. Hazel was bored with cooking for the family, but it never seemed to occur to Eleanor that she might occasionally take over the duties. And the only time Angus had ventured into the kitchen, when Hazel had been down with the flu, it had been a total disaster. His shepherd's pie had caught fire and he had run through the hall, billowing smoke and flames, and thrown it – dish and all – onto the drive. The experiment had not been repeated.

Eleanor suddenly dropped her fork with a clatter. The others looked at her in surprise. 'Perhaps he has left already,' she murmured.

'*Left?*' repeated Angus. 'Whoever said anything about his leaving?' He fixed a furious gaze on Eleanor. 'What have you done now?'

Eleanor dropped her head. 'I – I – just told him it might be better . . .'

'You threw him out? Your kith and kin?'

Eleanor began to tremble. 'We had words. He called me . . .'

Angus struggled to his feet and pointed an accusing finger at Eleanor. 'Well, you have your wish. The laddie is gone. An' I hope you are glad. I hope you are satisfied.'

25

Serpents Entwine

Duncan's entryphone speaker crackled into life. 'Who is it?'

'It's me. Calum.' The thin-faced boy glanced nervously over his shoulder.

The gate slid open and Duncan appeared in the doorway. He beckoned the boy inside. Calum entered the atrium, his eyes blinking in the light, and looked around him. Duncan eased himself into the leather sofa.

'So?'

Calum shifted his weight uneasily. 'I went to see Mary Kirkpatrick.'

'Did you now. And was she amenable to our little suggestion?'

'Was she hell! She fought like a tiger.' Calum sucked a knuckle. 'But she saw sense in the end.'

Duncan smiled. 'Of course she did, Calum. I'm sure you can be very persuasive when you want to. Did she sign?'

Calum produced a piece of paper from his jacket. 'Aye. Her writing's no' brilliant.'

Duncan snatched the paper and examined it. 'It'll do. It'll do just fine.'

He looked up at Calum. 'Good lad. Come sit down.' He patted the sofa.

Calum sat gingerly beside him on the soft leather. Duncan placed a hand on his shoulder. 'You are learning fast. I like that in a youngster. Shows you have potential, to go further. To go far. Is that what you want?'

Calum nodded. 'Aye. I do.' He looked around the room. 'I wouldn't mind some o' this, by the way.'

Duncan shook his head impatiently. 'These are just the trappings; the things that money buys. The important thing is power, control. That's what really matters. And to get power, you have to want it very much indeed. More than anything else in life. Be focused on it twenty-four seven. That's my advice to you.'

Calum looked up. His cold grey eyes met Duncan's. 'Aye, thanks. But that's not all, is it?'

Duncan removed his hand. 'Sorry?'

'What you *don't* tell me, or anyone else, is why you are bothering with this backwater. You can't really give a toss for Doran. Not an operator like you. You'd find far richer pickings elsewhere.' He paused. 'Unless of course there is something else here that you know about, something *really* valuable that you want to get your hands on – and that's another thing you're no' telling me about.' A thin smile crept across his lips.

For a moment Duncan looked taken aback. Then he threw back his head and laughed. 'Calum, you really are a remarkable young man. I must admit I underestimated you. I thought you were just another underprivileged thug looking for some easy cash. But there is a clever and calculating mind in there and, I shouldn't wonder, a heart of steel.'

Calum put his head on one side. 'So why not let me in – as a partner?'

Duncan regarded him over pressed fingertips. 'Now why should I want to do that?'

Calum sighed. 'Because it might be better to have me as a friend than an enemy.'

26

The Eye Shall Behold

Jamie shivered uncontrollably as he pressed forward through the rock caverns, holding the stone to his eye to find his way. At times the roof became so low he had to crouch to pass through, but at others it opened out so he found it hard to gauge its height. Occasionally he heard the sound of wings fluttering high above him, or the squeaking of a bat. The path was always uphill, though time and again it divided, presenting him with alternative ways ahead. On every occasion, Jamie would search the rough walls, looking for the unmistakable mark of the clasped hands. It was all he had to hold onto, a sure sign that someone had been there before him and bothered to mark the way. But when, and why, and to where? And what had become of them? Would he stumble upon a heap of dusty bones in some blocked tunnel?

It was 9 p.m. when the path finally ended abruptly. There were no bones – and nothing but a blank rock face before him. Jamie dropped to his knees in a panic, scratching at the surface with his hands as though he could somehow claw his way through. He cried out in frustration and pounded the rock with his fist. What was the point? Who had gone to the trouble of marking this lengthy climb only for it to end in a blind alley? Why place the Doran symbol on the walls to guide him to nothing? His mind raced. Maybe there was a mark somewhere that he'd overlooked. He searched the rock face feverishly but it was completely bare. Jamie hugged himself to try to get warm. His throat was dry and his stomach hurt. He didn't fancy having to pass the night in these conditions. The only alternative was to try to find his way back to the door in the cliff. The thought appalled him.

He sat down and leaned against the barrier wall, staring at the dull gleam from the stone in his hand. Somehow it comforted him. Whatever strange properties it possessed, they seemed to be benign. A force to help and guide him. Once again he pressed the stone to his eye and looked back towards the way he had come. The path sloped downwards and curved out of sight. Jamie transferred his attention to the wall on his left and froze. Beside him were two clear markings. He brought his face towards them and made out not one but two clan symbols, one pair of clasped hands placed directly above the other. Was it his imagination, or did they seem to be enclosed in a larger square of slightly darker rock?

Jamie ran his fingers lightly over the markings, feeling the etched lines in the surface. Then he pressed them with his hand, and felt the stone square move. He pushed harder and, with a grinding sound, the entire section slid backwards and then to one side, revealing a large hollow behind. Jamie felt a sudden gust of warm air on his face.

He dived through the opening and sprawled headlong onto some sort of woven floor covering. He sat up and brought the stone to his eye once more and gasped in astonishment. He was in a circular room with a high, domed ceiling. Around the walls were strange painted shapes and hieroglyphics. The floor covering, on closer inspection, was a light carpet with an intricately woven border. At the far side of the room was a dark and ancient wooden trunk with heavy brass hinges. The air was much warmer than the passage outside and, though slightly musty, smelled pleasantly of heather.

Jamie gingerly lifted the lid of the trunk and looked inside. There were rolls of material, some dusty books, a parchment map and some ancient regalia. There was also a tarnished but beautifully wrought silver flask which, when he shook it, seemed to contain some liquid. With some difficulty, Jamie managed to unscrew the top and sniffed the contents. It smelled like some kind of liqueur. He tentatively took a taste. Whatever liquid was inside was sweet and refreshing and he took a hefty swig.

The flickering lanterns held aloft by Murdo and Angus illuminated Jamie's made-up bed. There was no sign that it had been disturbed.

Eleanor stood by the door. She seemed suddenly to have shrunk and aged and her strident voice was reduced to a frail whisper. 'Have you looked on the roof?'

'Aye. He's not there. Nor has he been seen anywhere in town.'

Angus pulled at his beard. 'He had my old rod and we know he was off fishing. It's no' been returned.' He frowned. 'There's been an awful fierce high tide this after.'

'I'm sure Jamie can look after himself,' Hazel broke in. 'Malkie says he's a fine swimmer.'

Eleanor whispered again. 'We must make a search.'

Murdo nodded. 'Aye. But there's nothin' t' be done 'til first light.'

The sound of a lone piper fills the night air. Jamie has heard this music before, but not on the pipes. In the blood, hadn't he said? In the blood.

From behind the brow of a hill the majestic figure of a Highland warrior marches relentlessly forward. He is in silhouette, with the bright moonlight casting strange shapes onto the fir trees before him. Jamie can't see his eyes, but he knows the man is looking for him. As the warrior

comes nearer, the drums begin beating out their insistent
tattoo but his stride never falters, the kilt swaying with
the constant motion. His hand reaches for his claymore
and he grasps the hilt. The moonlight flashes on the silver
blade as it is suddenly drawn and held aloft, dazzling
Jamie . . .

Jamie's eyes snapped open and he sat bolt upright.
Something exploded in his head and he put a hand to his
forehead and groaned.

When the pain subsided, he noticed the flask standing
beside him and suddenly remembered where he was. He
looked around for the stone, but as he reached for it he
realized he could see perfectly well without it. Patterns
of light were flickering all around him. He looked up
and shielded his eyes. From the centre of the ceiling a
powerful light source was projecting beams into the
circular room. Jamie rose groggily to his feet and looked
down at the carpet where a brilliant circular pattern was
thrown onto its surface. It took him a moment to realize
that he was standing in the middle of a film. He stepped
backwards and took in the whole picture. No, it wasn't a
film, but an exact panoramic representation of an outside
scene. In this case, an eagle-eye view of Auchter Bay,
glinting in the early morning sun.

'Hey!' Jamie let out a whistle and crouched down to
examine the crystal-clear image. On the carpet, his
fingers traced the curve of the yellow sand and the gently
lapping waves. There was a boat drawn up on the beach
and Alistair and several islanders were systematically
searching the foreshore.

226

Jamie consulted his watch. 8 a.m.

Something stirred in his memory and he straightened and stretched his hands towards the light, breaking the beam. His fingers found an iron lever to one side, which he tugged. With a judder the lever swung down and the projected scene blurred. The harbour, village and then the castle swung into view. A figure wearing a pink sweatshirt and a hood from which amber strands escaped could be clearly seen cycling along the drive.

Jamie grinned in delight. 'A-maz-ing! A spy-cam. Hi, Hazel girl. I got my beady eye on you!'

A thought suddenly struck him like a thunderbolt. 'The eye! This is *The Eye*. The Eye of Doran!' From this viewpoint he could easily observe the whole island – just as the legendary clan chieftains had done.

He pulled at the lever again and the image panned crazily over the heather, trees and rocks. A wild and rugged terrain came into view, with no roads, only rocky cliffs populated with flocks of sea birds overlooking the ocean. Then more cliff and . . . *more* ocean? How strange. There seemed to be a double coastline.

Jamie reversed the lever and crouched again to inspect the image on the floor. What he had at first taken for the open sea was in fact an enclosed and tranquil inner lagoon. On the far side, beyond more rock cliffs, he could make out the white crested waves of the real ocean. As Jamie studied this wild seascape, a yellow shape moved swiftly into frame, trailing its creamy wake. Jamie muttered, 'Duncan!'

The speedboat was running parallel to the coast, but suddenly turned abruptly. It headed straight towards the outer rocks and promptly disappeared behind them.

Jamie whistled. 'What you up to now, Dunc? Nothin' good, I'll bet.'

27

Search

News of Jamie's disappearance spread quickly and became the main talking point among the islanders. By midday, the shops were shut and everyone was engaged in a desperate search. Farmers re-directed their tractors from gathering the harvest to drive down unused paths. Fishermen abandoned their nets and searched the coves and far out to sea.

Murdo commandeered one of the outside tables at the Doran Arms as an operational HQ. He fixed a large map of the island to a board, which Angus populated with pins of various colours. Eleanor, muffled in a thick coat, sat with an open exercise book at the table.

Occasionally she dabbed at her eyes with a lace hand-kerchief.

Every few minutes an islander would arrive and brief Murdo, who then reported on their search to Eleanor. She wrote slowly in her book as Angus placed another pin on the board.

A white-haired lady now strode briskly up to the table with her terrier dog panting at her heels. 'I've walked up yonder on the glen, towards the falls, wi' Gregor,' she shouted at Murdo.

'Thanks, Helen. Any trace?'

The old lady shook her head. 'We found nothing.'

Eleanor marked it in her book, and Angus put another green pin on an inland area of Doran.

There was a clatter of hooves, and Janet and Dougal arrived on horseback. Janet was flushed and breathing heavily as she dismounted. 'I'm no' in training for this sort of thing,' she announced. 'I think we've covered every road on the island.'

'No sign?' asked Murdo.

'Naw,' said Dougal. 'Though we did find some old jeans in a ditch. But they could have belonged to anybody.'

A thought struck Angus. 'Perhaps we should issue a description?'

Murdo chuckled grimly. 'There'll no' be too many black laddies roamin' the countryside, do you think?'

Eleanor motioned feebly to him. 'How are we doing?' she whispered.

Murdo pointed to the line of blue pins. 'All the

230

beaches thoroughly searched and' – indicating the green markers – 'we have reports in from most of the farms.'

Eleanor sighed. 'When was the last reported sighting?'

Murdo flipped back some pages of the book. 'We know for sure he headed off with a fishing rod early on. Oh, and Wee Malkie confirms they were fishing together down Spey Cove sometime later. He got chased off by Duncan.'

'We've searched the cove thoroughly?' asked Angus.

Murdo sighed and reached under the table. He produced a broken fishing rod. 'Aye. And we found this,' he said, holding it up. 'In the water.'

Angus examined it. 'Oh, the poor wee bairn.'

Eleanor leaned back heavily on the bench and covered her eyes.

Duncan rounded the corner and approached the group. He nodded curtly to Eleanor and Angus. 'Just got back into harbour and I heard the news. A bad business. Is there anything I can do?'

Angus looked at him sternly. 'It seems mebbe you were the last to see the lad.'

Duncan looked incredulous. '*I* was?'

'Aye. According to Wee Malkie. Had a go at them for fishing down Spey Cove. Yesterday morning.'

Duncan's mouth tightened. He spread his hands. 'Now why would I do that? The boy's a complete fantasist.' He paused and wagged a finger. 'Now I recall. I was out in the boat in the morning, and I did see them there from a distance, fishing off that big rock. I think I gave them a wave and a shout, but I had pressing business at home to attend to.' He moved closer to Angus and lowered his voice. 'Look, whatever the outcome, this must not affect the vote, you know.'

Angus recoiled and flushed. 'Haud your wheesht, man! Is that all you can think about when a fine young lad is lost?'

Duncan nodded. 'My concern is as great as yours, Angus. But there are even greater things at stake. Come what may, the Clan Meet must be held on Tuesday, as planned. In three days' time.'

The search continued throughout the day, and the map and the exercise book both became filled. But as the afternoon wore on, it became clear that Jamie had vanished without trace.

The members of Wee Malkie's gang organized themselves in relays to scour a large area of the moor. They worked nonstop, reporting regularly into the search HQ, and were now sitting dejectedly on some tree stumps in the wood clearing near Malkie's barn.

Donald pulled at his tangled blond hair and wiped his nose on his shirtsleeve. 'I'm fair puggled,' he announced.

'Aye,' agreed Wee Malkie. 'Ma pins are killin' me.' His thin shoes were split and caked in mud.

Andrew heaved a deep sigh. 'The poor wee fella.'

Wee Malkie dropped his head. 'An' it's all ma fault.'

Donald looked puzzled. 'How come?'

Wee Malkie kicked at the ground with his toe. 'If I'd

stayed by him – stood ma ground wi' Duncan, 'stead of scarperin' like a bauchle.'

Andrew got up. 'Aw, dinna fash yersel'. You're nae t' blame.' He looked around uncomfortably. 'Have t' gae haem for ma tea. Are you comin', Donald?'

Donald rose and they both stood awkwardly before Wee Malkie. 'Aye. See ya, Malk.'

The boys punched Wee Malkie gently on the shoulder and moved off. He felt hot tears welling in his eyes, and brushed them away angrily. He chewed on his lower lip.

'Yo, Malkie.' The hoarse whisper floated from the shrubbery.

Wee Malkie jumped up and looked around in terror. He raised his fists. 'Who's there?' he challenged, but his voice wavered.

'It is I,' said the whisper. Wee Malkie's eyes widened and he felt his heart hammering in his thin chest.

The bushes shivered and parted, and Jamie appeared. His clothes were torn, wet and filthy, his eyes stared sightlessly and his bloodied arms were stretched out before him as he staggered forward like a zombie. '*I am The Walking Dead,*' he intoned and then burst into laughter.

Wee Malkie gave a scream and then, with tears filling his eyes, he flung himself at Jamie, pounding him furiously with his fists.

Jamie was taken aback. 'Cool it, man. It was just a joke.' He trapped Wee Malkie's flailing hands. 'Easy there, dude, what's gotten into you?'

Wee Malkie wailed through his racking sobs, 'I thought you was dead.'

'Yeah. I guess I nearly was. Hey, bro.' Jamie looked curiously at Wee Malkie's tear-stained face. 'Were those for me?'

Wee Malkie dabbed roughly at his eyes with his sleeve and looked away. 'Och no. I couldnae care a docken for you.' He stifled a final sob.

Jamie put his arm around him. 'Sorry, Malkie,' he said. 'That was a pretty dumb move.'

Wee Malkie gave a sniff. 'No matter. I'd best go tell Angus you're found.'

'No!' Jamie looked intently into the boy's eyes. 'Listen, Malkie. No kidding now. I *really* need your help.'

28

Gathering Forces

Night had fallen, and with it all hope seemed to have been extinguished. Three figures sat huddled around the dying fire in the great hall in abject misery.

'I failed him,' said Eleanor at last, staring at the glowing embers. 'He came to us, his family, and I rejected him.'

Angus pulled miserably at his beard. 'You mustn't blame yourself.'

'I blame myself above all,' said Eleanor bitterly. 'I was his grandmother and I behaved like a foolish old woman, nursing my own wounds and taking out my spite on him. He was an innocent and I treated him like an enemy.'

Hazel stared into the fire. 'I was no better. Always putting him down.'

Eleanor turned to Angus in anguish. 'What are we to tell his mother? She will have to be informed. As if that poor woman has not suffered enough.'

Angus passed a weary hand over his face. 'Aye. But we'll not give up hope yet.'

There was a slight movement at the window and Hazel glanced up. Wee Malkie's grubby face appeared in the pane, spotted Hazel and signalled urgently. She gave a start, but Wee Malkie put a finger to his lips and bobbed down out of sight.

Hazel saw Angus regarding her curiously. 'What is it, girl?'

'Nothing. Just a shiver. All this sittin' around.' She got up and shook herself, like a dog. 'I think I need a breath of air.'

Eleanor watched her go, adding quietly, 'Don't forget your coat,' as the door closed. She sighed deeply. 'What's to be done about the vote? Tuesday, is it? I fear I have no heart for it any more.'

Angus murmured, 'Aye. Duncan can do his worst.' He watched the fire as a twig suddenly flamed. 'And yet . . .'

'What?'

'Och, I dinnae ken. There's no reason, and yet somehow, I feel . . . maybe all is not lost.'

Wee Malkie led the way in silence through the dark wood, pausing only to catch his rasping breath. Now they approached his father's tumbledown barn. Hazel was shocked. She had not been here for some months, and the change in the place was dramatic. In the moonlight she could see weeds growing right up to the door, which hung crookedly from its rusted hinges. Several of the windowpanes were cracked or missing. Indeed, the only sign of habitation was a wisp of smoke rising from the chimney.

Malkie refused to say anything as they walked through the woods, but now Hazel addressed the back of his head. 'Come on, Malk. Tell me. Is it your dad? Is he took bad or something?'

Wee Malkie gave a snort. 'He's as strong as an ox. It's the drink that protects him. No, he'll be down the Arms 'til closing.'

Hazel stopped. 'So what's with all the secrecy?' she demanded. 'Look, Malkie, this is just stupid.'

But Wee Malkie did not break his stride. 'You'll see soon enough.' He stopped before the door and gave two low whistles, then pulled it open.

In the gloom Hazel could just make out the large beamed room; she could see a table, the back of a decrepit armchair and a huge collection of bottles. A candle flickered feebly in a saucer. Hazel looked around her, bewildered.

'The leccy got cut off a week ago,' Wee Malkie said.

A dark figure rose from the chair. 'Thanks for coming, Hazel.'

Hazel's hand flew to her mouth. 'Crivens! Oh, Jamie, thank God!' Without thinking she rushed into his arms.

Jamie held her a moment. 'Never knew I was such a popular guy,' he said gently.

Hazel looked up at him. 'Lordy, where have you been? Do you not know the whole island has been out looking for you?'

Jamie nodded. 'Yes, I know. I saw.'

Hazel broke free and looked at him with contempt. 'You *saw*? And you never thought to say you were safe? You've had every man, woman and child breaking their heart for you. Well, if that is your idea of some sick joke . . .'

Jamie held her arms again and stared at her intently. 'I saw, because I was in a place where I could see *everything*.'

'Talk sense. What place? Where?'

Wee Malkie gave a gasp and sat down suddenly in the chair. His eyes were shining. 'You found it then?' he said.

'Yes.'

Hazel looked from one to the other. 'Do you both mind telling me what you are blethering about?'

Wee Malkie hugged himself and whispered, 'The Eye. The Eye of Doran.'

Hazel shook her head. 'Oh no, come on. Them's just stories . . .'

Jamie's eyes gleamed in the darkness. 'The stories are true. *The Eye shall behold, though the Head not see, 'til angels bring the key to understanding*. That's something Angus read to me and I didn't understand, then.'

Hazel tossed her head. 'Angus talks a load of rubbish.'

Jamie held out his fist and slowly opened his fingers to display the Stone of Doran. 'Angus gave me this,' he said, 'and although I can't exactly explain why or how, it has been real good to me.'

29

Taking the Shilling

The hard light snapped on and the loudspeaker crackled. 'Yes? Who is it?'

Alistair slunk back against the wall and hissed, 'Who do you think? Open up, unless you want the whole world to know our business.' The latch clicked and the gate slid open and Alistair hurried inside. A cap was pulled low over his brow, his clothes were muddied and torn and there were deep circles under his eyes.

Duncan was in the atrium, pouring a drink. He offered it to Alistair. 'You look as though you could do with this.'

Alistair grabbed the glass and downed the drink in

one. 'Aye. I shouldnae be here. We've been searching 'til just now for the wee bairn.'

Duncan sat down on the leather sofa and regarded his fingertips. 'Yes, tragic. A fine boy. A terrible loss.'

Alistair tore off the cap and gave him a wild look. 'He's no' been found yet. But if he is gone, seems tae me it would suit you just fine.'

Duncan looked hurt. 'Alistair. That is a terrible thing to say. But' – his eyes held Alistair's unflinchingly – 'we have to face up to realities in life and use them to our advantage. Or else we are fools.'

Alistair banged down the glass. 'Aye. A fool I was, ever to get mixed up with you.'

Duncan's eyes hardened. 'Let's get this straight. I seem to recall that it was you who came to me asking – no, *begging* – for help when you were up to your neck in debt. And out of the goodness of my heart I helped you.'

Alistair looked away. 'Goodness would be a stranger to your heart,' he said bitterly, 'and the only help you ever give is for your own profit.' He paused, then added in a whisper, 'I want out.'

'Really?' Duncan rose and crossed to the picture windows, and for a while contemplated the moonlit surf breaking silently beyond the triple glazing. 'And what precisely do you mean by "out"?'

Alistair shot him a troubled glance and paused before he spoke. 'I want to be my own man. I want to be able to look at myself in the mirror. I want to be able to face my friends, my fellow islanders, the folk who have been searching with me all day with no thought of themselves, and to stand up for their hopes and their dreams.'

Duncan turned and applauded. 'Bravo. Very noble. I must say I am touched.' He carefully lifted the pleats on his slacks and sat down again. 'And what is stopping you?'

Alistair swallowed. When he spoke again, his voice was so low that it was almost inaudible. 'They still want me to stand as their man. In the vote.'

Duncan grimaced impatiently. 'Yes, yes, we've been through all this. And we have agreed that you will stand, and then transfer their votes to me. What is the problem?'

Alistair murmured, 'The problem is that I would be betraying them, selling my soul.'

Duncan leaned forward. 'I don't know much about souls, and I think that yours must be pretty well discounted already. But this I do know. We only get given a few chances in our lifetime and we have to snatch them when they are offered.' He pointed an emphatic finger at Alistair, who seemed to have shrivelled within his coat. 'Look at yourself. What are you? Twenty-seven, twenty-eight? Soon be turning thirty, with a wife and kids, a failing farm and an overdraft at the bank. What have you got to show for your life? Eh? What have you achieved, for yourself or for this island? Then look at me.' He indicated the atrium. 'I don't ask you to like me, but you have to admit that I have achieved a fair bit. And why? Because I seized my chances.

'Now, listen, and listen carefully.' Duncan's face was taut and his lips drawn back, exposing the flawless white veneers on his teeth. 'Doran stands poised on the brink of disaster. It's five minutes to Armageddon and the clock is ticking. And who is to save it? Angus and Eleanor? Daft old fools in their crumbling castle. They represent the past. Jamie was a sweet kid, but an irrelevance, and now he's out of the picture. That leaves just you and me. You have many of the islanders behind you because they think you're one of them. They'd like to believe in you. But what can you offer them? You've made a pig's ear of your own life, and you imagine you are going to bring them a better one?'

'And you?' Alistair sneered at him. 'You'll save them? From the goodness of your heart, is it?'

Duncan sat back and pressed his fingers together once more. 'No,' he said evenly. 'I can't save them all. There will be – what is the buzzword? *Wastage.* The stupid, the blind, those without faith or vision – I can't help them. But those who want to embrace the future: I can offer them a share in it. And you, who will have helped to make it possible, will be rewarded above all.'

'And what's the guarantee? How do we know that this isn't all some scheme you've dreamed up to make yourself richer? That when you're chieftain you won't just sell us all down the river?'

Duncan nodded. 'You're absolutely right, of course. There are no guarantees. Except – consider this. I only get richer if my plans for Doran succeed, and if they succeed then Doran gets richer, and you, my good friend, if you keep your head and follow my instructions, will get *much* richer.'

Alistair reached for the bottle and, with a shaking hand, poured himself another large drink. 'And if I don't agree?'

Duncan shrugged. 'Well then, the deal is off. And after Tuesday's vote I will advise my powerful colleagues who are backing this enterprise to divert their very considerable funds to another project elsewhere. I assure you there's no shortage of candidates begging for our support. And you, I'm afraid, will be left holding the baby – without my support. You'll find every door closed to you and you'll have to be pretty sure you have all the answers when your friends turn on you.' He smiled. 'And of course' – he fished inside his jacket for an envelope – 'I need hardly add, there won't be any more of these.'

30

Truth and Consequence

Wee Malkie peered through the stone. 'Doesn't work,' he said flatly. 'I can't see anything.'

Jamie snatched it from him. 'Well, I tell you, it *did*.'

Hazel gave him a searching look. 'Jamie, this isn't another one of your fantasies, is it? 'Cos if it is, I'm no' in the mood.'

Jamie struck his forehead with a fist. 'Jeez. What do I have to do to persuade you guys that this is the honest truth? I nearly died out there. Had to swim round the headland out of Auchter Bay once the tide was low, and you think I'm into playing *games*?'

Hazel frowned. 'And you say you could see everything? From the Eye?'

'Yes. As clear as I can see you now. Real high-def. Look,' said Jamie, 'I saw you pedalling out of the castle on your bike. 'Bout eight a.m.? You had a shopping bag strapped round you and you had that stupid pink hood on your head.'

Hazel reached instinctively for the hood and found nothing. 'Yes,' she said, 'that's right. I did.'

Jamie warmed to his theme. 'And then they had some kinda meeting point, outside the bar. Big crowd. I could see Angus and Murdo and Eleanor – with a map? Just like in a movie, projected on the floor.'

'I wish I'd seen that,' Wee Malkie said sadly.

'Well, I actually remembered I *had* seen something like that before,' replied Jamie. 'When I was a small kid, my mom and dad took me to 'Frisco and we were down by the ocean, near Point Lomas, where they had this real fancy pier with all kinds of pinball machines and stuff. And there was this little round house you went in and it was all dark an' spooky, 'cept for this bright picture projected onto the table. You could see the seals and the gulls sunning themselves outside on the rocks, and even the Golden Gate Bridge in the distance.'

'But how?' Wee Malkie wanted to know.

'Seems like they came up with this glass prism way back, long before they discovered photography. They'd set it up on the roof when it was sunny and it projected the scene from outside. It was the neatest thing – I guess the IMAX of its day. *Camera obscura,* I think they called it.'

Hazel gnawed at a nail. 'And you saw Duncan, you say?'

Jamie laughed. 'Yeah, that was so weird. I still can't figure it out. I was lookin' at a really wild part of the island. No roads or nothin', just sea birds and cliffs – oh, and this hidden lake, sorry, loch. And Duncan was streaking along the ocean in that supercharged yellow monster of his, and, cool as a breeze, he just turned and drove it straight at the rocks. And then he disappeared.'

'Awa' you go!' scoffed Hazel. 'He may be puddled, but he's nae going to destroy his fine expensive boat. And anyway, he turned up right as rain at the Doran Arms after.' She thought for a moment. 'But what was he doing up there anyhow?'

'Up to no good, and that's for certain,' said Wee Malkie. 'My father says Duncan's in league with the devil. And I think he's right.'

Jamie looked grim. 'Well, he sure ain't number one on my hit parade right now. Forgetting to pick me up from Auchter Bay.'

Hazel tossed her head. '*Forgetting?* Wake up, Jamie. Duncan knew full well there's no way out from that beach. He also knows the tides like you know your two times table. No, Duncan didnae forget you. He wanted you dead.'

'Exactly. That's why I sent Malkie for you. 'Cos as far as Duncan knows, I *am* dead.'

Hazel was puzzled. 'So what? He'll find out pretty soon that you're alive and kicking.'

'Not if we don't tell him.'

Hazel frowned. '*Don't* tell him?'

Jamie rose and began to pace the room. 'Look, you may think this sounds weird, but then a lot of weird things have happened to me lately. And it's got me thinking about who I am, and why I'm here, and stuff like that. And I guess it's to do with my dad too, and the way I used to think he was really dumb, spending his free time trying to sort out the mess that some clan, on some faraway little island, had gotten themselves into.' He nodded before continuing. 'Yeah, and it's to do with *Macbeth* too, and witches and visions.' He looked around wildly. 'And stuff like ambition and murder.'

He caught the two of them staring at him blankly, and passed a hand across his eyes.

'Gee, I'm sorry. I guess it's been a pretty rough couple of days. Look' – he put a hand on each of their shoulders – 'what I'm trying to say is that, for better or for worse, I am the son of a chieftain. And I think I've just been given the opportunity, for once in my life, to do something important. I don't want to blow it. But I can't do it alone.'

Sunday morning, and Eleanor had not appeared for breakfast. Angus was slumped at the table, toying with his food, moving it around on his plate but not actually eating any of it.

Hazel had been up at dawn and, having made sure no one else was around, had slipped silently into Jamie's room and stuffed some items quickly into her shopping bag before setting off on her bicycle. She had returned, done her chores as usual and was now wiping the table. She glanced at Angus and, putting away her cloth, sat down opposite him. He glanced up sadly.

Hazel put her hand over his. 'Angus, dinna be sae dowie,' she said. 'I'm certain he'll be found. I really am.'

Angus nodded. 'Aye. That's what I keep telling myself and we're keeping up the search. But it's Sunday already, and still no news. And Eleanor is taking it awful bad.'

'Look, you know Jamie. He's probably gone wandering, got himself lost and is holed up somewhere. He's a right stookie, but he's muckle strong. He'll survive.'

Angus gave a thin smile. 'Aye, you're right. He's a fine lad. And he's the son of a chieftain.' He caught Hazel's strange look, and retorted, 'Well, is he no'? And a true MacDoran will always come through.' His face clouded. 'Only thing is . . .'

Hazel squeezed his hand. 'What is it?'

'I must go up now and telephone his mother. And I can tell you, I'm fair dreading that.'

Hazel patted his hand gently. 'Don't worry, Angus, I'll do it for you.'

'No, it's not a fit chore for a child.'

'But Marcia *knows* me. And, you know, coming from another woman . . . ?'

Angus brightened visibly. 'Oh, do you think so? Oh, that would be a real kindness.' He rose to his feet.

Hazel consulted her watch. 'Look, it's only nine o'clock and they're eight hours behind us in California, so Marcia won't welcome a call much before four o'clock our time. I'll come up to you then and we'll try to make a connection.'

Wee Malkie ran like the wind through the wood, his clenched fists punching the air and his thin, bony knees working like pistons. When he reached the clearing, Andrew and Donald were waiting for him in their usual spot.

'Michty me,' said Andrew, watching as Wee Malkie doubled up, coughing violently and fighting for breath. 'He'll be representing Scotland at the Olympics next.'

'What kept you?' asked Donald. 'We should be on our way.'

'The old fellow,' panted Wee Malkie. 'Had a skinful last night, and when he woke up he wis fairly gaun his dinger.'

Donald stretched and pulled on his rucksack. 'So, are you ready? I was thinking we could go search for our lad up the corrie. There's a load of caves I know that he could have got stuck in.'

Wee Malkie lifted his hand. 'No,' he said simply.

'What do you mean "no"?' said Donald indignantly, his round face flushed. 'There's a life at stake here.'

'Aye,' said Wee Malkie, 'I know that. But there is more important work to be done.' He looked around and lowered his voice. 'A secret mission.'

Andrew guffawed. 'You muckle sumph, Malk. Get real.'

Wee Malkie lifted his chin. 'Do you remember when

we made the rules of the gang?' he said. 'We cut our wrists and mingled blood and swore the solemn oath?'

'Aye,' said Andrew warily.

'And we said we would never divulge secrets, or let each other down?'

The boys nodded.

'Well, the oath is going to be tested.'

Duncan cradled the cellphone against his shoulder as he paced around the atrium. 'Yes,' he said, 'you'll be glad to hear that everything is looking good. We'll still do the business today.' He glanced at his watch. 'I could rendez-vous about midday. Yeah. Usual spot.'

There were some murmurings from the phone and Duncan nodded agreement. He caught sight of himself in the mirror and smoothed his hair with his hand.

'I think I can say the vote is pretty secure,' he said finally. 'Yes, day after tomorrow. Our friend will do what he has to do. He's a bit flaky, but he knows where his interests lie.' He listened as the voice on the other end ground on. 'No, there's no problem at all there.' He smiled contentedly at his reflection. 'You could say that particular entry has been scratched from the race.'

31

Interpret from Afar

Wee Malkie and Hazel jumped down onto the beach in Spey Cove to find Andrew and Donald waiting for them with a small dinghy. They wore dark jerseys and had woollen hats pulled low over their eyes.

'Well done,' Hazel whispered. 'Did you have any trouble?'

Donald shook his head. 'Naw. I told my dad we wanted to search some of the coves again and he was as good as gold.'

'Any sign?' Hazel asked anxiously.

'Not yet,' said Andrew. 'We took him some breakfast in our hideout in the woods and he said he'd make his own way down.'

Hazel looked at her watch. 'We don't have much time.'

There was a low whistle and a nearby clump of bracken shook and then rose slowly in the air. Jamie's face appeared beneath it. He smiled broadly. 'Dig the hat,' he said.

They all piled into the boat, and Donald fired the outboard engine. He pointed at Jamie. 'You'd better lie low,' he said.

Jamie crouched in the stern and pulled a tarpaulin over himself. 'How long do you reckon we got?'

'It's low tide now,' said Donald as he steered the boat out to sea, 'so I reckon four hours top whack.'

Auchter Bay finally swung into view, its deserted crescent of golden sand gleaming in the warm sunshine. Jamie scanned the cliff face and suddenly pointed. 'There,' he cried.

Donald ran the dinghy up onto the beach and Hazel, Jamie and Wee Malkie jumped down into the shallow water.

'I'll be back for you at two fifteen sharp,' said Donald.

'I seem to have heard that line before,' Jamie murmured.

They waited for the boat to disappear round the headland before Jamie fished the Stone of Doran out of his pocket. He put it to his eye and turned to face the cliff. A slow smile spread across his face. 'Ah,' he whispered. 'It wasn't a dream.'

Malkie reached eagerly for the stone. 'Please. Let me have a go.'

Jamie handed it over, and Malkie peered through it. 'Awa' you go. I can't see anything,' he said angrily, thrusting the stone at Hazel. 'You tell him.'

Hazel took the stone and raised it to her eye. There was a long silence.

'Told you,' said Malkie triumphantly.

Hazel ran forward until she reached the cliff, and then scrambled up onto the rock platform. She looked through the stone again and reached out to touch the chalk face. Jamie joined her and together they pushed at the cliff.

Malkie watched open-mouthed as the rectangular section swung inwards. 'Crivens,' he breathed. Then he glared fiercely at Jamie. 'So why does it nae work for me?'

An impromptu press conference had been called outside the Doran Arms. Being early on a Sunday, there was only one representative from the mainland media, a stringer from the *Highland News* who was scribbling in his notebook. A small crowd of islanders, most of whom had been involved in the search for Jamie, stood grim-faced as Murdo finished speaking.

'You could say that no effort has been spared to find the laddie, and every part of the island has been thoroughly searched. I only wish I had some better news to give ye.' Murdo sat down suddenly on the bench and covered his eyes. A chief constable who had come over from the mainland the day before rose to his feet. He shuffled some papers in his hand and cleared his throat.

'Aye, well, I am sure that we all echo those sentiments, and I would like to thank Mr, er . . .' He looked at Murdo and then peered at his papers. 'Well, everybody really, for the magnificent effort that you have made in this very upsetting case. No one could have asked for more.' He looked around at the crowd. 'I have my men here and we will of course be continuing the search. I'm expecting a helicopter. Shipping has been alerted, but each passing day obviously lessens the hope of a good outcome. This is now officially a Missing Person report, and' – he nodded to the reporter – 'I would be grateful if no names are disclosed, Iain, until the next of kin have been informed.'

The reporter nodded and raised his pencil. 'But would I be correct in thinking that the missing youth is the black lad from America who's been lodged at the castle?'

The chief constable looked uncomfortable. 'Aye, Iain, but as I say, no names at this stage.'

The pencil waved again. 'But could you confirm then, that he is the son of the late chieftain? And maybe was in line to inherit the title?'

There was a murmur from the islanders, and one of them stood forward. He glared at the reporter. 'If you were from Doran, you'd know that these things are put to the vote and there can be several contenders for chieftain. Any road, the lad was not even in the running.'

The reporter glanced at his notebook. 'Clan Meet's on Tuesday, isn't it?'

There was a murmur of assent, and the reporter tapped his pad with the pencil. 'I gather Duncan Wylie is odds-on to win.'

The islander spat. 'Over my dead body. Alistair MacDoran is our man.'

The chief constable spread his hands. 'Look, if we can keep to the point. We still have a missing person here, and that is what should concern us all.'

Wee Malkie rushed forward through the narrow, winding passage, with the beam from a powerful torch illuminating the way ahead. This time Jamie was able to take in the details: the dripping stalactites, the bats' nests wedged in the high crevices and the changing colours of the rock strata as they climbed upwards.

Their footsteps clattered around them and echoed back from the gaping darkness. At each division in the path, Jamie pointed out the carved pair of hands, and when they finally reached the blocked passage they paused, panting hard. Hazel looked enquiringly at Jamie, who directed the torch beam to the side wall. The twin emblems stood out in vivid relief. Jamie nodded to Hazel, who pushed gently at the rock slab. Once again it glided open, revealing the decorated chamber with its dazzling light display.

Malkie switched off the torch and clambered inside. He crouched on the floor, scanning the brilliant image, letting out low cries of amazement. Fingers of light danced across his thin face as he finally looked up at Jamie.

'It's real,' he gasped. 'The Eye of Doran is real. And to think that I should be allowed to see it!'

Hazel crouched down, studying the image of the harbour intently. 'Can you shift it?' she asked.

'Sure thing,' said Jamie. 'Which way?'

'Left a fraction.' The image slid across the floor. 'Whoa. Back, slowly. Stop.' She looked up. 'Duncan's boat's not at his jetty. Where is he off to today?'

'No idea,' said Jamie. 'But I told you, I saw the boat last time. Only up north, by some big rocks.'

'Can you find them?'

Jamie swung the lever and the lens rotated slowly, panning the image. Malkie kept exclaiming and recognizing places he knew, and at one point even identified his father making his unsteady way down to the village. The view flew across the glen and then rose high into the hills and finally skimmed the rocky peaks. Eventually Jamie located the inland loch, and beyond it the rock cliffs and the far ocean.

Hazel dropped to her knees and examined the image with narrowed eyes. 'That's Cape Wrath,' she said. 'I'm certain of it. Not a place you want to visit. The currents round there are something terrible, and there's plenty of submerged rocks too. Even the most experienced fishermen won't go near it. But this wee loch . . .' She traced the outline of the inner lagoon with her finger. 'I had no idea . . . nobody would know this was here. Hold on!' she cried, and the other two bent to see where her finger rested. 'There are some chains tied here and some sort of jetty, and a building hidden by the rock. Someone is using this place.'

'Maybe it's the government,' put in Malkie. 'Top secret.'

Hazel glanced at her watch. 'Look, we don't have much time,' she said.

Jamie was kneeling at the chest, lifting out leather-bound books, some swathes of material and a rolled-up map.

'What are they?' asked Hazel.

'I'm not sure,' Jamie replied, 'but someone obviously wanted to keep them safe.' He carefully turned over some of the ancient pages in one of the ancient books. 'Seems to be some kind of history. Of the clan, I think. There seem to be a lot of MacDorans.'

Hazel was unrolling the map. 'It's Doran,' she whispered, 'but long ago. Look, the village is much smaller, and the roads are not there, or just marked as tracks.' She brought the parchment closer to her face. 'There is a signature. Hard to make out. James . . . er, Malcolm, I think . . . Frazer?'

'What?' Jamie snatched the roll from her hand. Something nagged in his head. *Ask A if any truth in James Malcolm Frazer hoard.* 'Who was he?'

'Who?'

'This James Malcolm Frazer guy.'

'I don't know.' She hesitated. 'Well, maybe . . .'

'Yeah, what?'

Hazel scratched her head. 'I may be wrong, but I'm pretty sure he was the cattle-rustler I was telling you about who invaded Doran and tried to take over the clan ages ago. Led an armed uprising and captured the chieftain. Nearly pulled it off too. They looted the castle and most of the island, but one of his followers had a change of heart and released the chieftain, who gathered up the faithful clan members and drove James Malcolm Frazer and his thugs into the sea.'

'Drowned them?'

Hazel laughed. 'No. Worse. They were banished from Doran and last seen rowing hard for England. Remember I said that—'

There was a cry from Malkie, who was jabbing at the image on the floor. A familiar yellow shape had suddenly appeared in the ocean, to the right of the frame.

'Duncan!' they all exclaimed in unison.

'You gotta see this,' said Jamie. 'It's a really neat trick.'

Once again the speedboat turned and then headed straight for the outer cliffs.

'What on earth is he up to?' breathed Hazel as the boat disappeared from sight.

'The Great Vanishing Act,' said Jamie. 'Beats me.'

'There must be a reason,' said Hazel. 'There's no way he would risk bringing that boat so close to the shore unless . . .'

'Unless he knew his way around,' put in Jamie thoughtfully. 'Unless he was *going* somewhere.'

They gathered up the books and the material, and Jamie spent some time poring intently over the map again before rolling it tightly. He glanced at his watch. 'We really gotta split,' he said.

Something caught Malkie's eye and he crouched down again. 'Look,' he cried, and the three of them bent over his finger where it stabbed a small yellow shape that had suddenly materialized in the lagoon. 'It's Duncan. And he's *inside*.'

Angus was standing by the window of his office, wringing his hands and hopping agitatedly from foot to foot. They had waited an hour for a connection to the mainland operator. Now they were through, the signal was poor and kept fading in and out.

Hazel pressed the receiver to her ear and spoke loudly. 'A long-distance call to California. Yes, that is in America.'

Angus gnawed at his fingernails. 'What will you say? What can we tell her?'

Hazel turned away from him. 'Yes, a Mrs MacDoran. It is a three one zero number . . .' She glanced at a card as she read out the number, then put her hand over the mouthpiece and whispered fiercely to Angus, 'Look, I can't do this with you fretting there. Will you leave it to me? *Please?*'

'Aye, aye, sorry,' Angus whimpered, retreating through the door and closing it softly after him.

Hazel heard the long tone, then a click and finally Marcia's brisk voice.

'Good morning, MacDoran residence.'

'Hello, Mrs MacDoran. This is Hazel speaking.'

'Hazel?'

'From Doran. I'm calling from the castle.'

'Oh, *Hazel*! I am *so* glad to speak to you. I've heard nothing for ages and I was getting worried. You're pretty faint. Is everything OK?'

Hazel glanced at the door and lowered her voice. 'Can you hear me? There is something you should know ...'

32

Double Whammy

Monday dawned grey and damp, with a thick sea fog lying low over the island. It was impossible to see more than a few metres ahead, and the village and harbour were almost deserted. The fruitless search for Jamie, coupled with the impending Clan Meet, had cast a pall over everything and it seemed as though life was temporarily suspended.

Only someone with very sharp eyes and bold enough to be out in the murk in the early hours might have noticed Hazel cycling furiously out of the village, her basket crammed to overflowing, to where Janet was waiting on a horse at the crossroads. Or Donald and Andrew wheeling a barrow piled full of picks and shovels. Or Malkie leaving his house with his shopping bag. Someone with an interest. Someone like Calum.

He sauntered out of the bushes and blocked Malkie's path. 'Well well, what is this creeping thing? Is it a toad? Is it a skunk? Oh no, it's Wee Malkie. Now what can he be up to, slithering about on this foul morning?' Malkie put his head down and kept walking. Calum moved in front of him. 'Not so quick. I am talking to you. Don't you know it's bad manners to ignore folk when they are talking to you?'

Malkie tried to outpace Calum, but an arm gripped him firmly.

'Oh my, we are in a hurry.'

'I'm fetching some things for my father. Let me pass.'

Calum surveyed him warily. 'I've been watching you and your pals. Something's going on, isn't it? What are you up to?'

'Nothin'.'

Calum gave Malkie such a fierce shake that his teeth rattled. 'Don't give me that. You know something, don't you?'

'I dinnae.'

'What?' Another shake.

Malkie coughed. 'I haven't seen him,' he gasped.

'Who? Who haven't you seen?' Malkie's arm was twisted viciously behind him. Calum's eyes narrowed. 'Oh, is it that missing Yank?' Another violent twist.

'You're out of your heed. Let me pass.'

Calum landed a sharp slap across Malkie's face. The bag dropped heavily into the mud.

'What's in there?'

Malkie gave a cry and, snatching up the bag, raced back the way he had come. His thin shoes skidded on the ground as Calum pursued him. As he approached his father's dilapidated barn, Malkie looked desperately behind him, lost his footing and sprawled headlong. The bag flew open, revealing the rolled-up parchment map.

Calum reached down for it. 'Oh my, what have we here?'

Malkie struggled up. 'Give that to me. You have no business wi' that.'

'We'll be the judge o' that. Me and my business partner.' Calum unrolled the map, took a few steps towards the barn and whistled. 'But this is very interesting. In fact I would say it is *fascinating*.' He turned to Malkie, eyes hard like diamonds. 'Where'd you get this? Where were you taking this?'

Malkie pawed ineffectually for the map. 'Give it back, you—!'

Calum swung and landed a punch on Malkie's jaw. The boy went down again sprawling. Calum chuckled. 'Oh, Duncan,' he whispered gleefully, 'just look what I have found.'

The door behind Calum flew open so quickly he never saw the iron pan that struck him on the back of the head. He fell, pole-axed, into the mud.

Malkie sat up and his eyes widened. 'Dad?' he breathed.

His father put down the pan and grinned. 'That'll teach him. Trying to hurt my son.' He came over to Malkie and lifted him up. 'Are you all right, lad?'

Malkie rubbed his jaw. 'I think so.' Together they examined Calum.

'He's out cold,' said Malkie's father, 'but he's no' hurt real bad. We'd best get him back inside.'

Malkie faced his father. 'Dad, will you do something else for me? It's very important.'

His father's watery eyes tried to focus. 'Aye, son. What is it?'

'Do you think you can keep Calum here until after the Clan Meet tomorrow? He's in close with Wylie and he now knows something that mustn't get back to Duncan.'

'If he's a friend of Wylie he's no friend o' mine.' Malkie's father went back inside and emerged in a moment with a coil of rope. 'I used to be real good at knots,' he said, 'and I don't think I've totally forgot.'

'But, Dad, listen to me. This is for Doran, for us all, and I am relying on you.'

'Nae problem.'

Malkie's voice shook with emotion. 'Dad. Do you *understand*? There is a problem. This means no drink. *At all.* Please?'

His father reached out to touch Malkie's face gently. Then he nodded and turned to Calum, who was beginning to come round. He passed the rope deftly around his body and pulled it tight. 'This chicken is going nowhere,' he said.

In the castle, Eleanor and Angus sat gloomily in the draughty hall.

'So when do you say she will be here?' asked Eleanor, not for the first time.

'I've told you. Murdo will drive to the airport for her first thing in the morning and bring her back for the Clan Meet.'

Eleanor sighed. 'How can I face her? What will I *say* to her? And what will she make of all the clan business coming at such a terrible time? She will think us heartless.'

Angus shook his head. 'She will understand. She was married to a chieftain, after all.'

Eleanor gave another sigh. 'The clan. The burden that has weighed on all our lives. What use is it, Angus? Why do we go on with it? Why not just sell out to Duncan, like all the other rats, and be done with it?'

Angus cleared his throat and his eyes swivelled wildly. 'Because, madam, because it is our heritage and our duty . . .'

Eleanor shook her head sadly. 'I know. I know. But perhaps it's because we are stupid and old, clinging onto our past in this collapsing castle? The young won't thank us for it, they don't care tuppence for heritage and duty. They only want easy money and loud music and, what do they call them . . . ? *Skateboards.*'

Angus glared at her. 'Then indeed you are old and

stupid. That lad is young, yes, and he understands the modern world and its ways – skateboards and computers and things that vex my poor head. And he likes coffee and waffles and . . . er . . . burgers . . . that turn my stomach. But he is brave and bright and true . . .' A tear rolled down Angus's cheek and fell to the cold flagstones.

Eleanor touched his arm. 'There. It is myself that I am angry with, not that young lad.' She stared fiercely at Angus. 'And you are right. We must not let him down. We must do what we have always done and carry this through tomorrow with dignity. Face down that wretched Duncan and install you as the new chieftain, for this family and for Doran.'

Angus nodded. 'Aye. I dinnae ken whether I have the strength. But I'll try. I'll try.'

The chief constable peered out of the small window. 'It's a dreich scene all right,' he remarked to himself. Then, more loudly, 'Is that tea brewed yet?'

The sergeant bustled in with a cup and a digestive biscuit on a small tray. 'Aye, sir. Here it is.'

The chief constable returned to the table and sat heavily. 'I tell you, Sergeant,' he said, 'I won't be a bit sorry to get back to the mainland.'

The sergeant nodded. He wouldn't be sorry either, he thought to himself. The station house wasn't big enough for both of them, and he had been forced to move into the small outer office. And brew the tea.

The chief constable took a sip. 'No news, I suppose?'

'No, sir. Someone thought they saw something in a ditch up on yon brae, but it turned out to be a scarecrow. You cannae see much in this dreep.'

The chief constable sighed. 'Aye. I had to call off the boats. My men are freezing to death in that barn. And I've not even got the chopper off the ground, having had it brought all the way from Glasgow.' He gave the table a decisive thump with his fist. 'I think the time has come to draw a wee line under this sad business.'

'Aye.' The sergeant hesitated.

The chief constable blew on his tea. 'Yes, Sergeant? You have something to add?'

'Only, sir, that tomorrow is the Clan Meet.'

'Not expecting trouble?'

'No, sir. Just that maybe it might be prudent to wait until it's done and dusted.'

The chief constable chewed his lip. 'A bit tactless to pull out when their future hangs in the balance? You could have a point there.'

There was a tap at the door and the sergeant crossed to open it. Hazel stood outside, holding her bicycle. 'Ross, do you have a minute?' she asked.

'We're a wee bitty tied up just now.'

'Who is it?' boomed the chief constable.

'It's young Hazel MacDoran,' said the sergeant.

'Well, fetch her in,' said the chief constable. 'There's an awful draught in here.'

Hazel propped her bike against the station house and ducked inside. She pulled down her hood and shook her hair free.

'Make it quick, lassie,' said the sergeant. 'The chief constable here is a busy man.'

'I think I know where he might be,' said Hazel.

The sergeant's eyes lit up. 'Jamie? You've found him?'

Hazel shook her head. 'Not found him. But I've seen signs of life.'

The chief constable put his head on one side and peered at her. 'We've searched every inch of this island. Where are these signs?'

'Near Cape Wrath.'

'Cape Wrath!' The sergeant exploded. 'Now, my girl, you and I and everyone else on Doran knows there is nothing living up there but sea birds and fish.'

'Sergeant, haud your wheesht. Now, Hazel' – the chief constable stared intently at her – 'you saw these signs of life from a boat, at sea?'

Hazel shook her head. 'No. You couldnae. Not from the sea. From on high.'

The sergeant guffawed. 'Ham-a-haddie! Now, Hazel, don't play the loun. There's no earthly way you could get up on those crags. Even the goats gave up trying.'

Hazel reached into her coat and withdrew Jamie's cellphone. She punched a couple of buttons and held it out.

The chief constable looked from Hazel to the sergeant. 'I don't understand. These things don't work over here. My boys have had to use their satellite radio.'

Hazel gave him a pitying look. 'It's a camera too. See . . .'

The two men peered at the small screen and the sergeant's mouth dropped open. 'Well, help ma boab!' he exclaimed.

Hazel switched off the cellphone and smiled sweetly at the chief constable. 'You have a helicopter?'

33

The Meeting of the Clan

A team of volunteers laboured all morning preparing the hall for the ceremony. A huge log fire was blazing in the grate and rows of chairs were set out across the stone floor. The long table from the library had been placed at one end, along with several high-backed chairs. Clan banners hung unfurled from the high beams. Eleanor, dressed entirely in black, walked to and fro, supervising the arrangements. Her hair was tied back and she had applied powder to her face. She held herself erect and from time to time pointed imperiously with her stick and issued curt instructions to the helpers.

The fog had seeped away in the early hours, leaving a

clear but cool sunlit day. Just before noon the church bell began to toll, the mournful peals ringing out across the island. Gradually figures began to appear, clad in their dress kilts or best clothes and shined shoes, making their way slowly towards the castle. Some had dogs with them, while others carried babies.

There was a blast from a ship's horn, and the tiny ferry rounded the headland and nosed into the harbour. Several lads ran down to tether it, and Murdo's ancient Rolls drove onto the quayside, emitting its customary explosions from the exhaust. When it left the quayside Marcia was sat in the rear, solemn-faced and dressed in a grey, tailored suit with a dark shawl draped across her shoulders.

When the car entered the castle drive, it was soon surrounded by a silent crowd that pressed tightly against it. Faces stared at Marcia through the antique glass. Murdo sounded his horn, but the way was hopelessly blocked. He hopped out and opened Marcia's door. 'I think we'd better walk,' he muttered. There was silence as Marcia stepped out, then a sudden chorus of shouting voices.

'We're hert gled to see you . . .'

'He's a braw laddie . . .'

'Jamie will be fine, you'll see . . .'

'We won't give up . . .'

Marcia looked around and smiled. 'Thanks so much. I can't tell you how grateful I am to you all for looking out for my boy.'

Hands reached out to her, and she grasped them

gratefully as she walked slowly up the drive. At the great doors, Eleanor was already waiting, her head held high. Marcia stood before her.

Eleanor swallowed. 'My dear,' she said. 'I am so truly sorry. Can you find it in your heart to pardon a foolish, obstinate old woman?' She held out her arms. Marcia hesitated before stepping forward. The two women embraced.

Overhead a blue and yellow helicopter clattered across the sky and headed up the glen.

Refreshments had been served and now the hall was thronging with islanders and clansmen. There was a palpable air of excitement and anticipation as they chatted nervously together or gazed around at the unaccustomed surroundings.

The younger members stood together, slightly awed by the occasion. Gordon was critically inspecting the insides of a paste sandwich and Janet was unusually silent, playing with a needle and thread that she eventually pinned on her coat.

Alistair was at the centre of one group, who frequently clapped him on the back, but he seemed withdrawn, his face pale and tense. Angus, too, was surrounded by many of the older members and engaged in earnest discussion.

Eleanor and Marcia stood to one side, talking intently. Occasionally clansmen would approach and Eleanor would make introductions.

Duncan made a dramatic late entrance in a fine

tartan kilt and full dress. He paused for a moment, caught in a shaft of sunlight, and then passed through the throng in regal style, with a remark here, a joke there, a smile, a wink or a nod. He seemed supremely self-assured and made his way over to Marcia. He gave a slight bow.

'We are honoured to have you back. I only wish we had some positive news.'

'Thank you.'

'Jamie was a fine lad. I had become terribly fond of him. We were great chums. A dreadful loss.'

Marcia looked at him coolly. 'Not lost yet, Mister Wylie. I prefer the present tense. Jamie is a very resourceful boy.'

'Of course. You echo our hopes and prayers.' Duncan made another bow and moved away.

Eleanor watched him with undisguised contempt. 'My dear, I cannot abide that man.' She caught Marcia's eye and gave a tight smile. 'Now, where is that Hazel? I've not seen hide nor hair of her all day.'

Andrew ran across the drive and flattened himself against the shrubbery. When he was certain no one was around, he climbed swiftly up the creeper and peeped into the hall.

Everyone was now seated or standing pressed against the walls. Marcia was in the front row, facing the large library table behind which sat Angus, Alistair and Duncan. Eleanor was in her high-backed chair, and when the hubbub subsided she gave a nod to Murdo,

274

who walked to the front to face the audience. He was dressed in an extraordinary outfit that made him look like a cross between a soldier and an elf. A threadbare green cloak was drawn around a scarlet tunic with gold buttons. He wore a kilt but his feet were enclosed in fur boots. He shuffled some papers and raised his hand for silence.

Someone called from the back, 'Murdo, you bauchle. Could you nae have worn something special for the occasion?'

Murdo ignored the laughter. 'Clan members and fellow Doraners, I want to welcome you to this place on behalf of our host, the Lady Eleanor.'

There was applause and Eleanor gave a slight nod of recognition.

Murdo cleared his throat. 'This is an historic day for this island, for today the Clan MacDoran meets to vote for its new chieftain. Since the sad passing of our fine chieftain, James MacDoran, in a motor accident in America, this highest position has remained vacant.'

Marcia gave an involuntary shiver and pulled her shawl around her.

Murdo went on. 'By clan custom, the vote is normally open to all islanders, and also, traditionally, the next of kin can be nominated if they wish to take on this great honour, but also great burden. Most of you will have got to know young Jamie MacDoran and will also be aware of the sad circumstances of the past few days. Most of you too will have spared no effort in searching for the laddie, but to date he has not been found. His mother is with us today and our hearts go out to her.'

Heads turned to look at Marcia, who studied her hands.

Murdo shuffled his papers and continued. 'Clan lore says that within two calendar months of the death of the chieftain another must be selected by vote of the clan members and the islanders. Three worthy candidates have now presented themselves and are sitting behind me. You all know Alistair MacDoran, whose family can boast eight generations who have lived here in Doran.'

There was a roar from a section of the crowd. Alistair gave a curt nod, but didn't smile.

'Angus MacDoran here probably knows more about the clan than any of us, and he represents the direct line of the MacDoran family.'

There was polite applause and Angus rubbed his eyes vigorously.

'And finally, someone else who needs no introduction. Mr Duncan Wylie.'

There were some cheers and a few boos and Duncan smiled broadly.

'Each of the candidates will now have the opportunity to speak a few words, to put their case as to why they should be the next chieftain. Then you will get your chance to vote.'

Wee Malkie gazed down at the wild landscape that tilted beneath the chopper. Sheep scattered across the sparse grass in fright as they roared overhead. Malkie's eyes gleamed with delight and he clapped his hands round his earphones. 'This is great,' he shouted into his intercom. 'I dinna ken Doran was so big.' He turned to the two crewmen and yelled, 'I never flew 'til now. What's this machine called?'

'It's state of the art, this is,' replied the pilot. 'Our very own Eurocopter.'

The chief constable, strapped into his seat, chuckled and clicked on his mike. 'Now, Malkie, can you guide us?'

Malkie nodded and shielded his eyes from the sun. 'Aye.' He spoke to the pilot. 'You'll need t' head for yon mountains. Take a right, and then mebbe you can make out a wee clump of rocks beyond in the sea?'

The chopper banked again, and Malkie watched the grass give way to brown shingle and then dark volcanic rock. Before long they were flying alongside the jagged teeth of the mountain range and then suddenly hovering over the northernmost tip of Doran. Giant waves whipped by a fierce easterly wind were submerging a group of evil-looking rocks before slapping against the slate cliffs. Gulls wheeled in the air.

Malkie pointed a bony finger. 'Cape Wrath,' he said.

The chief constable frowned. 'Well, I don't see anything.'

Malkie scratched his head. 'But it must be there. Can you go closer?'

The pilot pulled a face. 'Bit tricky with these thermals,' he said. Gradually the chopper moved closer, its skids almost touching the tops of the cliffs, and Malkie could hear the hiss of the retreating waves.

The pilot glanced anxiously at the chief constable. 'That's about it,' he muttered. 'Don't see any break in the coastline.'

Malkie looked down desperately. 'If we could just peep over . . .'

The chopper rocked as the tops of the cliffs inched beneath them. And then suddenly, hidden deep in the cleft between mountain and coast, the lagoon was revealed – its calm blue water now ruffled by the down-draught from the rotor blades. Malkie let out a whoop of joy.

There was a concrete jetty on which stood several metal containers. Chains were fixed to mooring rings and a low brick building ran alongside. A receiver dish was mounted on the roof with a thicket of aerials.

'Michty me,' breathed the chief constable. 'What have we here?'

Alistair did not speak well. Sweat stood out on his brow and his hands shook as he tried in vain to make out his scribbled notes. He mumbled some platitudes about representing the ordinary islanders, with their trad-itional crafts, and serving their best interests, but his eyes kept sliding towards Duncan. Finally he muttered that he hoped he deserved their vote and collapsed back onto his chair.

Angus fared little better. Nervous tics pulled at his mouth, and his arms and legs were occasionally racked by involuntary spasms. A large pair of bandaged spectacles perched precariously on his nose, magnifying the large eyes that skittered around independently. He rambled on about the clan's proud history, producing a huge file of yellowed documents, most of which spilled out onto the floor. He spoke of destiny and magic and prophesies. Muttering sprang up within the crowd, then laughter and taunts.

'Gi' on wi' it, man. We'll be sat here 'til sunset.'

Answered by: 'Dinna be sair on the man, he's trying his best.'

'If that's his best, I shouldnae like to hear the worst.'

Eleanor's mouth tightened into a thin, hard line.

Duncan was the last to speak. He sprang lightly to his feet, placed his hands on the table and gazed intently around at the expectant crowd. Everyone in the hall fell silent.

'Enough of this tomfoolery,' he snarled. 'I have not come here to talk of the misty past, of dead warriors and blind seers, but of a brilliant future for this island. Today we stand poised at a crucial moment in our destiny. There is a signpost here and it points only two ways – backwards or forwards. The other contenders are obsessed by what has *been*. I represent what *can be*.' Duncan's eyes glittered as they swept the hall. 'Look around you and what do you see? People struggling to make do, make ends meet – to survive. Their shops are shutting down, the roads are a mess of holes – even this place is a pathetic ruin . . .'

Eleanor stiffened in her chair.

'It's time for a new broom, for younger, stronger leaders – above all, leaders who know the modern world and its ways. And yes, there is a new world out there. We either join, or we die.'

Andrew turned from his perch by the window and inserted two fingers into his mouth. He let out two blasts of a low whistle.

Duncan was in full stride. 'I mourn our past chieftains. I mourn James MacDoran, who was a close friend even though circumstances required him to live far away. I mourn for Jamie, his son, who in the short time he was with us entered our lives and our hearts. He was a fine youth with so much ahead of him. Who knows what he might have become had he . . .' Duncan's voice faltered with emotion. 'Had he been spared.'

Marcia stared ahead, her eyes unfocused.

'But' – and Duncan suddenly struck the table, making everyone jump and sending more of Angus's papers spiralling to the ground – 'the time for mourning is over. This is the time for action, and either we vote to take Doran into a brilliant future or we let it limp back into a dismal past. There is *no – other – choice*.' With each of the three last words Duncan hit the table with a corresponding sharp blow. He sat down, breathing heavily.

The islanders sat in stunned silence until Murdo shuffled back to address them.

'Well, you have heard the three candidates and now it will be time for you to vote by raising your hands. But first, by the custom of our clan, I have to ask this assembly if there is any other consideration to be heard before we decide who shall be the new Chieftain of the Clan MacDoran? This is your last chance to speak.' He looked around the hall.

There was a moment's silence and then the distant skirl of the pipes. The playing was far from expert, but gained confidence as it grew louder. An excited murmur ran through the crowd as they recognized that the melody, however imperfect, was 'Hail to the Chieftain'. Eleanor looked enquiringly at Angus, and Duncan half rose, staring ahead.

With a crash the great doors were flung open and everyone turned to look at the intruders. Silhouetted against the strong sunlight was a small procession, which began to make its way into the hall. The crowd parted to let them through and a gasp went up as the piper was revealed to be Hazel, dressed in her clan finery and red-faced from the exertion. Behind her came Donald and Andrew in their customary ragged clothes, but with their hair plastered down and carrying a shopping bag between them. Bringing up the rear was a tall warrior in kilt and full Highland dress. He carried a ceremonial claymore sword before him, and wrapped around his head he wore a swathe of ancient tartan that revealed only a glimpse of his flashing eyes. Eleanor stiffened in her chair and leaned forward intently.

As the group approached the table, they halted and Hazel let the bagpipes deflate with their usual mournful sound.

'Is this some sort of sick joke?' demanded Duncan, his knuckles white against the table.

The tall figure slowly unwound the cloth from his face. 'No joke, Duncan,' said Jamie. He laid the sword carefully on the table.

There was complete silence in the hall as everyone stared open-mouthed at Jamie. He turned to face the audience.

'I did joke with these duds once,' he said, indicating the dirk and chieftain's garments. 'My dad caught me and my buddies playing kids' games with them and he went ballistic. Told us they could only be worn by someone who had the right – by birth, by history and by duty. My dad could be a pretty scary guy when you crossed him, but he had a heart of gold and he loved this island. Told me it was the most beautiful place on earth, and you know something? I guess he was right.'

There was a murmur of approval.

'And not just the place – the most beautiful people too, who searched day and night to find a lost kid who they hardly knew. They made me realize the meaning of "kith and kin".'

Someone called urgently from the back, 'Where were you, Jamie? We feared you were dead.'

Jamie gave a tight smile. 'Yeah, me too. And of course I should have been if all had gone to plan.' Jamie glanced at Duncan, who had sunk back in his seat and turned very pale. 'But things don't always go the way you figure, do they? I got lucky, and of course, thanks to Angus, I had this.' Jamie fumbled in his sporran and produced the Stone of Doran. He turned it over thoughtfully in his hand. 'Sure saved my bacon.'

He shook himself and looked up. 'Gee, I'm sorry, I guess I didn't answer your question. *Where was I?*'

Jamie looked around the sea of upturned faces. 'With the help of this ancient stone, I managed to reach a place where I could see but not be seen. I could watch everyone busting a gut to find me, but I couldn't communicate. A secret place where chieftains of old could keep a beady eye on this island.'

Angus gave a cry. 'The Eye of Doran!'

Jamie nodded. 'I bet those crafty old chieftains used to sneak up there and snoop on the whole scene. Things they knew about' – and again Jamie turned to look at Duncan – 'and things they weren't meant to know about.'

Duncan laughed hoarsely and attempted a smile. 'Do we have to listen to fairy tales? The boy has obviously played a very stupid and costly practical joke on us all – and not for the first time, I might add. I seem to recall him climbing the castle tower not so long ago in an attempt to plant the American flag on the weather vane.'

Marcia gave Eleanor a quizzical look.

'Everyone knows the Eye of Doran is a figment of folklore,' continued Duncan. 'Surely this is another Yankee attempt to mock our clan business today? This is plainly a foolish child who has abused the hospitality he found here. He should go home to California and leave serious matters to the grown-ups.'

Jamie nodded ruefully. 'Right on, Duncan. I am just a kid. And my mom is always bawling me out for rushing into things, when I should hold back and bide my time.' He caught Marcia's eye and grinned. 'But, you know something? I like to believe what people tell me. I figure most times they're telling me the truth. It's a kid thing.' Jamie's expression hardened. 'So when a grown-up takes me fishing in his expensive power boat, and drops me off in Auchter Bay, saying he'll be back in a couple of hours, I believe him. Stu-pid! When he says all roads lead back to town, I believe him. Stu-pid! There ain't no roads out of Auchter Bay, as any islander knows. Oh, and there is one other little bit of information this grown-up forgets to give me. It'll be high tide in an hour. Now, fancy forgetting a thing like that.'

Duncan gave another bark of laughter. 'Enough of your fantasies, Jamie. Just apologize for the trouble you have caused and let us get on with our business.'

'I do apologize,' Jamie continued, 'to each and every one of you for all the trouble I caused. And I swear that when I finally got back to Auchter Bay, and the tide was low enough to let me swim round the headland . . .'

A gasp went up from the crowd.

'Yeah, it took a while – of course I was aching to deliver the good news to you all. But then I asked myself, why would some grown-up care so much about a kid that he would want to get rid of him? That's plumb crazy, ain't it? Now, what possible threat could little old Jamie MacDoran be to a real big-shot grown-up?' Jamie's eyes widened innocently. 'It couldn't be the fact that Jamie just happened to be the son of the chieftain, could it? Well, fact is, no one even knew he existed 'til he showed up at the funeral, and then they reckoned he'd be a pushover to sign away any claim and vamoose back to the US of A.' Jamie shook his head.

'But stupid Jamie didn't sign, and he stuck around trying to toss the caber, and climb the tower and stuff like that. Really digging this place, just like his dad had. Well, that really got up the big-shot's nose, 'cos he reckoned Doran kind of belonged to him. I mean, he had already bought up half of it, closing down businesses and moving people off land they had held for generations. He said it was for the good of the island, to make everyone richer, to give Doran a kick into the twenty-first century. And you know something? Jamie believed him, 'cos this was a grown-up with a flash pad and an at-ri-um and a neat set of wheels, not to mention a real hi-tech boat. But when they're out on the ocean, the big-shot tries to buy Jamie's support in the main game – a wad of banknotes, and more to come if he'll transfer over onto his team. Wow! Big league! Now, Jamie – 'cos he's just a stupid kid – doesn't play ball. Which is when he is left to explore Auchter Bay.'

Duncan exploded. 'Lies, lies, there's not a shred of evidence—'

Alistair rose to his feet and silenced Duncan. 'Aye, it's the truth. And I am ashamed that it takes a wee braw bairn to speak it. For it should have been me standing before ye who owned up. Who'd have told ye what this nyaff was up to. For I have taken Duncan's shilling – not wanting to, at first – just to clear a bad debt. And then another and another, until I was in over m' heed with

285

no way out. And when you sell your soul there is nothing you will not do. You'll even ask for the votes of your dearest friends and be prepared to . . . sell them on.'

There was a sudden clatter of a rotor, and through the hall windows the blue and yellow Eurocopter could be seen gently descending in a cloud of dust onto the drive. Within moments Wee Malkie ran into the hall, followed by the bulky form of the chief constable and a couple of his men. Malkie pointed at Duncan and the chief constable approached the table.

'My apologies for intruding into your meeting,' he said. 'But I'm afraid this is a matter that cannot wait.' He turned to Duncan. 'Are you Duncan Wylie?' he asked.

Duncan nodded and dropped his head.

'Then I have to inform you that I am arresting you in connection with serious charges that include attempted murder and trafficking in prohibited drugs.'

Duncan, his eyes wide with terror, backed away from the approaching officers and then, in desperation, vaulted across the table. A solid rank of islanders blocked his way. 'Let me pass,' he cried. 'You fools, let me through.'

When Duncan had been handcuffed and taken away, all eyes turned to Wee Malkie. He grinned at Jamie and his small frame seemed to swell with pride.

'I went up in the Eurocopter an' we found it,' he said. 'Duncan's hideaway, his wee private loch up at Cape Wrath. The perfect hidey-hole where he could stash all the stuff before he brought it into the mainland. Tons of drugs, the cops reckon, and you'd never know it was there.'

Malkie turned to Hazel. 'You were right,' he said. 'Duncan had it all fitted out – a dock with all his hi-tech equipment. The jammy—'

'But how did he get in and out?' said Hazel. 'Even Duncan doesnae run to a helicopter.'

'Aye. When the guys dropped down inside they found this enclosed loch with no way out to the sea. But there *had* to be a way that Duncan could get in and out.'

'Because we saw Duncan's boat in there,' insisted Hazel.

'We saw a yellow *craft* in there,' corrected Malkie, 'but even Duncan Wylie can't sail through a cliff.'

Jamie suddenly understood. 'But a submarine can go *beneath* a cliff if there is an underwater entrance that would also fill the loch . . .'

Angus had risen to his feet, holding an opened book: '*Turn aside from Wrath and from the depths you shall find a way to the sanctuary of light.*' He prodded the page. 'You see, the ancients knew about that place. They used it as a hidey-hole when things got rough, or mebbe just when they sought some peace and quiet. They had no submarines, but they must have had mighty lungs and dived deep to pass through.'

Pandemonium broke out in the hall, with groups of islanders waving their arms and shouting. Murdo tried to silence them.

'Will ye keep a calm sooch?' he cried. 'We have serious business to attend to.' He climbed on a chair and yelled,

'Will ye haud yer whisht? For the sake of Doran?'

Gradually the crowd settled, but one of the clan elders, a stooped and kilted figure leaning heavily on his stick, rose painfully to his feet. His voice was faint and shook with emotion.

'Dinnae forget we are here to appoint our new chieftain. Jamie, you have done us a great service and your father would have been right proud of you. You are descended from a great line of chieftains. Might you have it in your mind to take on this duty?'

Jamie stepped forward and looked around him. He was aware of his mother gazing up at him. 'Nothing would make me more proud than to accept that honour,' he said quietly.

The crowd erupted with a roar of cheering and stamping.

Jamie held up his hand. 'But, as Duncan said, I am still a kid. An American schoolkid, and I got unfinished work back there. That don't mean I can't keep closely in touch. I can be over every vacation, and with a bit of investment we can have the Internet up and running. Angus here is comin' on pretty well with his computer studies, and we can get more of you hooked up and get cellphones working. With a bit more effort, we can start to turn Doran around – get some healthy tourism going, open up the stores again. We got plenty of local talent and energy – some real strong guys, as I found out to my cost at the Games . . .'

There were shouts and cheers.

'And I tell you, the kids are no slouches either. Dougal

has already shown his skill as a horsebreeder – and as a brilliant musician. I know Gordon here would love to start up his own restaurant, and if he does I'll be first in line, 'cos that guy has really got the gift.' Janet let out a whoop of approval, which ended abruptly as Jamie pointed to her. 'And Janet too is ace at dressmaking and I know she can't wait to start her own business. Look what she ran up for me in a few hours with the old clan tartan we found up at the Eye.'

Jamie did a quick twirl that raised the pleated kilt. Wolf whistles and stamping broke out from the youngsters.

Jamie quietened them. 'I know, I know, it all costs money. Many of you may have asked yourselves where Duncan's readies came from. I think we have found the answer today. He had some pretty powerful friends in the underworld, and that hidden loch was a very handy base for their operations. But that doesn't entirely explain why Duncan wanted to become chieftain so bad and to get total control of Doran. I think I know why.'

The hall had, once again, become very silent. Jamie looked around. 'When, centuries ago, Duncan's ancestors tried to seize power, they were beaten and thrown out of Doran. While they were on the run they buried their stolen wealth somewhere in the hills, hoping to return someday to claim it. They were led by James Malcolm Frazer, and he kept a record – actually it was quite a hefty book – that contained details of his claim, and a map of the island. The book and the map were discovered by the chieftain, who was fed up to the back teeth with rebellion, so he kept them hidden in a chest at the Eye of Doran. And there they remained until today. Well, a few days ago, to be exact.'

Jamie motioned to Andrew, who opened the shopping bag and brought a leather volume over to Angus, who seized it and leafed eagerly through the pages. Then Andrew handed the map to Jamie and he unrolled the parchment.

'This is a real neat map of Doran as it was centuries ago,' he said. 'It shows the castle, the village, some tracks and farms, but here' – he jabbed a finger – 'out in the hills, there is something really weird – a peacock standing in front of a tall, triangular-shaped rock.

'Well, I know I ain't been here too long, but I know that rock. I was taken there not long ago.' Jamie paused. 'By a horse called Arion. It's a creepy, awesome place and the rock has a name. Ain't that right, Donald?'

Donald blushed furiously, tugged at his blond hair and looked nervously to Jamie, who nodded with encouragement.

'It's . . . er . . . that is, many folk round here call it Bobantilter . . . the icicle . . .'cos it's got such a funny shape.' Donald paused and cast another agonized look at Jamie.

'Now I seen some strange birds around here,' Jamie continued, 'but I ain't never seen any peacocks. And I'm pretty sure there weren't any around in James Malcolm Frazer's time neither. I had an idea this peacock was trying to tell us something.'

There was a murmur of laughter.

Jamie turned back to Donald. 'And what did you do?' he asked.

Donald's hand flew nervously to his hair once more. 'Eh? Oh, you mean with the picks?'

Jamie nodded again.

Donald took a deep breath. 'Well, there is this big, bare patch of earth in front of the rock, where nothing wants to grow. Andrew and me took some tools and had a wee dig around the base. We didnae have much time, but pretty soon we found . . .' Donald fumbled in the bag and brought out a tarnished silver cup, a large salver and a fistful of golden rings.

A gasp came up from the crowd.

Jamie held out his hand. 'Look, I don't know how much stuff is buried there. But the thought of it sure fired Duncan's imagination, and if we do find there is something of real value, then let's put it safely in the bank as the first instalment of Doran's new account. It will be a start, but it won't solve all our problems. To do all that we gotta work together, like a true clan and a united island, stop the in-fighting and use the strengths that we have.'

Jamie turned to look at Alistair, who dropped his head and stared at the floor.

'I know Alistair feels he's goofed badly, but I reckon deep down he's a tough and brave guy. And so did my dad. I think if he was given another break, he could do great things. If I were chieftain I'd want to appoint him to be my lieutenant and I know he wouldn't fail me or Doran.'

Alistair looked up, his eyes suddenly bright. Jamie held out his hand, and after a moment Alistair grasped it.

Jamie turned back to the crowd, who now hung on his every word. 'But you're gonna need more than that. When I was Stateside, you'd need to feel the chieftain was here among you. You'd need someone around who shares your heartbeat and your soul and has sussed this place inside out. Someone who, if things had turned out different, would have *been* chieftain. Someone who gave me a real hard time when I first came here, but who I would now trust with my life. That person is right here beside me.'

Jamie turned to Hazel, who was staring at him in shock. 'Yeah, I know, Hazel's a girl, and girls can't be chieftains. Well, personally I think that's pretty stupid, but I have a proposition for you. Well, if I own up, I guess it's more of a *condition*. I'd want Hazel here to be the deputy chieftain in my absence. Any rule in your book, Angus, that says she can't?'

Angus scratched his head. 'No. I dinnae ken . . .' And then his face brightened. 'I suppose we could always make a *new* rule.'

Jamie grinned. 'You got it, Angus. Lateral thinking.' He was aware of Eleanor watching him from her high-backed chair, and he walked over to her and dropped onto one knee.

'I hope you'll forgive me, Grandma,' he whispered. 'For giving you so much grief.'

Eleanor's eyes filled with tears as she reached out to

touch Jamie's face. 'No, it is you who must forgive a stupid, proud old woman who treated you so poorly. It will not happen again.'

Murdo came forward to address the crowd. 'Well, it only remains for us to take a vote. All those in favour of Jamie MacDoran as Chieftain of the Clan raise your right hand.'

A forest of hands punched the air, and with a roar the throng rushed forward. They seized Jamie and Hazel and hoisted them onto their shoulders, carrying them in a cheering procession around the hall.

34

Laddie, Come Home

Jamie entered the graveyard and approached the mound of turned earth. It was still without a headstone, but was covered with a counterpane of drifted leaves. He knelt and placed a hand on the ground.

'Oh, Dad,' he whispered, 'I wish you'd been there. Or maybe you were there, 'cos I felt you so strongly, and I suddenly saw all those people as my people, as my family, and this beautiful place as my place too. And I felt I belonged. Sure, I love the States and Mom and my friends, and I'll always have them too. But this I never knew I had, and it was here all the time. As Dougal said: in the blood. Yeah, in the blood.'

The ferry waited at the quayside, the Rolls-Royce once more strapped securely to the deck. Murdo was wearing his captain's cap, and he whistled as he polished the brass. It seemed as though the whole of Doran had turned out at the harbour, chatting animatedly in the bright morning sunshine. A pipe band sent jigs and reels skirling into the fresh breeze that fluttered the flags and bunting.

Eleanor held tightly onto Marcia's arm. 'We will miss you, my dear. We have to make up for so much lost time.'

Marcia smiled. 'We'll be back real soon, Eleanor. But meantime, can we persuade you to visit with us in California?'

Jamie broke in, 'It's all fixed, Mom. I've signed Grandma and Angus up for a surfing course.'

Angus laughed. 'I've nae time, laddie. I'm fully engaged wi' ma computer studies!'

Jamie noticed Wee Malkie and the gang standing nearby. 'Now, you guys. You did a great job and I'm relying on you to keep an eye on things while I'm gone.'

Malkie stood up tall. 'We'll let you know if there's something we can't handle, but there should be nae problem.'

Jamie gave them all high-fives, and then went to embrace Alistair. 'You won't let me down?' he said.

Alistair shook his head vigorously. 'Never.'

There were hands to be pumped, and big bear hugs

for Craig and Gordon. Dougal stood to one side with Arion, holding his bridle. Jamie patted the stallion's neck, and Arion turned to nuzzle his hand. 'See you later, pal,' said Jamie.

Janet stood before him, her hand on her hip. 'Aw, come here, ya beauty,' she roared, and enveloped him in a huge embrace.

And then there was only Hazel, standing on her own, chewing her lip. She was wearing a freshly ironed white linen shirt and her hair, almost tamed, glowed with a deep amber sheen. She eyed Jamie suspiciously. 'You're quite sure you'll be back then?'

''Fraid so. Do you mind?'

'No. Remember I'm only the deputy, by the way. You've got to give the orders.'

Jamie raised an eyebrow. 'And will you obey me?'

Hazel's eyes flashed for a moment and then she laughed. 'Suppose I've got a wee bit used to you hanging around. Bit of excitement in our boring lives.' She slid her arms around Jamie's neck and they kissed. A huge cheer rose up from the crowd and Hazel, blushing furiously, flapped her hands at Jamie. 'Now, away wi' ye. We've work to do.'

The ferry hooted twice, and then headed slowly out towards the open sea. Jamie and Marcia stood waving at the stern, and the whole mass of islanders standing on the quayside waved back, finally breaking softly into song that drifted over the water long after they vanished from view.

'There's a storm making,
And waves breaking,
A leave-taking, carry you back
To where your heart has dreamed of,
A place far off,
Your folk are waiting – Laddie, come home.

There's a voice heard crying,
And a soul dying,
And you, trying to find your way home
Back to the glens and the mountains
Where pipes are playing
And folk praying, saying – Laddie, come home.

In this time of times
We'll stand right by your side,
For this land is strong
And this land is wide.
And we need a voice
And we need our pride
And the strength to carry on . . .

There's a moon rising
And the clouds are parting
And hope starting, can't you hear?
All the pipes playing
And people praying, saying,
Come back, Laddie – Laddie, come home.'

About the Author

Ken Howard divides his time between London and California, where he loves the ocean and hiking in the desert. He has written and directed many award-winning TV dramas and documentaries, as well as composing million-selling records for major artists and West End musicals. *The Young Chieftain* is his first novel.